PRAISE
for the
RED HAND ADVENTURES

"O'Neill has an eye for detail, atmosphere, and action...this is a rousing period piece that ends on a cliffhanger."

—*Publishers Weekly*

"Whether intended for a YA or adult audience, this is a book the entire family can enjoy reading...The book reads like a Boy's Own adventure and is filled with action involving bandits, pirates and rebels, reminding the reader of such grand entertainments as Rudyard Kipling's *Kim*, Michael Chabon's *Gentlemen of the Road* and John Milius' *The Wind and the Lion*...Four Stars."

—Kenneth Salikof for *IndieReader*

"Debut author O'Neill incorporates a great deal of cultural and historical context in his story...and will make the readers feel as though they have traveled back in time and fallen into that world. An exciting, exotic tale...The cliffhanger ending all but demands that readers jump to the next installment of the series."

—*Kirkus Reviews*

"Block out the next few hours, because you won't want to put this book down!"

—Kevin Ma 's Magazine

D0980802

The
RED HAND ADVENTURES

Rebels of the Kasbah
BOOK I

Wrath of the Caid
BOOK II

Legends of the Rif
BOOK III

MORE PRAISE
for the
RED HAND ADVENTURES

Selected as a *Publisher's Weekly* indie select book
(Rebels of the Kasbah)

Selection for the 5th/6th and 7th/8th grade categories
for the 2014/2015 National Battle of the Books Contest
(Rebels of the Kasbah)

Silver Medal Winner for the 2013 Mom's Choice Award
(Rebels of the Kasbah)

Bronze Medal Winner for Best Book Series—Fiction
in the 2013 Moonbeam Children's Book Awards
(Red Hand Adventures)

Gold Medal Winner of the 2013 Independent
Book Publisher's Living Now Award
(Wrath of the Caid)

Black Ship

PUBLISHING

Adventure Novels with a Shot of Wry

EX LIBRIS

The
RED HAND ADVENTURES

BOOK II

Wrath of the Caid

JOE O'NEILL

A portion of proceeds from the sale of all *Red Hand Adventures* books will be donated to help the many impoverished and enslaved children in the world.

Wrath of the Caid

COPYRIGHT © 2012 BY JOE O'NEILL
Cover Art and Design by Kristin Myrdahl
Graphic Design by Anna Fonnier
Edited by Sara Addicott
Copy Edited by Bedelia Walton
www.RedHandAdventures.com

Black Ship

PUBLISHING

ISBN   978-0-9851969-6-7

This book is dedicated to the team that made it possible.

SPECIAL THANKS

This is the second book in the Red Hand Adventures series. What was once just an idea has now morphed into something more amazing than I ever could have hoped for, or imagined. I have been fortunate to work with so many dedicated, hard-working, and amazing people and I am humbled by their talent and efforts. In particular, I want to thank my lovely wife Kristin for her tireless effort on all design aspects of the series. I don't think there's anyone in the world who could have done a better job at creating the world of The Red Hand. I am also grateful to Bedelia Walton, for her sage advice and tireless editing; to Anna Fonnier, for her illustrious graphic design skills and patience with our many, many changes and re-designs; and to Sara Addicott, for her great suggestions and keen editing skills. It's been an adventure working on this book, and I am so excited to begin working on the next one with all of you.

—Joe O'Neill

JOIN THE RED HAND!

The Red Hand isn't just about reading books,
but also having a sense of adventure,
being curious about the world, where we've been,
and how we've gotten here.

It's giving back to those less fortunate and
having a sense of justice in our everyday life.

At Red Hand we are constantly holding writing contests;
trivia contests; sponsoring sports teams
(such as soccer and others);
teaching new adventure skills, and much, much more.

In addition, you'll be privy to new books and
other cool stuff before the general public.

To join The Red Hand, please go to
www.RedHandAdventures.com

TABLE OF CONTENTS

ALL THE WORLD'S A STAGE

All the world's a stage,
And all the men and women merely players;
They have their exits and their entrances,
And one man in his time plays many parts,
His acts being seven ages. At first, the infant,
Mewling and puking in the nurse's arms.
Then the whining schoolboy, with his satchel
And shining morning face, creeping like snail
Unwillingly to school. And then the lover,
Sighing like furnace, with a woeful ballad
Made to his mistress' eyebrow. Then a soldier,
Full of strange oaths and bearded like the pard,
Jealous in honor, sudden and quick in quarrel,
Seeking the bubble reputation
Even in the cannon's mouth. And then the justice,
In fair round belly with good capon lined,
With eyes severe and beard of formal cut,
Full of wise saws and modern instances;
And so he plays his part. The sixth age shifts
Into the lean and slippered pantaloon,
With spectacles on nose and pouch on side;
His youthful hose, well saved, a world too wide
For his shrunk shank, and his big manly voice,
Turning again toward childish treble, pipes
And whistles in his sound. Last scene of all,
That ends this strange eventful history,
Is second childishness and mere oblivion,
Sans teeth, sans eyes, sans taste, sans everything.

—William Shakespeare
As You Like It, Act II, Scene 7

CHARACTERS RETURNING FROM *REBELS OF THE KASBAH*

Tariq (tah-reek): An orphan; kidnapped and sold to Caid Ali Tamzali to race in deadly camel races

Fez: A friend of Tariq's; fellow slave to the tyrant Caid Ali Tamzali

Aseem (ah-seem): A friend to Fez and Tariq; fellow slave to Caid Ali Tamzali

Margaret Owen: An English girl; kidnapped and sold to Caid Ali Tamzali

Mister LaRoque (la-rohk): A shadowy French underground figure; had Margaret kidnapped

Aji (ah-jee): Tariq's best friend on the streets of Tangier; killed by a street thug named Mohammad

Sanaa (sah-nah): A beautiful Moroccan assassin; part of the resistance, instrumental in prison escape

Malik (ma-leek): A respected tribal leader; part of the resistance

Zijuan (zee-wan): A gifted Chinese woman and sage martial artist; rescued Tariq from streets of Tangier

Jawad (juh-wad): A slave and camel jockey; betrayed Tariq, Fez, and Aseem

Charles Owen: A decorated colonel in the British army; kidnapped by pirate crew; father to Margaret and David

Louise Owen: A devoted wife to Charles; mother to Margaret and David

Captain Basil: An Algerian pirate captain; kidnapped Charles Owen

Lieutenant Dreyfuss: A corrupt lieutenant in the British navy; tried to kill Charles Owen

Caid Ali Tamzali: An evil warlord; feared ruler of the Rif Mountains

Note: For definition in this book, a Caid (k+aid) is a warlord in Morocco who answers only to the Sultan, the sovereign ruler of Morocco. He controls his own territory, but pays taxes and owes all allegiance to the Sultan. However, a more common definition of a Caid is a Muslim or Berber chieftain, who may be a tribal chief, judge, or senior officer.

CHARACTERS INTRODUCED
IN *WRATH OF THE CAID*

The Black Mamba: The most ruthless assassin in Morocco; a loyal servant to Caid Ali Tamzali

Melbourne Jack: An Aboriginal adventurer and treasure hunter; formerly a member of a mystical circus in Australia

Foster Crowe: Born in Belgium, becomes a circus director in Australia; has important plans for Melbourne Jack

Amanda: A teenage girl; takes care of young Melbourne Jack in the circus

Cortez/Sharif Al Montaro: A notorious bounty hunter; hunts Charles Owen and Captain Basil

Matthew Hatrider: An army friend of Charles Owen's; offers to help Louise find Charles

Alice Fitzgerald: A new friend of Margaret's from Ireland

Hillie Dansbury: Margaret's oldest friend in England

Henri: A revolutionary and anarchist; rebel to the French government and loyal to Napoleon Bonaparte

Miss Cromwell: Headmistress at Margaret's school in England

Timin: A former betting parlor boss, imprisoned and left homeless; friend of street boys

Sister Anne: Head of St. Catherine's School in the south of France

The French Students: Sophie, Etienne and Inez; roommates of Margaret's at St. Catherine's

THE BALLAD OF GUNGA DIN

You may talk o' gin and beer
When you're quartered safe out 'ere,
An' you're sent to penny-fights an' Aldershot it;
But when it comes to slaughter
You will do your work on water,
An' you'll lick the bloomin' boots of 'im that's got it.
Now in Injia's sunny clime,
Where I used to spend my time
A-servin' of 'Er Majesty the Queen,
Of all them blackfaced crew
The finest man I knew
Was our regimental bhisti, Gunga Din.
He was "Din! Din! Din!
You limpin' lump o' brick-dust, Gunga Din!
Hi! slippery "hitherao"!
Water, get it! "Panee lao"!
You squidgy-nosed old idol, Gunga Din."

The uniform 'e wore
Was nothin' much before,
An' rather less than 'arf o' that be'ind,
For a piece o' twisty rag
An' a goatskin water-bag
Was all the field-equipment 'e could find.
When the sweatin' troop-train lay
In a sidin' through the day,
Where the 'eat would make your bloomin' eyebrows crawl,
We shouted "Harry By!"
Till our throats were bricky-dry,
Then we wopped 'im 'cause 'e couldn't serve us all.
It was "Din! Din! Din!
You 'eathen, where the mischief 'ave you been?
You put some "juldee" in it

Or I'll "marrow" you this minute
If you don't fill up my helmet, Gunga Din!"

'E would dot an' carry one
Till the longest day was done;
An' 'e didn't seem to know the use o' fear.
If we charged or broke or cut,
You could bet your bloomin' nut,
'E'd be waitin' fifty paces right flank rear.
With 'is "mussick" on 'is back,
'E would skip with our attack,
An' watch us till the bugles made "Retire",

An' for all 'is dirty 'ide
'E was white, clear white, inside
When 'e went to tend the wounded under fire!
It was "Din! Din! Din!"
With the bullets kickin' dust-spots on the green.
When the cartridges ran out,
You could hear the front-files shout,
"Hi! ammunition-mules an' Gunga Din!"

I shan't forgit the night
When I dropped be'ind the fight
With a bullet where my belt-plate should 'a' been.
I was chokin' mad with thirst,
An' the man that spied me first
Was our good old grinnin', gruntin' Gunga Din.
'E lifted up my 'ead,
An' he plugged me where I bled,
An' 'e guv me 'arf-a-pint o' water-green:
It was crawlin' and it stunk,
But of all the drinks I've drunk,
I'm gratefullest to one from Gunga Din.
It was "Din! Din! Din!

'Ere's a beggar with a bullet through 'is spleen;
'E's chawin' up the ground,
An' 'e's kickin' all around:
For Gawd's sake git the water, Gunga Din!"

'E carried me away
To where a dooli lay,
An' a bullet come an' drilled the beggar clean.
'E put me safe inside,
An' just before 'e died,
"I 'ope you liked your drink", sez Gunga Din.
So I'll meet 'im later on
At the place where 'e is gone --
Where it's always double drill and no canteen;
'E'll be squattin' on the coals
Givin' drink to poor damned souls,
An' I'll get a swig in hell from Gunga Din!
Yes, Din! Din! Din!
You Lazarushian-leather Gunga Din!
Though I've belted you and flayed you,
By the livin' Gawd that made you,
You're a better man than I am, Gunga Din!

—Rudyard Kipling

SHIP ROUTES

Angelina Rouge

– – – – – – – – – – –

Route from the Canary
Islands to Ile d'Yeu

Dreyfuss

• • • • • • • • • • • • • • •

Route from the Galite Islands

French Naval Ship

Pirate watch

POINTS of INTEREST

Where Alice Grew Up

Margaret's House

Hillie's House

**Saint
Catherine's
School**

**The Black Mamba
Leaving Prison Cell**

Gypsy Casts Spell

**Melbourne
Jack's Hot
Air Balloon**

Napoleon's Grave

The Chicken

Tariq Hides Here

Kasbah

Cortez

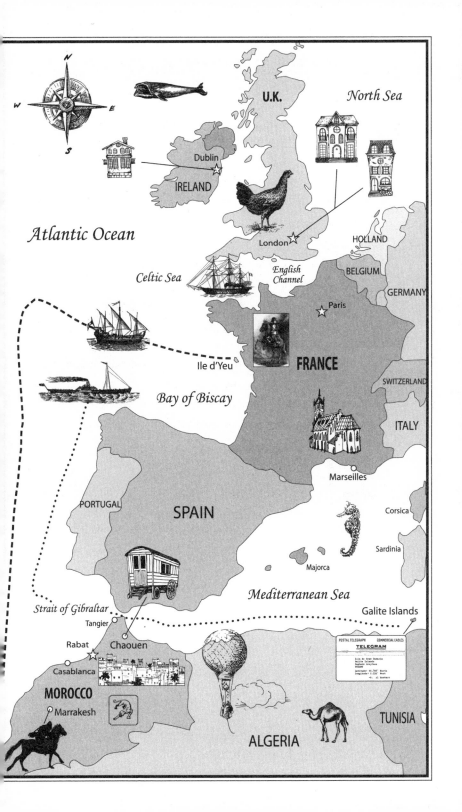

PREVIOUSLY, IN BOOK I
REBELS OF THE KASBAH:

Tariq is kidnapped from his home in a Tangier orphanage and sold to the evil Caid Ali Tamzali to become a camel jockey. The orphanage is owned by the venerable Zijuan, a mysterious and able martial artist from China.

En route to the Caid's kasbah, Tariq meets Fez, Aseem, and Margaret, who are also sold into slavery. Tariq is injured in a race and tortured by the sadistic Zahir.

Meanwhile, Margaret's father, Charles, watches as his yacht is stolen by the rogue pirate Captain Basil. However, Charles sees that Basil is actually forced into piracy by the corrupt and ruthless Lieutenant Dreyfuss of the British Royal Navy. In a fit of desperation, Charles joins Basil to fight against his native England.

Margaret, Fez, Aseem, and Tariq all escape from the Caid with the help of the assassin Sanaa, who helps them join a rebel resistance in the Rif Mountains. There they meet the leader of the resistance, Malik, who then launches a daring raid against the evil Caid.

PROLOGUE

A full moon hovered over the Sahara Desert.

A gypsy woman stared at it for an eternity, unable to move her eyes from the pale orb.

She was rumored to be over eighty years old and the wrinkles on her face showed her age. They were deep and craggy, and gave her face the appearance of a dark raisin. Her prominent cheek bones stuck out from her skinny face, and her magnificent green eyes were full of passion and mystery.

To stare into her eyes was like staring into the eyes of a wild cat.

She was stooped over, and her bony hands held a wooden cane made of cherry and walnut. A silk scarf covered her gray hair and a burgundy shawl covered her shoulders. She walked slowly, but deliberately. Somehow, her feet never left a trail in the sand. Staring up at the full moon, she couldn't keep her eyes off of it.

She was worried.

Some said she was a witch and could foresee the future.

"You seem concerned, Mother," her eldest son remarked.

She looked at him, feeling the smooth handle of the cane in her hand.

"There are dark times ahead, son. There is blood on the moon," she slowly answered.

Hearing this, her son felt a tingle go down his spine. When his mother spoke of dark times, it usually meant hardships that few could survive. He stared at the moon but could not see what his mother saw. He did not inherit her gifts for the supernatural.

"I am going to put my grandson to bed. I am tired," she told him and made her way to the tent her favorite grandson called home.

The tent smelled of jasmine and myrrh and the floor was covered in fine Moroccan rugs. He was a boy of ten and was already being groomed by his grandmother to be a leader in the tribe.

A solitary candle burned next to the bed.

"Can you tell me a scary story?" he asked, always pleased when his grandmother told him a bedtime story.

"I shall tell you a true story. The story of a monster," she replied, sitting down next to the boy and stroking his brown hair, worry in her eyes.

"What monster?"

"A monster by the name of The Black Mamba. A man so evil that even Hell would not have him."

"Is he a real man?" he asked.

She swallowed hard and took a deep breath.

"Oh yes, child, he is very real," she answered.

The Black Mamba was, indeed, a monster.

And he was very real.

The tears from Margaret's expressive brown eyes rolled down her cheeks and eventually soaked her blouse. Some of them landed on her lips, tasted salty and made her swallow hard. The bitter taste made its way down her throat.

Tariq, Fez, and Aseem were crying as well. Tariq looked solemnly at the ground, trying to hold back his sorrow, but watched as his tears hit the dirt below.

"Okay then, I guess this is it," Margaret said, trying her best to be stoic and strong as a good English girl should be.

All three boys nodded their heads in agreement.

Fez looked up and met Margaret's eyes.

"I will never forget you, Margaret Owen. You are my friend for life," he said.

Margaret smiled as best she could and wiped the tears from Fez's cheeks.

"And you will always be in my heart, Fez."

They hugged for a long time. Finally Fez let go, and then Aseem stepped forward.

"You are the only white person I have ever known. But, if all English people are like you, then I would very much like to visit your country someday."

Margaret laughed a little at this.

"You will always be welcome as my guest, Aseem."

The two hugged as Tariq stepped forward, tears streaming from his eyelids.

The two stared at one another for a few seconds, unable to find any words to say their goodbyes.

"You saved my life, Tariq. If not for you, I would still be a slave in the Caid's kasbah. I can never repay you."

"You already have, Margaret. You are my family, and I shall never forget you."

He stepped forward and gave her a long embrace, which made her cry even more.

Malik, not wanting to disrupt the final goodbyes, finally stepped forward.

"Margaret, you belong with your people and your family. Besides, it is too dangerous for you in Morocco. The Caid's spies are everywhere, and you make an easy target. We must deliver you back to your family in England."

She nodded in acknowledgement, as she knew this was true. A pale girl in Morocco stood out like a red grape in a bunch of green ones—especially in the countryside.

Sanaa brought two horses, one for her and one for Margaret.

Pulling herself onto her horse, she promised, "I will deliver her to the ship in Tangier. Do not worry, she will be safe." Looking down at her friends, she drew back the reigns, still a little uncomfortable at such a display of emotion.

"Stick to the countryside, as the Caid will have patrols at every road and town," Malik ordered.

"Of course, I'm not an idiot!" she answered, and this made Malik smile a bit.

Margaret mounted her horse, wiped the tears from her eyes, and waved at the boys, who waved back. The two women descended down the mountainside, eventually disappearing into the thicket and trees.

Tariq stepped forward to Malik. "Will they be safe, just two girls?" he asked.

"I hope so. It is a very dangerous journey, but two women present a much less interesting target than a posse of men. Remember, Sanaa is equal to the force of twenty of the Caid's soldiers," Malik said.

Tariq watched and worried for Margaret. The Caid and his men were everywhere, and would be on the lookout for any fair-skinned girls.

Margaret was being hunted, and she was now heading right into the belly of the Caid's nest.

Caid Ali Tamzali sent for the one person in the world he could trust, his only son, Abd-El-Kadar.

Abd-El-Kadar's name meant "servant of the powerful" in Arabic, and most certainly described his son's position in his father's kingdom.

"I want you to release him," the Caid instructed.

"It will take a king's ransom," his son replied.

"The ransom is in this chest. You are the only person I trust with such a fortune."

His son, a man of twenty, went to the table and opened the chest to discover it filled with gold coins. Shoving his hands deep into the bounty of gold, he slowly brought them up again, enjoying the weight of the coins sifting through his fingers. Abd-El-Kadar was tall and slender, but had the face of a rat. Most felt he was weak, not knowing he inherited his father's ruthlessness toward all of humanity.

"I will leave immediately, Father. And what are my instructions to him?"

The Caid walked to a window and stared out at his desert. Placing his hands behind his back, he slowly turned and walked back to face his son.

"Instruct him to hunt down Malik, the one called Sanaa, and the four who led the escape—Tariq, Fez, Aseem, and the white girl named Margaret. Hunt them down like dogs, and then crush Malik's entire tribe. Make an example of them, so that no one dares to defy me again. Take a small protection of soldiers with you, along with that boy Jawad."

His son bowed and quickly left the room.

There was no time to waste.

Wrath of the Caid

CHAPTER
— *I* —

ENTER THE BLACK MAMBA

Prison du Marac, just outside of Marrakesh

The jail cell stank of mold, body odor, rat feces, and rotten meat. Water dripped from the roof, splashing down on a large mud puddle in the middle of the dirt floor. The cell was small—very small—and there was only one inhabitant.

He sat in the dirt, leaning against a rock wall, his ankles chained together with a strong steel link. His wrists were chained as well, and the sores on his skin had long since scabbed over and formed calluses where the shackles had been tightened much too tightly.

On his back, fresh wounds from his daily whippings created a red smear against the rock wall.

The man's face was deformed. His right ear had been chopped off in battle and only a nub like cauliflower was left in its place. Burn scars covered his massive neck, as well as much of his chest—the result of nearly being burned to death by an angry mob.

He stared into the darkness, as he did each and every day and night. Light was not a luxury afforded to him. In spite of living in this cell for twenty-four hours a day, seven days a week, his entire body was still a mass of muscle. He stood six foot six inches tall and not one hair grew on his bald head.

He heard the sound of footsteps walking down the hallway that stopped at his jail cell door. A key clumsily opened the lock, and a figure appeared in his cell.

"Come with me," the voice whispered.

The man couldn't see the face in the darkness until a match was lit, illuminating a face to the voice. It was a guard the man had never seen before.

"Come with me now," the guard instructed.

The man stood up and slid over to the guard, only able to walk in the baby footsteps his shackles would allow.

"We don't have much time. You must hurry," the guard said, as he leaned down to unlock first the ankle shackles and then the ones to his wrists.

The two men walked out of the cell, down a hallway, up some stairs, down another hallway, finally reaching a steel door. The guard unlocked the door, swung it open, and urged the prisoner through it.

"Quick, go to that building across the street," the guard instructed before closing the door and locking it.

The door closed behind him, the guard made a cross with his fingers and said a silent prayer, *God forgive me for what I have done.*

The man walked quickly to the building as instructed. Turning a corner, he stared into the face of Abd-El-Kadar.

He smiled slightly.

"I suppose I owe your father a great debt," the man said.

"You do," came the reply.

The man said nothing to this, preferring to stare at Jawad and the group of soldiers.

"Who is this boy?" he asked.

"He is why you are now free. There was an assault on the kasbah; many of my father's soldiers were killed and they continue to attack our patrols. This boy knows of the rebels and their whereabouts. He will escort you and you will exterminate them."

The man stared at Jawad, who was doing his best to look fearless, and doing a very bad job of it. Even on his horse, Jawad was tall and handsome, with olive skin and short, black hair. Yet there was blankness in his eyes, the look of someone who had seen a tough life.

Abd-El-Kadar nodded to one of the guards who stepped forward with a giant black horse complete with an exquisite leather saddle. A burlap bag hung from the side of the horse, and a sword was sheathed on the back. It was this man's horse. Putting on his clothes, the man jumped on the back of his ride and looked at Jawad and the soldiers.

"These soldiers are mine to command?" he asked.

"Half are yours, the other half will escort me back to the kasbah," Abd-El-Kadar answered.

The man brought his horse around and stopped in front of Jawad.

"Come boy, I want to know everything about these rebels. You will tell me as we ride."

Jawad gulped and started to feel himself sweat. His heart pounded in his chest. The man was even more frightful in person than Jawad ever could have imagined.

Jawad followed the black horse into the fog of the night.

He was now the servant of The Black Mamba.

CHAPTER
— 2 —

A NEW PASSENGER

The *Angelina Rouge* held steady at eight knots, cutting through whitecaps and bobbing up and down with the rhythm of the waves.

Charles Owen stood at the wheel, surveying the ocean, enjoying the breeze at his face. His stature was erect and perfect, and his blond hair tossed back and forth over his eyes. From months at sea, his skin had turned from fair to tan and crow's feet were now prominently featured around his eyes.

Charles Owen was a pirate.

In his former life he'd been a colonel in the British army. That seemed like a lifetime ago. Now, along with Captain Basil and the crew of the *Angelina Rouge,* he captured ships and gave their wares to poor villagers who needed the bounty for survival. Basil was seen as a saint by the peasants and citizenry along the African coast.

Even Charles was gaining a reputation with the locals; they had started to call him "Abyad Amir," which means "White Prince."

What Charles also learned was that there was a bounty on his head from the British navy. After scuttling an English cruiser, one of that ship's crewmembers had whispered to him that they had received orders to kill Charles Owen on sight. Charles didn't know if this news had reached the civilian papers or press, as he didn't have access to any newspapers in his travels. He only knew that he couldn't return to England under these circumstances.

His biggest concern lay with his family. Months ago, Charles sent a letter to his wife, but doubted it had ever been received. There was no way he could send a telegraph without alerting the British authorities to his whereabouts. Every night Charles felt a pit in his stomach from the pain of missing his wife and children. He had not seen them since he sent them overboard all those months ago, hoping to ensure their safety. Through various contacts, he did get word that they had made it to the hotel in Tangier, but that was all he knew. He had no idea of their where-abouts or if they remained safe.

Charles especially missed his daughter Margaret. She was at such an impressionable age, and he felt she needed her father.

As he scanned the ocean, he noticed a boat far ahead, just off the port bow. It was a small boat, probably that of a fisherman, and the sails were luffing in the wind.

"Aquina, there's a boat up ahead just off the port bow, do you see it?" Charles called out.

Aquina, the first mate, took out his monocular and aimed it at the spot where Charles was pointing.

"Aye sir, just a wee fishing boat, shall we take a look?"

"Yes, prepare a crew to board her."

Charles turned the wheel just slightly, in order to head upwind, and prepared to bring the *Angelina Rouge* about to board the small vessel.

"What's all this fuss about?" Basil asked, emerging from below, still buttoning his shirt.

Basil wore a white cotton shirt covered by a burgundy frock coat with large black buttons. The coat went down to just above his knees, and his gray trousers were held up by a large black leather belt with a thick silver square for a belt buckle. A large dagger, about twelve inches long, lay safely tucked into his belt. His hair was long, falling down his neck in the back, and peppered with streaks of gray on the sides. He'd grown a goatee in the last two months and it made him look the part of a Spanish nobleman rather than a wanted pirate. If there were a word that could describe his physical appearance, it would be "distinguished." His manners and speech were impeccable.

"Some kind of fishing boat that looks to be abandoned," Charles replied.

Basil took the monocular as the boat grew closer. He didn't see any-one aboard, but did see some fishing nets dragging over the side. Other than that, it looked unremarkable.

The *Rouge* sailed within one hundred feet of her and came to. Then Basil, Charles, and three other crewmen rowed to the boat's stern. All were armed with pistols in the event of any unpleasantries.

Tying off the dinghy, all boarded the tiny boat—only to be met with a most miserable scene.

Blood streaked across her deck. A bloody knife lay in the middle, the area splattered with blood on both sides. The fishing nets were untied; half lay on the deck with the other half dragging in the water.

Charles immediately went to the door of the hold. With his pistol raised in front of him, he walked down the five steps into the cabin. It was dark, but not dark enough to blind him. Small and cramped, the hold would only have room for four or five crewmembers. To his left he saw the galley, with a small table, one counter, and some cupboards. To his right was a door that he assumed led to storage, and two beds lay on either side directly in front of him.

On the floor, lying face down, was the body of a man.

"Basil, look at this!" Charles cried out.

Charles went to the man and immediately felt the pulse in his neck—he was alive! Charles gently turned the man over. He appeared to be unconscious, but was breathing normally. Blood covered his shirt and Charles could see a nasty knife wound on his shoulder.

"Let's get him back to the boat. It looks like the handiwork of the British navy," Basil ordered.

Charles rummaged quickly through the hold but found nothing of consequence. The crewmembers and Basil loaded the man into the dinghy and prepared to return to the *Rouge*.

"What about his boat?" Charles asked.

"We have to leave it. We are too far out at sea. Besides, I don't want to split up the crew—these are dangerous waters!" Basil replied.

Charles quickly joined the others and was soon back on the deck of the *Angelina Rouge* with the injured man, who was taken to the medical hold, where his bloody clothes were replaced with fresh ones and his knife wound was stitched up. There was an angry welt on his head.

After ten minutes he came to.

"Where am I?" the man asked, groggily.

"On the deck of the *Angelina Rouge*," Basil answered.

"How did I get here?"

"We found your boat floating in the sea. You were unconscious down below."

"What of the rest of the crew?"

Basil and Charles looked at one another before Charles replied.

"There was no sign of your crew. There was some blood on the deck. I am sorry."

The man looked away and tears formed in his eyes.

"British navy?" Charles asked.

"Yes," the man replied.

"What is your name?" Charles asked, gently.

"Cortez."

"Cortez, we had to leave your boat. You're in no shape to single-hand her and we're too far out at sea to command her into port. Unfortunately, you'll have to join our crew for a bit before we can find a way to return you to your home," Basil explained.

Cortez nodded in agreement and tried to get up.

"No, no, you stay down here for today. That's a nasty wound and it looks like they hit you good on the side of the head. They probably took you for dead. It's a miracle you're alive," Charles explained.

"I don't remember much. A British warship boarded us. We are just simple fishermen, and we didn't think they would want anything. That's when they started beating the crew. I was hit upside the head and that's all I can remember."

Charles cringed. Unfortunately, it had become an all-too-familiar story: the British navy killing innocents.

"Get some sleep, my friend," Charles told him and left the room.

Cortez nodded in appreciation. He was a younger man, about thirty. He smelled of fish and wore simple peasant clothes. His face was completely ordinary and it seemed there was nothing remarkable about him at all.

Only, there was something very, very remarkable about Cortez.

A Month Earlier

Lieutenant Dreyfuss of the British Royal Navy stood in a pub called The White Whale. The interior of the pub was dark and foreboding, with shadows casting an eerie atmosphere from candlelight. The air stank of ale, whiskey, and fried fish. A rat, nibbling stale bread, stopped to observe Dreyfuss. The Lieutenant was dressed to the nines in his British naval uniform, and openly showed disdain for such a dank establishment. The collection of rogues, pirates, cutthroats, and thieves staring at him made him sick. He had called this gathering here, because this particular pub was a known as a waypoint for seafaring criminals who congregated here for meetings, traded bounty, and even shanghaied crew.

There was one thing most of them had in common—they were bounty hunters, desperate men who would hunt down criminals for a price.

Dreyfuss was flanked by six British soldiers as a show of force.

The pub was packed. A steady murmur increased in pitch as everyone speculated on what the Great British Empire would want with their brand of scum.

"OK now, I'm sure you're all interested in what I have to say, no doubt for the profit involved," Dreyfuss began.

"Is there any other reason we'd be here?" a voice rang out from the back, and everyone laughed.

Soon the pub grew silent, and all eyes were fixed on Dreyfuss.

"We are seeking two fugitives from justice—two vagabonds who must be brought to justice by the British crown. We are offering a bounty of 100,000 British pounds for each individual."

There was a gasp from the crowd. This was ten, or even twenty times the amount usually offered as a reward.

"Dead or alive?" a voice asked.

"Alive, with half the amount if they're dead."

"Who are they, then?" asked one man.

"A man who goes by the name of Basil, and another by the name of Owen," answered Dreyfuss.

"We all know Captain Basil, but who is this Owen?"

"Don't concern yourself with who Owen is. Just concern yourself with how you're going to capture both of them."

"Okay then, any idea what they look like?"

"We've prepared wanted posters with descriptions of both men and the boat. This should answer all of your questions," said Dreyfuss, holding up the poster for all to see.

"What do we do once we've captured them? Take them to a British embassy?"

"No, you must bring them to me directly. Do not take them to an embassy or any other British establishment."

The crowd murmured some more and took in the information they'd been given.

"And how do we find you?"

"I've included a list of ports that my ship will be in, and approximate dates. Bring the bodies to me and you'll get your reward."

As Dreyfuss surveyed the crowd, a question came from the back from a man dressed in a black velvet cloak, with greased-back brown hair. A Spanish piece of eight played between his fingers.

"You want the *Rouge*?" the cloaked man asked.

Dreyfuss shifted on his toes so he could see to the back of the room where the man stood.

"You know of the *Angelina Rouge*?" he asked the stranger.

"Everyone knows of the *Rouge* and 'er captain. My question is, do you want her?"

"If you can deliver her to me, then, yes, I'll offer an additional 100,000 pounds for the capture of the *Angelina Rouge*."

Dreyfuss stepped a couple of steps closer to get a good look at the man. It was Cortez!

"What is your name, sir?"

"My name is Sharif Al Montaro."

All eyes in the pub shifted to the man called Sharif Al Montaro, who would go by the alias of Cortez.

Even Dreyfuss was impressed.

"I have heard of you, Mister Montaro. Your reputation as a bounty hunter is renowned across the Mediterranean."

"As is yours, Lieutenant Dreyfuss," Montaro smiled and lifted his glass of red wine towards Dreyfuss.

Dreyfuss smiled at this gesture. Secretly, he was completely satisfied that one of the most ruthless criminals in the world was now working for him.

The other patrons shifted in their seats and couldn't keep their eyes off of Mister Montaro. They all knew his name, his reputation, and his legend. This was a man who had hunted and killed French generals, African warlords, Chinese opium smugglers and, most recently, a Spanish prince.

He was a man as cunning as he was ruthless.

The meeting adjourned and Montaro quickly went to work.

To launch his plan into action, Montaro went to a neighboring village and quickly changed from his regular outfit into that of a simple fisherman. In the dead of night, he stole a fishing boat and supplies, and began to crisscross the Mediterranean, along routes he knew to be frequented by the *Rouge*. He carried out this meticulous work for a full month, checking in with fishing villages along his routes, asking his network of spies if they'd seen the *Rouge*.

Three days earlier, one of his informers had told him the *Rouge* had been to their village and was headed across the water to France. Montaro knew they usually took a circular route to avoid running into British patrols. If he took a straight route he could probably catch them.

He was fortunate enough to spy them through his telescope one day before they saw him. This small stroke of good luck gave him enough time to splash some tuna blood on the deck to make it look like his crew had been murdered.

His plan worked to perfection.

"Cortez" was now a passenger on the *Angelina Rouge* and a guest of Captain Basil and Charles Owen.

Resting in the hold, he started to put his plan together, dreaming of how he would turn in Basil, Charles, and the *Rouge* for more bounty than he'd seen in his entire life.

CHAPTER
— 3 —

THE EYE OF LAROQUE

Margaret and Sanaa rode fast and hard through the darkness. They avoided all roads and towns and kept to mountain trails and obscure valley passages. Normally a three day ride to Tangier, their trip would take five days with such long routes.

Margaret was silent during most of the journey. There were so many things going through her mind that she had no time for words. She felt melancholy and regretful at leaving the tribe and her friends, but she knew Malik was right; it was too dangerous for her in Morocco. Still, it didn't feel right, leaving her friends in such danger.

She thought about how it would feel the first time she finally saw her mother and brother and, hopefully, her father. She thought of her home in London and her best friend, Hillie Dansbury. How she and Hillie would have sleepovers and make little tea parties together. She wondered how it would feel to sleep in her own bed again, in her own house.

Margaret yearned to feel normal again.

Sanaa was not much for conversation, which made it much easier for Margaret to get lost in her thoughts. Since the escape from the kasbah, Sanaa was even more silent and withdrawn, almost like a wild animal who knew it was being hunted.

On the final night of their journey, Sanaa thought they were being followed by the Caid's soldiers. She led Margaret up a steep mountain pass and zigzagged for hours through the forest. A river passed through the valley, and she made a point of crisscrossing through the river to throw off their scent. The equestrian skills Margaret learned in England were really coming in handy—Sanaa couldn't begin to imagine such a trip without that background.

They never saw any soldiers, and after a long day, Sanaa finally felt safe enough to set up camp. She continued to be nervous and wary, and scouted the area just to be sure they were safe. They did not make a fire, to avoid signaling their location.

At last, Sanaa sat next to Margaret, and together they enjoyed a dinner of smoked lamb and apricots.

"When we are in Tangier, please keep your face covered. We do not want to attract attention to ourselves," Sanaa ordered.

"Do you know if my mother is in Tangier?" Margaret asked.

"I do not know, Margaret. We will try and send word for her, but we must get you on that steamship as early as possible. It is very dangerous for you to stay in Morocco and we must return you to England right away."

Margaret listened intently and felt the seriousness in Sanaa's voice. It was true. She was wanted by the Caid, and he would stop at nothing to capture her.

"Get some sleep, Margaret. It will be long day tomorrow," Sanaa said, and the two of them fell fast asleep under the watchful sky of stars. After the hard day of riding, Margaret immediately fell into a deep sleep.

They awoke the next morning and made the final journey to Tangier. Margaret covered her face beneath a veil and did her best to look inconspicuous. It was the first time she had been in a city since the day she was kidnapped, and she was overwhelmed by the smells and sights and sounds. She had grown accustomed to life in the mountains and the tranquility that went along with such a simple life. She enjoyed the peace of simply walking among the trees, feeling the grass at her feet, and listening to the sounds of the forest. Her favorite time of day was always the morning, when she would awake with frost still on the ground. Wrapping herself in a blanket, she would walk to a cliff edge and watch as the sun came up over the horizon. Sipping some herb tea, she would dream of her home and her family, enjoying the silence and the beauty of the world.

The two rode through the many streets and alleys of Tangier until they came to an old building. Tying off their horses, they went inside and quickly shut the door behind them.

They were in Zijuan's orphanage.

"There is not a moment to waste," Zijuan urged, coming in from the outside, and hurriedly taking their possessions.

Zijuan was probably close to fifty years old, but didn't look a day over thirty, with skin almost entirely devoid of wrinkles. She wore a black shirt that hung over her arms and simple white pants that draped over her bare feet. A mane of black hair was pulled back in a ponytail, accentuating her Asian features and eyes. Zijuan had a presence that was calm, yet firm and authoritative. Sanaa was instantly deferential to her and seemed to completely relax in her company.

"A steamship leaves at seven o'clock tonight, and you must be on it, Margaret. There are inquiries about you everywhere," said Zijuan.

Margaret, shocked that anyone would be interested in her, felt an immediate rush of panic. She was also a bit surprised that Zijuan had completely dispensed with the pleasantries and was getting right down to business. Margaret had heard so much about Zijuan from Tariq that she was very curious to know more about her.

"I must see if my mother is still at the Hotel Continental," she answered.

"It is impossible, you would be spotted immediately, and I don't know if I can protect you there," Zijuan answered sternly.

"I can go," Sanaa volunteered.

Zijuan stared at Sanaa. How she had grown into such a brave warrior from the orphan she had rescued all those years ago.

"You must be discreet," she replied.

"I will go now. Please prepare Margaret for her journey."

Sanaa made her way back out of the orphanage, onto her horse, and back into the streets of Tangier. She rode directly to the Hotel Continental without wasting so much as a minute.

The hotel was opulent, a magnificent sight on the banks of the Mediterranean. It was usually full of tourists, but over the last two weeks, as rumors grew that France would send more troops into Morocco, most of the tourists had left in a rush.

Sanaa tied up her horse and walked quickly to the concierge. She did her best to look anonymous.

"I am looking for an English woman," she said to the man.

He appeared fastidious and neat, and wore round spectacles. He was accustomed to attending to rich and spoiled Europeans, and was unimpressed with the peasant woman in front of him.

"What is the name?" he asked.

"Louise Owen."

He stared at Sanaa for a long time. What could she possibly want with Louise Owen?

"I'm sorry, we don't have anyone by that name," he lied to her. He didn't like some poor woman bothering one of their most popular guests.

Sanaa quickly and quietly grabbed his wrist and started to bend it backwards. The pain immediately shot up his arm and he winced.

"I have no time for your games. I believe you do have someone by the name of Louise Owen at this hotel, and it is vital I talk with her right now," Sanaa hissed at him.

The man immediately understood the gravity of the situation. Sanaa looked him straight in the eyes while maintaining her grip on his wrist, and there was a seriousness in her voice that could not be misinterpreted.

"I am not here to hurt or hassle Louise Owen. I have a message for her and I am in a hurry," she calmly explained.

The man nodded and Sanaa released his wrist. He looked over for a bellboy, whispered in his ear, and he quickly disappeared through a door.

"Mrs. Owen will be down momentarily," the concierge assured her.

"Thank you," Sanaa said, and waited patiently by the stairs.

Moments later, Louise Owen walked down the stairs, looking confused as to who could be asking for her.

"Louise Owen?"

"What is this all about?"

Sanaa whisked Louise over to a more secluded area and sat down at a table. Louise was still apprehensive as to why this fierce-looking woman wanted anything to do with her.

Sanaa lowered her voice to a whisper.

"My name is Sanaa. I have Margaret. She is safe, but in much danger. We must get her out of Morocco immediately. There is a steamship departing for England tonight at seven o'clock on Dock 8, can you meet her there? I will write down the exact instructions for you."

Sanaa began writing down the time and place of the rendezvous and then handed the information to Louise, who held the piece of paper in her hand, too paralyzed to absorb the news that had been given to her.

The look on Louise Owen's face was one of both shock and joy. She had been frantically searching for her daughter for over six weeks and had nearly given up hope. Now, this strange woman appeared from nowhere telling her that Margaret was safe?

"But how? Where is she now? Where has she been?"

"I don't have time to explain to you. Can you purchase her ticket and meet us there?"

"Yes, yes of course. Do you really have Margaret?" Louise finally asked, almost pleading that this was the truth.

"Yes, I have her. She is safe and misses you very much. Just meet us at the dock and she can explain everything to you. I must go now. There is no time to waste."

Sanaa stood up and, without so much as a handshake or hug, briskly left the building and got back on her horse, leaving Louise dumbfounded as to what had just transpired.

Louise immediately walked to her room and began to pack for the journey.

What neither Sanaa nor Louise had noticed was a man watching the two of them from across the room. He was thin, dressed in a white suit with a black tie, with his black hair greased back. He casually smoked a cigarette while drinking a gin and tonic, trying his best to not appear interested in their conversation.

When they had gone, he went to the tablet of paper that Sanaa had used to write the note upon. At first glance, there was nothing on it. He produced a pencil and scribbled over the blank page, which caused a faded inscription to appear on the page. The message was only partly legible, but it gave him all the information he needed.

It read, "Dock 8, 7:00pm."

Immediately the man went to his room.

His name was Mr. LaRoque. He was the same man who had targeted Margaret for abduction from the hotel. As a shadowy individual who lived and thrived in the Moroccan underground, he was more than aware that Margaret was wanted by the Caid.

Now he knew just where and when to find her.

Abd-El-Kadar sat on his horse, flanked by a dozen soldiers. He was at the gates of the kasbah, about to embark on yet another raid on a village. He had been making these raids frequently, as a way to impress his father.

His father, the Caid Ali Tamzali, stood by as his son prepared to ride off.

"It would be better if you stayed in the kasbah, my son. It is dangerous in the countryside."

Abd-El-Kadar circled his horse around.

"Do not worry, Father. I want to find these rebels more than anything. I will make you proud!"

"Do not worry about such a thing. I am always proud of my only son."

Abd-El-Kadar smiled and led the charge out of the gates.

The Caid walked back to his chambers flanked at all times by a security of six soldiers. Secretly, he was very worried about his son. While willing, his son was not a capable swordsman and he wasn't with the usual number of troops. Normally, he would send fifty or one hundred troops with his son as protection.

However, since the raid by the rebels, and his ransom of the Mamba, the Caid was actually having financial difficulties. He couldn't continue to support his usual army and had let go of half of his troops. His rifles had grown rusty and his ammunition supply was low.

The Caid knew he had to think of something to gain back his strength.

France had maintained a limited presence in Morocco for decades. Mostly, they had a couple of forts along the coastline. They didn't really do much, but there were rumors that was about to change. Already, the Caid had word that the French were preparing an all-out invasion of Morocco.

The Caid sent word to his contact in the French ministry about a potential alliance. If he could become partners with the French, his strength would increase and he could repair the damage he suffered during the raid on his kasbah.

It was a risky strategy, but he didn't have a choice.

He was becoming desperate.

The Mamba, as he was known, reserving "Black Mamba" for more formal occasions, sat at a campfire, roasting a rabbit on the end of a stick, mesmerized by the flames.

"Tell me of Sanaa," he instructed Jawad.

"Their most able assassin. She is beautiful and deadly. She is the one who freed Margaret from the prison."

"And this Margaret, just a simple English girl who was captured to be a slave in the kasbah?"

"Yes."

"And the three boys—Tariq, Aseem, and Fez—you know them well?"

"Yes."

The Mamba spat disgustedly onto the sand.

"It is an embarrassment to have some children and a woman escape from the kasbah. If I had been in charge, it never would have happened."

Jawad didn't know what to say to the Mamba. He was afraid of him and hoped his words wouldn't insult him.

"If you don't mind, Sire, why were you imprisoned?" Jawad asked.

The Mamba smiled at the question.

"Some French soldiers mistook me for a simple peasant and tried to make a servant of me. I taught them a lesson that cost them their miserable lives. It took forty of them to finally surround me in a shack in the hills."

Jawad gulped hard and didn't know how to continue.

The Mamba looked at him. He didn't usually like boys, but he liked Jawad. He was mature for his age and he had ambition. He could see that Jawad was a natural-born killer.

"So you wanted to be in the Caid's cavalry? Why? Usually slaves just want one thing—freedom," the Mamba asked.

"I don't have a home, so where else would I go? Besides, I can see the power and riches of the Caid."

"So, that is what you want? Power and riches?"

"Doesn't everyone?" Jawad answered.

The Mamba smiled even more, pleased with Jawad's answer.

"Have you ever killed anyone?" he asked the boy.

Jawad thought about how to answer this. He didn't want to appear weak, yet he knew the Mamba would see through him if he told a lie.

"No Sire, I have not."

"Power and riches only come to those who can be absolutely merciless. This is a hard country for hard men."

Jawad listened intently. He was impressed with the Mamba and was attracted to his strength. The Mamba, in turn, thought that Jawad reminded him of his younger self.

He only needed a bit of seasoning.

"People don't respect reason. They don't respect anything except force. Show one ounce of mercy and you will lose their obedience. This is why we must hunt down and kill these rebels. We must show everyone in the land they will be subjected to the same fate if they defy our authority."

Jawad nodded with understanding.

"I want you to be the one to kill Aseem, Fez, and especially Tariq. It must be you. If you can do that, then I will allow you to be my apprentice," the Mamba told him.

His eyes widened; Jawad was amazed to hear this! Up to this point, the Mamba had just glared and grunted at him. To be offered an opportunity to be his apprentice was more than he ever could have hoped for. He was the second most powerful man in their region, next to the Caid, and to be his apprentice would be to touch the sweetness of true power.

"How do we find them?"

"No doubt they have moved their camp. Malik sounds like an intelligent enough man, a rarity in these parts. We will send out a network of spies and begin setting traps for them. But first, there is an order of business we must attend to."

"What is that?'

"I need to visit a witch who may be able to bring them to us."

At precisely six thirty in the evening, a fog rolled in on the docks of Tangier, giving the entire harbor an eerie and forbidding feeling. Sanaa, Margaret, and Zijuan were waiting in the shadows, still wary of being identified.

That's when they saw Louise Owen and her son David walk to the front of Dock 8. A long ramp led to a walking platform that went to the ship. A few passengers passed them; otherwise, it was completely desolate.

Sanaa, Margaret, and Zijuan quickly ran to Louise and David. Margaret didn't have a thing packed! Once Louise saw her daughter, she dropped her bags and sprinted to her with her arms outstretched.

Mother and daughter embraced, both crying. Louise held Margaret's face in her hands. She couldn't believe she was actually holding her daughter.

"I can't believe it's you!" she exclaimed, laughing, and held her daughter some more.

"I have so much to tell you, Mother!" Margaret laughed. She grabbed and hugged her younger brother David, who was still a bit awestruck in seeing his sister.

"Come, you must go now!" Zijuan instructed, picking up two of Louise Owen's bags and starting to walk down the walkway.

"I don't think little Miss Owen will be going anywhere just yet."

The voice came from behind them. It was a man's voice, dark and husky.

All of a sudden, four men surrounded them, each holding a stick. All looked rugged and dirty, like men who would do anything for a coin.

"Come quietly now, little girl. The Caid would like to have a word with you," the man sneered. He was Moroccan and a gold tooth shone front and center in his smile.

As he reached for Margaret, Zijuan deflected his arm, turned in a one-eighty, and broke his nose with her elbow. Stepping forward, she placed her right leg in front of his torso and flipped him over her, holding his left wrist as he fell, breaking it on impact.

Sanaa took the man closest to her, stretched her palms out wide, and brought them together on the sides of his head, immediately smashing both of his eardrums. He went to the ground in a ball, shouting and crying, the pain so excruciating.

Another man made a charge at Zijuan, who simply brought up her foot to his groin, doubling him over, then broke his jaw with her left knee.

Sanaa, not wanting to be outdone, produced three quick kicks to the man closest to her; the first kick knocked the stick from his hand, the second buckled his knee cap, and the final one smashed and shattered his wind pipe.

It was over in a matter of seconds.

"Come, we must go, the Caid knows of Margaret's whereabouts," Zijuan ordered and each woman grabbed a bag and began running to the steamship.

"Margaret, who are these women? Where did they learn to fight like that?" Louise asked, thoroughly impressed with the display of deadly martial arts she had just witnessed.

"No time to explain, Mother, I'll tell you everything on the boat!"

They made it to the ticket taker, where Louise immediately produced three first-class tickets. He checked their passports and checked them in.

Margaret stopped to hug Sanaa.

"I will never forget all you have taught me, Sanaa. You are the most powerful woman I have ever met."

Sanaa, never one for emotion, nonetheless returned her embrace.

"I don't know you very well Zijuan, but Tariq thinks of you as his mother and talks so much of you. I can't thank you enough for helping me escape," she said, hugging Zijuan as well.

"Be safe Margaret, I am glad you are with your family."

Running up the ramp, the Owen family disappeared over the deck, leaving Sanaa and Zijuan alone.

"Do you think she will be safe?" Sanaa asked.

"I think so. The Caid wouldn't have a need to chase her to England. Besides, he wouldn't want to make a scene by abducting her on a busy steamship. Come, we have much to discuss," Zijuan replied.

The two women left the docks and returned to Zijuan's orphanage.

In the shadows, Mr. LaRoque watched as his henchmen were defeated by two women. Hiding behind a garbage bin, he was helpless as Margaret and her family left on the steamer, his prey on her way to England.

He would make it a point to keep an eye on Zijuan to find out more about this woman who interfered in his business.

CHAPTER
— 4 —

UNPLEASANT NEWS

Tariq, Malik, Fez, Aseem, and twelve other resistance fighters lay crouched on a hill overlooking a village. They had been in this position for over two hours, barely moving, spying on the horizon. The boys carried bows and arrows, which lay at their side, ready to pounce into action. They all felt nervous and excited at the same time. This was the first time that Malik had allowed them to join on a raid, as a rite of passage of sorts. They would be allowed to attack the Caid's soldiers—that is, if they ever showed.

Spies told Malik that a raid was planned on this village, this very morning. The Caid's men usually attacked at dawn, taking advantage of an element of surprise. Malik had moved his men into position in the dark of night and camouflaged them by caking their face with mud and covering their bodies in leaves and grass. Even from twenty feet away, they were almost invisible to the naked eye.

The village had yet to stir as the sun came up over the horizon. Slowly, smoke began to fire from various chimneys as the villagers prepared for their day.

That's when Malik felt it.

It was only a little shake, a rhythmic, thump-thump-thump far off in the distance.

The distinct sound of horses, probably fifteen or more, about half a mile away.

"They are coming," he whispered.

Aseem and Tariq looked at one another and smiled. Yes, they were nervous, but they were also anxious to taste battle for the first time. They had been training for months and months. They were happy because finally, Malik felt they were ready. He had specifically instructed all three boys to hang back and observe, more than to engage. He didn't want them in the thick of it.

He let out a whistle that sounded like a crow—a signal to the other dozen resistance fighters that were hidden on the opposite side of the village.

The Caid's men would be surrounded.

After five minutes, the Caid's soldiers rode into the village, with conch blowing, dust spitting up from the horses' hooves, and men yelling. There were about sixteen of them, all on horseback, all carrying rifles.

They rode around the village, yelling and terrifying the villagers; one man tried to run out of his tent and a soldier shot him in the back. A family came out: a father, mother, and two young boys—bowing to the troops and begging for mercy.

After much fanfare, the riders stopped and dismounted. As was their custom, they left their rifles on their horses, in order to save bullets. Each carried a sword for their dirty work.

All were dressed in the usual colors of the Caid—crimson and black—all except one. He wore white, with a gold veil over his face. The other soldiers deferred to him and allowed him to talk to the villager.

"Where is your village chieftain?" he asked.

"I am the chieftain, my lord. Please, as you can see, we are poor people and can barely survive. I have a bushel of figs and some dried fish. I know it is nothing, but it is all I have to offer," the man begged.

"I do not care for your food, peasant. I want information. Information on the whereabouts of the rebel filth that dot these mountains," the leader yelled at him.

Before the leader could continue, he heard something whizz through the air; without warning, one of his men let out an oomph sound and stumbled forward in the sand, an arrow shot clean through his neck.

Six more arrows found their mark and six more soldiers fell to the ground.

The man in white ducked for cover behind his horse as more and more of his soldiers fell. He tried to mount his horse but was tackled and sent to the ground.

Soon, only four soldiers remained, surrounded by Malik and his men. Tariq, Aseem, and Fez were part of the group, although they stayed a bit to the rear. It was a complete onslaught by their group—the Caid's men never had a chance. A dozen of them had been struck down and not one rebel had died.

The battle had lasted only ten seconds, and it was over.

"Looking for us?" Malik smiled and taunted.

"You must be Malik," the man in white answered.

"I am, and who might you be?" Malik asked.

"Abd-El-Kadar," the man hissed.

Malik stared at the man. He was young and tall and carried himself as a noble. Could it be that he had actually captured the Caid's son?

"Abd-El-Kadar? I'm surprised you would do the miserable deed yourself. I thought you a coward, just like your wretched father," Malik spat at him.

"Enough!" Abd-El-Kadar screamed, raising his sword and swiping it at Malik, who easily parried it and moved away.

"Not bad with a sword, but your anger will be the best of you," Malik coolly answered.

"Fight me like a man, not like a coward who shoots at me with an arrow!"

"Or like a jackal who slaughters innocent unarmed villagers," Malik answered.

"Fight me, so I can feel my steel run through your miserable body!" Abd-El-Kadar screamed.

The two men circled one another with drawn swords, each sizing the other up.

"Malik, enough with this nonsense. Let's kill him and be done with it!" one of the rebels screamed.

"No, for this one, I will take my time," Malik answered.

Abd-El-Kadar sprang first, swinging in a three-sixty, using his robe to disguise his sword, and stabbing straight toward Malik's heart.

Malik simply stepped aside, out of danger.

Next, the Caid's son brought his sword straight down, like he was chopping wood, lunging to meet Malik's skull. Malik merely stepped backwards and allowed the blade to hit the ground.

"It's quite different fighting someone who can defend himself, isn't it? Not like slaughtering innocent women and children who are defenseless," Malik said with ice in his voice.

Abd-El-Kadar thrust at him with four wild swings that met nothing but air.

"Your technique is sloppy. You telegraph your moves. You are slow and clumsy, just as your father is fat and stupid," Malik laughed at him.

Abd-El-Kadar let out a giant scream and continued to flail wildly at Malik, with each swing being met or deflected with ease.

"Fighting against the living is quite different from fighting against a tree—the living fight back!" Malik scolded and, with a flick of the wrist, brought his blade down on Abd-El-Kadar's left arm, causing a four inch gash that spurted blood.

Abd-El-Kadar looked at the wound and went a shade of white. This was the first wound he had ever encountered in battle. None of his former battles had really been battles—they were more like massacres.

"Shouldn't the Caid's son be traveling with a much larger garrison? Is that because your father's kingdom is crumbling before his eyes?" Malik mocked him.

"My father will have his revenge. The Mamba will have you gutted and killed, you dog!" Abd-El-Kadar hissed.

Malik stepped back a few steps to take in this information.

"When I meet the Mamba, I'll be sure to tell him that," Malik said, and with two moves, drove his sword into the belly of Abd-El-Kadar.

His white robe soon turned a dark shade of red as blood soaked the fabric. Dropping to his knees, his mouth fell open and he desperately gasped for air. Falling forward, he reached out with both hands and fell to the ground—dead!

Fez, Tariq, and Aseem all gasped with awe. Malik had destroyed the Caid's son in a matter of seconds. This was the Caid's son! The entire group stared at his dead body, still unbelieving of Malik's accomplishment.

"Finish the others, take their weapons, and head for the mountains," Malik ordered.

"Malik, you killed the Caid's son. That is amazing!" Tariq exclaimed.

"It is a moral victory and nothing else. The truth is, Abd-El-Kadar was as stupid as he was incompetent. I have stirred the hornet's nest, but I have not weakened him. Abd-El-Kadar was never a military leader—he was just a spoiled child," Malik answered.

"What of the Mamba?" Aseem asked.

Malik took a moment before answering.

"The Mamba is a different story," he replied, looking Aseem in the eyes, and then walking off.

Tariq followed him, interested to hear what Malik had to say about the Mamba.

"Malik, is the Mamba really free?"

Malik stopped, adrenaline still rushing through his veins from the sword fight. It gave him no pleasure to kill a man, but the Caid's son was most definitely deserving of such a fate.

"I imagine he is."

"But, I thought he was sentenced to die by the French?" Tariq asked.

"I'm sure the Caid figured out a way to free him," Malik answered, clearly exasperated by this news.

"What does this mean for the tribe?"

"It means we must be that much more careful and clever. The Mamba is as smart as he is vicious, and I have no doubt that he will be coming for us."

Tariq nodded his head, sobered by such news. Malik saw the worry on his face and lifted his chin up with his index finger.

"Tariq, this was a very good day. It was a successful ambush and we weakened the Caid. We will defeat the Mamba one way or another. Please, do not trouble yourself with this. Celebrate with the others."

Tariq looked up and felt much better hearing the confidence in Malik's voice. Turning, he joined Aseem and Fez in loading the loot and making their way back to camp.

Malik, however, was anything but confident upon hearing this news. The Mamba would be looking for him, as well as the boys, and would stop at nothing until they were all dead.

He made the decision to move the camp yet again and begin doubling his sentries. He did not want to be caught off-guard.

Zijuan and Sanaa sat at a table in Zijuan's orphanage. They had quickly made their way back after seeing off Margaret and her family, and Sanaa had stayed at the orphanage for a week to help Zijuan.

"You must return to the tribe," Zijuan instructed her.

"When?" Sanaa asked.

"Immediately. Tell Malik to begin making peace with the other tribes. Like a wounded animal, the Caid is now more dangerous than ever."

Sanaa took a sip of her tea. She enjoyed being with Zijuan and being back at the orphanage. She could truly relax in the presence of her mentor, and enjoyed the relative peace it provided her.

"Okay," she answered.

"I will keep my contacts in the city and try to obtain as much information as possible. It is a very important time...either we damage the Caid right away, or we allow him to become even more powerful."

Zijuan's voice was serious and stern. Sanaa understood she had a kind of psychic gift and was in tune with the happenings and energies around her. She was tranquil, and her voice was little more than a whisper.

Sanaa could not tell if Zijuan was worried or simply very focused. Either way, she would depart in the morning and return to Malik and the tribe.

Cortez needed a way to get the *Angelina Rouge,* and Basil and Charles, into the hands of Dreyfuss.

Basil offered to drop him at a nearby port so he could find a ride home. But Cortez convinced Basil that he would make an excellent crewmember for the *Rouge.* Captain Basil didn't take much convincing.

Somehow, he needed to get word to Dreyfuss to set sail to follow the *Rouge's* course and intercept them. Cortez knew Dreyfuss would be at the Galite Islands' main port in a week's time. He had to get a message to him.

He had one opportunity.

The *Rouge* had one last stop to make before departing for France, at Lanzarote, the easternmost island in the Canary Island chain. It was only about eighty miles off the coast of Morocco. The *Rouge* was being forced to take a very roundabout route to France, as British patrols frequented the Strait of Gibraltar. They would make their way over to Spain, then stick to the coast in hopes of avoiding British patrols.

The port at Lanzarote was little more than a single pub and store in a protected cove. It was a haven for pirates and criminals looking to avoid the more popular ports.

Cortez made his way among the pub's many occupants. He was looking for a ship headed for the Galite Islands. Unfortunately, the room wasn't very full and it didn't look like any ships were headed anywhere.

He approached the bar. The bartender, a tough and ready looking Ivorian, eyed Cortez suspiciously.

Cortez did his best to look unintimidating and pathetic.

"Sir, I was wondering if you could get a message to my grandmother. She lives in the Galite Islands. Unfortunately, I have to embark this night and I don't have time to find a proper ship to deliver the message," Cortez asked as pleasantly as possible.

The bartender, a thuggish and thick man, stared directly at Cortez.

"Parcels and packages are fifty dirhams," he answered.

"Oh, I see! No problem. In fact, here is 100 dirhams to be sure it is delivered," Cortez answered faithfully, producing both a letter and coin from his pants pocket.

It was common to have pubs deliver letters and parcels to various destinations lacking a telephone or mail service. Many ships carried mail to various ports as a matter of necessity.

"Any idea when a ship might be heading out?" Cortez asked.

"Probably in the next few days. Fishing fleet is coming in and usually a few head that way. We drop those parcels at the Salima Gull," the bartender answered, looking at the letter.

"Your grandmother's name is Dreyfuss?" he asked suspiciously.

"Yes, her last name. She married a British gentleman—my grandfather, rest his soul."

The bartender shrugged his shoulders and went about cleaning his glasses.

Cortez left the pub and headed for the *Rouge*. With any luck, Dreyfuss would receive the letter and intercept them.

And Cortez would be a very, very rich man.

CHAPTER
— 5 —

MARGARET TAKES HER TEA AT THREE

Two months had passed since Margaret departed from Morocco. She sat in her mathematics class, dressed smartly in a school uniform, listening to one boring lecture after another. Her long, blond hair hung down her back in a tight ponytail. Her naturally fair skin no longer showed any sign of her tan from the Moroccan sun. She was quite a pretty girl, but not a raving beauty like some of her friends. She was confident, but presented an air that could be construed as being a little snobbish. Margaret, however, was no elitist and no snob.

At first she loved being back home in her big house with her sheepdog and all the trappings of modern English life.

Lately, however, she had grown increasingly agitated with all those around her. After being a slave, and being part of a rebellion, and living with such simple people, she became disillusioned with the English way of life. She witnessed the arrogance and ignorance of her peers and their parents. They knew nothing of life in other countries, yet they walked around as if they could solve the world's problems.

They had an impossible amount of food and clothing, and more luxuries than they could ever possibly need. Why did they all want more, more, more? The latest dresses and perfumes, an automobile, or beautiful ivory hair brushes from the trunks of elephants. Who cares if these brushes are all the rage in her school? Don't they know they had to kill the elephants to get the ivory?

Her father was another story.

They still hadn't heard a word about Charles Owen and it was presumed he was dead. That news had devastated Margaret.

She couldn't believe her father was actually dead. In her mind, he was indestructible. He had always been so strong, and so assured of his abilities. She always felt safe in his presence and now he might be dead! It just didn't seem possible.

Her teacher, Mrs. Cloverfield, continued to lecture about equations and fractions, putting numbers up on the chalkboard at a dizzying rate. While the other girls frantically tried to write down the equations, Margaret merely looked busy. The fact was, mathematics didn't interest her. Where once she had been the best student in her grade, now she was making mostly C's in all of her classes, and even a D in Societal Behavior.

Societal Behavior was a mandatory class of every English schoolgirl from the first grade all the way through secondary school. Its purpose was to teach young English girls of a certain stature how to behave within society or, more importantly, how not to behave within society.

Girls were never to play sports.

Girls were never to show their ankles or wrists.

Girls were to sit properly, knees together with feet positioned perfectly to one side at all times.

Young women must never drink alcohol or smoke in the presence of men.

There were lessons on how to drink tea, what kind of tea to drink, and what time of day tea should be drunk.

Girls learned how eat a croque-monsieur sandwich with a knife and fork, were instructed on which fork to use for which meal, and were shown which dishes should be eaten in their proper order.

Margaret studied how to write thank you notes on the proper stationery for every occasion.

Margaret was convinced that Miss Cromwell, who was also the headmistress of the school, had it in for her. Even though Miss Cromwell was frail and thin, with a pointy nose and hardly a chin at all, she walked around with a ruler in her hand, quick to punish any students she thought were disrespecting the school or church.

Miss Cromwell never let anyone forget that one of her ancestors was Oliver Cromwell, considered by many to be the most brutal tyrant in English history.

Obedience, at all times, was the order of the day. On this particular day, Margaret was in no mood to be obedient. How could she concentrate on lectures when all she could think about was her father and the safety of her friends in Morocco? How could she care about memorizing a verse when there was so much poverty in the world?

Each time she fumbled a definition, or forgot a word, Miss Cromwell was by her side whacking her with the ruler. After each lesson she returned home with her knuckles red and swollen. Miss Cromwell had even taken to calling her names when she made mistakes. It was getting so Margaret thought her nickname was "idiot," "imbecile," or her personal favorite, "ingrate."

Yet, she was instructed never to disobey her teachers. To complain was a sin in itself. Besides, her father never would have approved. He detested whiners and complainers and would have told her to keep her chin up and try harder.

It was a daily occurrence that Margaret spent the afternoon in detention after school. Generally, Miss Cromwell had her write definitions from a dictionary for three hours without a book. Margaret was not allowed to speak, to look up from her desk, or even to take a bathroom break. She was simply forced to write page after page of definitions until the three hours were up, at which point she would walk home, usually just as it was getting dark.

Today was no exception.

Margaret had fallen asleep during mathematics and was, once again, given detention.

There was only one other girl in detention class—an Irish girl by the name of Alice Fitzgerald.

Margaret stared at Alice occasionally when Miss Cromwell wasn't paying much attention. Alice had a dubious reputation around her school and was, for the most part, a complete outcast. The other girls gossiped about her constantly and teased her unmercifully about her clothes, her looks, and her Irish heritage.

Studying her, Margaret didn't think she looked the part of a malcontent. Her brown hair was cut short (not the fashion of the day), but she was not altogether unattractive. Her face was a bit round, with brown freckles on her nose and big brown eyes that were undoubtedly her best feature. Margaret noticed that she nervously bit her fingernails almost nonstop. As far as Margaret knew, Alice didn't have one friend in the entire school.

Finally, mercifully, detention ended and the girls were allowed to leave under the disdainful gaze of Miss Cromwell.

Outside, it was a bit darker than usual and a strong wind had come up. Margaret noticed Alice buttoning up her jacket and shyly looking at Margaret.

Margaret made up her mind to at least be civil to Alice.

"I can't stand detention. I think Miss Cromwell hates me more than anything," Margaret said, trying to be as pleasant as possible.

Alice immediately perked up that somebody would even speak to her.

"Yes, I can't stand her either. I think she has her own personal crusade against me," she said and Margaret immediately noticed the difference of her Irish accent.

"What were you in for?" Margaret asked.

"Hmmm, I disagreed with one of the teachers about Brian Boru."

"Brian Boru?"

"He was Ireland's greatest king and defeated the Vikings in several battles. He used taxes to build schools and libraries and hospitals."

"So what's wrong with that?" Margaret asked.

"The teacher referred to him as just another Irish pig, and I took exception," Alice replied.

Margaret laughed at this and Alice smiled a bit, still awfully nervous as Margaret was definitely considered one of the more popular girls in her school and she didn't want to mess up.

"Well then, would you like to walk with me? It's getting dark and I'd rather walk with someone," Margaret asked her.

Alice's eyes lit up at this invitation.

"Of course, I mean, yes, absolutely. I live on Cork Street, just at St. James's Square. How about you?'

"I'm at Savile Row—we're practically neighbors," Margaret replied, and the two girls went off walking down the London streets.

It was dark now, and fog rolled in from the English Channel. The only light on the street came from the occasional pub or the omnipresent oil burning to illuminate the streetlights. Buildings cast shadows along the narrow streets and gray clouds kept any moonlight from helping the girls to see clearly.

"Didn't Jack the Ripper live around here?" Alice asked.

"Alice! What a horrible thing to say! He most certainly did not. I mean, he did all his horrible deeds in the Whitechapel district, which is far away from here."

"I heard he killed his victims and then dissected them like frogs."

"What do you mean, like frogs?"

"Well, I heard he was some kind of doctor and the only way anyone could possibly dissect a person was to have a medical background."

"That makes perfect sense," Margaret agreed.

"You know, they never did discover him. He could very well be alive and well and watching us right now!" Alice said.

"Alice! Are you trying to scare me to death? Jack the Ripper has been dead and gone for some time."

Alice smiled and Margaret had to smile back at her little joke.

"Okay, no more Jack the Ripper jokes."

They continued to walk for twenty minutes and Margaret learned all about Alice and Dublin and that her father was a wealthy banker who wanted to fit in with London society. Her parents were almost as outcast as Alice in London society circles. Being Irish was, most definitely, looked upon as being a second-class citizen. Most of their weekends were spent alone at home reading and playing the violin.

In all their chattering, they had taken a couple of wrong turns and, suddenly found themselves in a completely unfamiliar part of town.

"Which way?" Alice asked.

"I'm not sure. I thought we would have hit Hanover Square by now."

Trying to find a familiar landmark, the girls walked for a few blocks, only to become more disoriented.

Margaret stared at the street addresses but nothing was familiar. Even the street names were strange. For a few moments she walked up and down a couple of streets as Alice followed behind her, keeping quiet, allowing Margaret to find their way.

"Margaret, I think there's something you should know," Alice said.

"What is it?" Margaret asked, absentmindedly.

"I think we're being followed."

Margaret looked at Alice who was pointing with her right thumb. Margaret glanced over and saw two men leaning against a building, smoking cigarettes, and watching the girls like a hawk watches a mouse.

"Alice, we need to get out of here now!" she whispered.

Margaret had been warned by her mother on several occasions not to stay out past dark, as there was a crime epidemic in London associated with the arrival of masses of immigrants, most of whom were, coincidentally, of Irish descent. Every manner of thief, pickpocket, burglar, and criminal prowled the London alleyways and streets just looking for their next victim.

The girls immediately began walking in the opposite direction as quickly as they could without running. In this part of London at night, two schoolgirls walking by themselves would have attracted any number of criminals. They would be easy and defenseless targets.

As they walked, Alice did her best to glance back without drawing attention to herself.

"Are they following us?" Margaret asked.

"Yes," Alice whispered.

Panic began to set into Margaret's steps. Glancing back, Margaret saw that the men were definitely following them and keeping up with their pace. One was skinny and the other was considerably larger. Margaret couldn't exactly see what they were wearing, but they looked very shabby. Their footsteps echoed in the alleyways and were the only sound the girls could hear besides their own breathing.

"We've got to find some kind of public place, Alice. I don't think those men are looking to ask us to tea."

"Where is everyone?"

"Nobody comes out at night," Margaret replied.

"Except criminals, of course," Alice whispered.

The two girls kept walking, but could hear the footsteps drawing closer. Continuing to look back, Margaret saw that the bigger man had a handlebar moustache and the younger man was wearing a top hat. Both were dressed like common vagrants.

"Margaret, we've got to escape. I think we're in a lot of danger," Alice said, with genuine fear in her voice.

Margaret looked at Alice and she knew she was right.

They were in tremendous danger.

The gypsy woman stared into the eyes of the monster.

The Mamba had come across their caravan only an hour prior and demanded to see the woman. Her reputation as a necromancer was renowned throughout the desert. In fact, that was one reason why the Caid was hesitant to be too harsh on her clan. He gave her caravan a wide berth when it came to flaunting the laws of the kasbah.

"I have need of your dark arts, woman," the Mamba hissed at her, sitting at her campfire.

The gypsy, not accustomed to being spoken to in this tone, took a hit off her water pipe and allowed the apricot flavored tobacco to resonate in her lungs before answering.

"And what deed do you desire, Mamba?"

"We are hunting a group of rebels."

The gypsy woman took another long hit from her pipe and stared at the Mamba. He cut an imposing figure with the fire reflecting off his bald head and squared face. His black eyes rarely blinked and he stared right through her. His face seemed to be chiseled from granite. She noticed that his right ear was a mess of flesh and hideous burns had left scars across his neck.

"In return for my help, I want free passage for my clan," the gypsy woman said.

"For how long?"

"For eternity."

The Mamba almost laughed at the proposal.

"I cannot promise that."

"Yes, you can."

"How about if I simply wipe you and your clan clean off the earth right here, right now?"

"Then you lose any chance of catching these rebels."

The Mamba thought over the offer. He really didn't care if the gypsies had free passage or not. Since they didn't pay any taxes, there would be nothing to lose.

"And if I agree to your terms?"

"A curse will be placed on these rebels. A dark curse."

"A curse?" the Mamba asked.

"Although these people can run from you, they cannot hide from a curse, especially one brought on from a witch such as I."

The Mamba was a huge believer in curses and dark magic. Although physically massive, he was extremely superstitious and followed a routine each morning to ward off evil spirits. Ironic, since most people thought the Mamba himself to be an evil spirit.

"I like that idea," the Mamba said, grinning to show his pleasure.

"The more you can tell me about this clan, the more it will help me. Do you have any of their artifacts or clothing?"

"They reside in the Rif Mountains. Their leader is a man named Malik, and they are joined by a woman named Sanaa."

The old woman sighed as this would make her job very difficult.

"I have something," Jawad interrupted.

The Mamba looked over at Jawad, irritated that he would join in the conversation.

"What is it?" he asked.

"A panther pendant from Tariq. I stole it from him when I was their prisoner."

The old woman perked up at this news.

"Oh, that is good…very good. Was it precious to him?"

"It belonged to his best friend. He said it was the most precious thing he owned."

Jawad presented the medallion to the witch, who rubbed it between her fingers for almost thirty seconds. A body of a black panther was molded from bronze and hung from a thick leather strap. Scratched from years of wear, the metal was cold in her palms, and she warmed it with her hands by rubbing it back and forth.

"Oh this is good! This piece has much to tell me."

The Mamba nodded with satisfaction towards Jawad. Jawad, not wanting to smile, secretly beamed with pride at this simple nod from his master.

"What kind of curse will this be?" the Mamba wondered.

"The worst kind. There are many evil spirits in those mountains. This curse will draw them to those people. It will open the gates for the worst kind of ghosts."

The Mamba was overjoyed at this news. If they couldn't defeat this rebel filth in the physical world, then he would defeat them in the spiritual one.

"When will this curse happen?"

"In three days' time, and then I must rest for three full moons."

The Mamba produced a bag full of dirhams and tossed it to her. He liked the witch—she was one of the few who showed him no fear.

"For your troubles."

The woman picked the bag up off the sand and threw it to one of her gypsy sons, who stood right behind her.

The Mamba stood up, bowed slightly to the woman, who did not return this gesture, and ordered his soldiers to move out. In a moment, their horses were heard riding off into the darkness of the night.

The woman waited until the Mamba and his riders left before she puffed again on her water pipe, staring into the dark night air. Her heart felt heavy at the task before her. To aid an enemy was difficult enough, but to harm folk who had never caused any trouble for her people was especially difficult. Although her gypsy clan was extremely hostile towards outsiders, they had good relations with quite a few of the mountain tribes. In fact, some of them sheltered the gypsies and fed them when times were especially tough.

Her first allegiance, however, was to her people.

She looked at one of her sons and gave the orders.

"I will need a full grown rooster, a stone made of amethyst, blood from a lizard, and sprigs of rosemary. Tomorrow the moon will be full and I will begin."

The son, who never questioned his mother, bowed slightly and went about making the preparations.

Margaret and Alice continued to walk. They could hear the footsteps behind them drawing closer and closer. Margaret felt genuinely afraid, as there was nobody on the city streets. Turning a corner, she was sure the two men were going to grab them when...

The two girls literally bumped into a policeman, that is to say, a copper. A large man, maybe six foot four inches tall, with a bushy moustache and a barrel chest, he was swinging his nightstick, whistling a modern tune, when Margaret almost bowled him over.

"Sir, sir..." she started, eyes wide and scared.

He was immediately concerned.

"Sir, those two men behind us..." she stammered.

The copper immediately looked behind the building and saw the two men running away, obviously scared off by the police.

"Okay, okay, you can relax now. Come, let's get the two of you home."

The policeman was a kind man with two daughters of his own. He scolded Margaret and Alice for being out so late in such a tough neighborhood. However, he also understood how the minds of teenage girls could wander, allowing them to get so turned around. He first escorted Alice back to her house, a pretty little Victorian house with a green door and a fresh lawn in the front.

"Well, that was an adventure," Alice said, not knowing if Margaret would want to see her again.

"I'll say. I haven't had that much excitement since Morocco! I'm glad it all turned out well, Alice," Margaret said, smiling.

"Me too, I really enjoyed walking with you Margaret. Um, I guess I'll see you around," Alice replied, sheepishly looking at the ground, knowing that Margaret couldn't be her friend in school.

"Alice, would you like to go to the arcade tomorrow? I heard they have this amazing new film called *The Mystery of Temple Court*. Would you like to see it with me?"

Alice practically jumped out of her shoes!

"I'd love to! My mother has the most delicious toffee and I'll bring a bag for us."

"Okay, I'll see you after school. Only this time, we'll make sure to get home before nighttime."

Alice ran up the stairs to her house, beaming with excitement! Shutting the door behind her, she hugged her mother, danced in circles, and told her parents all about the adventure of the evening, along with every detail of her new friend.

Margaret was escorted home, so glad she had met Alice. The entire experience had been thrilling! It had been so long since she'd done anything out of the normal obligations of British upper-class existence, and it made her feel alive.

Up the stoop she went, skipping her black school shoes on the brick masonry of her steps. Waving goodbye to the nice policeman as she opened the front door, she was in jolly spirits.

"Mother, I'm home!" she yelled.

"In the dining room darling," came the reply.

Margaret, expecting to see just her mother, was entirely casual and at ease until she stepped into the dining room.

There, having tea with her mother was Miss Cromwell.

And Miss Cromwell was not happy to see Margaret.

CHAPTER
— *6* —

THE GHOST OF MOUHHAK

The wastelands are where the dead go to wander. They walk and wander through the physical world, yet cannot freely communicate with the living. They are ghosts, walking among the living.

Some of the ghosts cannot yet leave for the spiritual world; they must wait for loved ones to die and join them before moving on. Others are simply evil and must walk and wander until a sentence is handed down.

The evil ones spread much anger and hatred among the living. They can inhabit a living being and spread darkness and anger throughout that person's soul. Their mere presence around a village can bring bad luck to everyone there.

One such ghost was named Mouhhak.

He was especially drawn to the insecure and the confused, to the angry and the lost souls on earth. Loners and wanderers were especially susceptible to evil spirits such as him.

For thirty years he walked the desert—a rotten and evil soul with no purpose. Six times he managed to enter a person's soul. Each time, that person took on his evil and rotten self until somehow he was exorcised. Usually, Mouhhak's evil was driven out simply because the person found love, which conquers evil. Or, very infrequently, a priest or priestess might perform a ritual to draw him away.

When he occupied another person's soul, of course that person had no idea they had been touched by evil. Slowly, they began to see the world differently. They began to distrust those around them, to be envious and jealous of others and view the world very negatively. They suddenly had the craving for power and the desire to have others bow down to them. They felt the world was against them—and that the world deserved to be destroyed. They enjoyed humiliating those less fortunate, different, or weaker than themselves.

When he wandered, his entire formless body and soul was shrouded in pain and darkness. It was, indeed, a living hell. However, when he finally did inhabit a soul, the pain ceased. It was as if he had found a home. Although he didn't directly control a person's actions, his presence in their soul meant they were much more inclined to do evil and to be satisfied with evildoings.

If he inhabited a soul long enough, eventually evil consumed that soul completely and he could move on—but to where? He didn't exactly know, except to understand that he would no longer be required to wander the wastelands endlessly.

In his travels, he never ate, slept, or drank. His soul simply walked among the living, unseen and unheard. There were, of course, signs to the living that his evil presence was in their midst. Most had a slight chill on the back of their neck or a sudden feeling of melancholy or dread. However, over the past few days, he felt a calling. As if he had a homing beacon within himself, he felt drawn to a certain place or person, without knowing exactly where to go or who to seek. For a week he walked in the sand, wandering towards this calling.

Finally, around midnight one evening, he came to a ridge overlooking the camp of Malik's tribe. He wandered among the tents until he came to one in particular—the one that kept calling him. Creeping inside, he looked over the soul that caused him such hunger and longing. He looked upon it the way a crazed and thirsty man looks upon a bucket of cool water.

Beneath him, Tariq lay in a fitful sleep, his sixth sense warning him of an evil presence, but powerless in his slumber to do anything about it. He tossed and turned but never awakened.

Mouhhak looked upon Tariq and knew his was the body he was to enter, whose soul he was meant to inhabit. He let out a primordial scream that could only be heard by others in the underworld—falling upon deaf ears to those in the physical realm.

He started to enter Tariq's soul. He felt his spirit being joined with Tariq's spirit. Soon, he would be at peace.

Then something happened.

A cat. A tiny white cat with gray whiskers jumped on Tariq's bed, hissing at Mouhhak! The fur on the cat's back stood on end. Mouhhak instantly felt himself being drawn backwards, away from Tariq. The cat continued to hiss at Mouhhak, driving him away.

How evil spirits hated cats.

Cats were the only animals with the ability to see into the spiritual world. They could sense a spirit's presence and hiss to alert their owner. Most of the time, cats could actually see the spirit and follow its movements.

Suddenly, Tariq woke up with a start, feeling his heart beating fast and sweat on his palms. Allowing his eyes to adjust to the darkness, he spied the tiny cat between his legs.

"Where did you come from?" he asked.

The cat began to purr, crawling up Tariq's chest and gently rubbing his chin against Tariq's.

"Hey, hey, you're a friendly guy. I shall name you Aji after my best friend in the whole world. Do you like that, little Aji?" Tariq asked, stroking the cat's white fur.

Aji purred with appreciation and began to knead Tariq's skin with his paws.

"Ow, hey, that hurts. Where did you come from Aji? I've never seen a cat in these mountains."

Aji continued to purr, looking Tariq in the eyes. Tariq scratched him behind the ears until Aji was fast asleep between Tariq's legs. From then on, Aji slept between Tariq's legs each night. During the day, he followed Tariq as best he could during the day, always watching out and protecting him.

It was as if Aji was sent by someone to look after Tariq.

Yet the Ghost of Mouhhak did not disappear entirely.

He continued to stalk the area around the tribe, searching for indecisive souls to inhabit. He was drawn to Malik's tribe, and although he was unsuccessful in entering the soul of Tariq, undoubtedly there would be someone else to play the perfect victim.

He would stalk the tribe and wait for exactly the right opportunity.

Over time, other evil spirits would be drawn to the tribe as well.

CHAPTER
— 7 —

NOT A BEST FRIEND IN THE WORLD

The *Angelina Rouge* had been sailing for three weeks. Cortez had turned out to be a wealth of information and easily navigated between the British and Spanish patrols. He was a hard worker and a credit to the crew. Once every few days they might encounter a fishing boat and make some trades, but other than that it was peaceful and easy sailing.

"This is beautiful, eh? Nothing like the ocean to calm my spirits," Basil said to Charles on the deck one night.

"Yes, quite peaceful," Charles agreed, albeit somewhat apprehensively.

"Is there a problem my friend?"

"Things have been a little too easy. We've been hunted and hounded for months and now we're like a family on a pleasure cruise. And Cortez seems almost psychic in his ability to know the timings of the patrols. It all makes me very uneasy."

"You worry too much, Charles. We finally caught a break, so relax and enjoy it."

Charles smiled and nodded his head. He was a worrier! His wife had often nagged him about it. He was always double- and triple-checking knots on his boat, returning to check the doors at his house to ensure they were locked, and fastidiously cleaning the chimney to prevent any kind of backdraft from happening. That worrying nature made him a good leader, a good sailor, and a great pilot.

But tonight, something just didn't feel right to him. He couldn't put his finger on it, but it kept gnawing at him.

They would soon set foot on French soil, but he still had not figured out a way to contact his family or return to his native England.

The pressure weighed heavily on his shoulders.

"Miss Cromwell has been so kind as to drop by for a visit, won't you join us for a cup of tea."

It wasn't a question from her mother, nor a request, but an absolute order. In a second, Margaret was plunged back into the hierarchical and puritanical ways of her family and her country.

But what did Miss Cromwell want at her house?

"Of course, can I get any biscuits or sandwiches?" Margaret politely asked.

"No, we're all set, dear, please have a seat," came the response from Miss Cromwell.

Margaret sat down next to her mother and straight across from a scowling Miss Cromwell. Trying to look demure, she stared at the table while Miss Cromwell stared directly at her.

"I've been talking with your mother about your disobedience in my classes, Margaret, and what can be done to alleviate the situation."

Her tone was smug and condescending, and altogether superior. Margaret stared at her skinny face and long nose. She didn't have much of a chin at all, but a small little button that seemed to disappear into her neck. Her face was elongated and narrow, and in Margaret's opinion, she looked like a malnourished little weasel.

"Yes, ma'am."

"I've asked your mother if you could come in on Saturdays for extra lessons and she's agreed."

Margaret hadn't expected anything of this sort. She looked at her mother for reassurance, yet her mother refused to return her stare and deferred to the sound judgment of Miss Cromwell.

"I want you to arrive at school promptly at seven o'clock each Saturday morning. I think, over time, perhaps we can drive this rebelliousness and insolence from you and return you to the good-natured girl we all know and appreciate."

"Yes, ma'am."

"How are your studies Margaret?" the always stern Miss Cromwell continued, but asking the question in an entirely obvious way. She waited for an answer.

"Not bad, ma'am."

"Not bad? If you call two C's, a D plus, and three B's not bad then I think you should entirely re-evaluate your standards."

"Yes, ma'am."

"Your mother has been through a great deal with you, all while her husband is missing. I think you can do better as a supportive daughter, and I will help you find your way."

"Yes, ma'am. Sorry, ma'am."

Miss Cromwell stared at Margaret, who still refused to meet her eyes. She had been taught always to honor and obey her elders, even when she thought they were wrong.

Margaret's mother continued to say nothing and allowed Miss Cromwell to run the meeting.

"Very well, then. Mrs. Owen, I thank you for the tea and I look forward to seeing Margaret this Saturday."

"Thank you, Miss Cromwell, and thank you for your visitation and respects for my family and missing husband."

"I'll see myself out. Thank you again."

Miss Cromwell politely shook the hand of Mrs. Owen while completely ignoring Margaret. She walked to the front door in dainty steps, like the walk of a proud peacock. Once the door was closed, Margaret launched at her mother.

"You've got to be kidding! Every Saturday morning? At seven o'clock? What did I do to deserve this? She hates me. She has always hated me and now I have to see her once more a week?"

"Margaret, your grades have been slipping and…" her mother's voice trailed off.

"My grades aren't that bad, and I know I can bring them back up. It's only first term."

"Margaret, Miss Cromwell wields a considerable amount of power, and I must be sensitive to that."

"What do you mean?"

Louise Owen poured herself another cup of tea and sat down.

"All the children within our circle go to her school. She sees all the parents and they all see her. If, for any reason, she thinks we are being unreasonable, then..."

"Then what?" Margaret demanded.

"Margaret, I don't want to go into it."

"What is it, Mother?"

"You just don't understand certain things, Margaret."

"Then explain them to me."

"Our life, this life, isn't by accident. We know the right people. We're invited to the right parties. Our children go to the right schools. That's how we maintain our place. If we start going against the grain, then..."

"Then what?" Margaret asked, frustrated.

"Then it all comes crashing down."

Margaret's mother said the last sentence with an icy tone. She had been so flustered and so despondent over Charles's disappearance that she had grown more and more impatient with Margaret. She didn't understand Margaret's decline in grades and moodiness and, truthfully, just didn't have the time or energy to deal with a difficult teenage daughter.

Margaret looked incredulously at her mother and couldn't believe her ears. Yes, she understood that their place in society had a price but had never heard it vocalized in such a frank manner.

"So I suppose that's the end of that," Margaret said firmly.

Margaret turned on her heel and left her mother drinking tea by herself. Up in her room, she sat on her bed and held a pillow against her chest. It was only a few short months ago that she and her mother and brother had jumped from their sailboat to escape attacking pirates. How close Margaret had felt to her mother then—when she was held captive in the Caid's palace, she wanted absolutely nothing more than to have her mother back. She would cry herself to sleep at night, just wanting to be with her mother.

And now they couldn't be in the same room together.

Margaret felt sorrow in her soul and began to cry again. She wasn't sure why, other than her world seemed to be spinning out of control.

Tariq was trying to camouflage himself from Aseem and Fez. It was a game they played where one was the prey and the others were the hunters. The boy who was the prey tried to hide from the others for as long as possible. Tariq had covered himself in black mud and pasted dead leaves and twigs all over his body to blend in with the environment. As he lay prone in a small field, completely invisible to the naked eye, Sanaa and Malik came and sat less than six feet from him on a stump. Their conversation was animated and excited.

Malik spoke first.

"I have received word through our spies that the Caid is trying to align himself with the French. A French general is due to visit Chaouen in three days' time. The only intelligence I have is that he should arrive in the early evening, and that the purpose of the visit is to negotiate an alliance with the Caid. If that happens, then he will become more powerful than ever."

Sanaa stared at Malik, digesting all the information.

"We don't have any spies in Chaouen. Perhaps I could go to gain some information?"

"No, it is far too dangerous for either of us. I would send some of our other scouts but we are already cut thin. I will try and use our contacts at the harbors to see if a French general has arrived and his destination. Perhaps we can glean some information that way."

"I agree. There is only one way the French would enter our country and that is through our ports. We will know soon enough if they are planning to send more troops, and if they are in alliance with the Caid."

Malik nodded in agreement.

"Good, let's keep this between us. We don't need to start a panic in the tribe."

"Agreed."

The two walked back to the village, never knowing that Tariq had heard this entire conversation. Once they had gone, he quickly stood up and went running for Aseem and Fez. It didn't take long as he almost ran into them just around the bend.

"That's not a very good job of hiding, what kind of prey almost runs into its hunters?" Fez asked.

"Forget about that, I know of a secret, and how we can help the tribe," Tariq said, breathing heavy from the run.

"What is it?" Aseem asked.

"A French general is going to Chaouen. He may have vital information we can use against the Caid. If we can find that information, we can help the tribe and Malik."

Aseem considered this for a moment.

"How would we know how to find him?"

Tariq thought about this, but it was Fez who answered.

"The Caid always has an outpost in a city. If we find the outpost, then we find the general."

"Good, so you will go with me?" Tariq asked.

Fez and Aseem looked at one another, smiled, and nodded their heads in agreement.

"Excellent, we will leave early tomorrow morning. I will draw a note and leave it for Malik."

The boys made their way back to their tent, more than excited that they had an actual adventure on their hands—something that would make Malik proud of them. They wanted so badly to help defeat the Caid and this was their opportunity. They began forming their plans.

Hillie Dansbury was Margaret's age. She was tall and thin and beautiful. Her skin was as delicate as porcelain, and her long, dark hair shimmered down past her shoulders. For years she and Margaret had been friends, complete with sleepovers, birthday parties, play days, and other activities. They had known one another as long as either of them could remember.

Hillie was part of a group of girls who had all grown up together. Their parents were of the upper class and socialized with one another. They frequented the same private clubs, restaurants and polo grounds. It was an amazingly insular group, specializing in the fine art of gossip. No detail was too small to nitpick. They took apart a manner of speech to determine the class of a person, the type of tie knot they used, the lineage of their ancestry, and even the type of bread used in cucumber sandwiches.

The daughters mimicked their parents.

Gossip at Margaret's school was as prevalent as writing and math. The girls gossiped about everyone, such as who had the best dress or the newest shoes, who had been with a boy, who was thin or fat, or most importantly, who was in the group or out of it.

Hillie was the undisputed leader of Margaret's class. She was never given the official designation, or voted into the position, or even acknowledged as such. It was simply known. The other girls deferred to Hillie and sought her approval on everything. They clung to her and followed her the way baby chicks follow a hen.

Margaret had been part of this group for as long as she could remember. She and Hillie had been best friends since before they could walk. Margaret had always taken it for granted that she was part of the group.

Until now.

It all started two weeks ago when they were at lunch, eating together, as always, in the school refectory, or cafeteria. The usual banter was going on and the subject of Alice Fitzgerald came up, again. She'd been the primary target for gossip for months, so this was nothing new. However, Hillie was becoming unusually mean, precisely because Alice seemed completely unaffected by their gossip and abuse. She was always smiling and replied to their insults with a witty response that usually left the antagonizer with a silly look on her face. Although Margaret and Alice had been spending time together outside of school, within the school grounds their relationship remained very distant. Margaret understood the rules of her clique and its feeling towards outsiders.

"Did you see her shoes? I guess they're new, but they look like something a soldier might wear," Hillie said in her proper British accent and the other girls laughed.

Margaret never participated in such gossip, but she didn't deter it, either. It was a delicate balance she had to play. To be in the group was to get along always, and to accept whatever the group thought on a particular subject. She didn't go along with the nasty cutting down of Alice, but she didn't protect her either. It's not something she was especially proud of, and she struggled between loyalty towards the girls she had known forever and the newfound friendship of an outcast.

It wasn't easy to go against the grain with girls she'd known her entire life and considered her best friends. Nonetheless, she recognized how absolutely horrible they could be to anyone outside their group.

Alice was sitting by herself at the far end of the cafeteria—as she did every day. She generally read a book or did homework while munching on a lunch prepared by her mother. In four months, she hadn't had lunch with one other girl in the school. Margaret felt bad about this but hadn't made the effort to sit with Alice. The most she could muster was a smile between classes and a brief "hello" in the hallways.

Hillie decided that merely gossiping about Alice or insulting her to her face wasn't enough—something drastic had to be done. Alice had to understand her place in this school and get that stupid smile off of her face. Hillie looked at the other girls, shook her bottle of milk, and laughed.

"Watch this!"

The other girls giggled with excitement as Hillie stood up and began walking towards Alice, whose back was facing the cafeteria.

"What are you going to do?" Margaret hurriedly asked.

"Pour this all over her stupid Irish head, of course."

Hillie began walking closer to Alice, who was completely oblivious to the scandal happening behind her. Even girls at other tables stopped their chattering to see what Hillie was about to do. Once they saw she was walking towards Alice with an open milk bottle, the whispering and chattering and gawking increased to a new decibel level.

Margaret felt a pit in her stomach. She didn't want to see Alice embarrassed and she, quite obviously, didn't want to stand up to Hillie as that was a battle she couldn't win.

She would be ostracized from the group.

Then, for an inexplicable reason, the images of Tariq and Aseem and Fez came into her head. She remembered their friendship and how they had helped her in her time of need. She remembered, quite vividly, how Sanaa had rescued her in the kasbah and the great danger Sanaa had put herself in to ensure Margaret's safety.

Without another thought, Margaret picked up her lunch and began racing after Hillie. Her lunch consisted of warm shepherd's pie, milk, and an apple crisp.

Hillie was only six feet behind Alice, with her milk jug raised in the air, about to pour it on Alice's head when....

Margaret dumped her entire lunch on Hillie!

The shepherd's pie landed on her head and the gravy covered her whole scalp. Milk dripped down the entire front of her face and body, and the apple crisp splattered all over her perfect school uniform.

There wasn't a spot anywhere above her neck that wasn't covered in gravy, chunks of lamb, apple crisp, or farmer's milk. Hillie looked as if she had gone bobbing for apples in a pig trough.

A hush came over the entire cafeteria. Alice turned around to see the carnage behind her and started giggling in Hillie's face.

Hillie turned around to see Margaret's face. Margaret wasn't gloating or giggling or anything else. In fact, she had a look on her face of immense determination. At once she remembered the warrior she had been in Morocco and, if the situation had called for it, would beat the living snot out of Hillie on the spot.

Hillie saw the look of determination in Margaret's eyes and was immediately scared. She wasn't accustomed to anyone standing up to her. Margaret didn't show an ounce of fear and Hillie immediately knew to back down. In fact, she was terrified by the look in Margaret's eyes.

She tentatively looked at the other girls, all of whom were staring at her, and then she burst out in tears and ran out of the cafeteria.

That's when Margaret started laughing along with Alice.

"Mind if I join you for lunch?" Margaret asked.

"Not at all, but it looks like you'll have to share mine because yours is all over Hillie."

Both girls giggled even more and Margaret sat down across from Alice and immediately felt relieved. The fact was, she genuinely liked

Alice. She was tired of having to be popular and fashionable, and no longer needed to be part of that ridiculous clique.

The Caid stood over the body of his dead son. The body was laid to rest on a stack of sticks and twigs—waiting to be set aflame.

He blamed himself for his son's death.

He should have sent more soldiers with him. He should have insisted he stay in the safe confines of the kasbah where he could be protected. He knew that Abd-El-Kadar had been so upset with the Caid for releasing the Mamba that he had foolishly tried to prove his valor to his father.

It had cost him his life.

Like most fathers, Ali Tamzali had not fully seen the limitations in his son. If he had, he never would have allowed him to venture out on patrols, as Abd-El-Kadar was no warrior.

His son was a cold-hearted butcher, yes. A murderer, definitely. But against someone who knew his way around a sword, he was as useless as a duck with one wing.

The Caid asked one of his generals, who was also in the room, about the death of his son.

"You are sure it was Malik?"

"Yes, Sire, we have confirmation."

The Caid nodded solemnly in understanding. Malik and his tribe had grown into the biggest threat against the Caid.

The general stepped forward.

"I have word that the Mamba is making progress and is almost on Malik and the tribe. A little more time, Sire, and we will have them."

The Caid nodded in agreement.

"Good. I want them to suffer as I suffer now," he said and, with one final look at his son, took a torch and lit the kindling under the body.

Soon, the body was engulfed in flames, as the Caid stared at the burning remembrance of his only son. His legacy would not be passed onto another generation.

Immediately after lunch, Margaret was called to the office of Miss Cromwell. She had been expecting the call since the cafeteria episode, as it was doubtful that something this glorious would go unnoticed.

Outside Miss Cromwell's office, her assistant scratched letter after letter that awaited the signature of her boss. The letters were addressed to various parents and politicians, informing them of their child's performance and even included mild threats over donations. Margaret felt very alone in the waiting room, sitting in a hard wooden chair with no cushion, listening to ink scratch over stationery. She knew that she was in for a thrashing.

After five minutes, the door to Miss Cromwell's office slid open and Margaret was pointed to the door by the assistant. She didn't even have the courtesy to say, "Miss Cromwell will see you now." She just pointed with a smug look on her face.

Margaret bravely left her seat and entered the office. Miss Cromwell was at the door and immediately closed the door behind her.

"Have a seat, Margaret."

Margaret took a seat opposite Miss Cromwell's desk. The desk was huge—enormous, even—and Miss Cromwell looked tiny sitting behind it. On the bare white wall behind the desk hung a small wooden cross. It was the only decoration in the room. All the walls were completely barren and white, and the only furniture was the hideous, massive wooden desk and two chairs. On the desk was a small oil lamp, exactly one sheet of paper, an ink bottle and a pen holder.

It was cold in the office, as if a draft were coming in through the walls.

"I understand there was some trouble in the cafeteria."

"Yes, ma'am."

"Do you care to provide me with your testimony of the events?"

"Just a disagreement among girls."

Miss Cromwell didn't like Margaret. Since her return from Morocco, there was something different about her. Miss Cromwell liked girls who were deferential and completely obedient. She would not stand for any kind of childish rebellion or outward mocking of her authority. She could sniff out a "bad girl," as she called them, the way a hound could sniff out a fox.

And Margaret was most certainly a bad girl.

Margaret, on the other hand, knew exactly why she was in the office. It wasn't because she had dumped her food on a girl—it was because she had dumped her food on the *wrong* girl. Hillie Dansbury was not only a favorite pet of Miss Cromwell's, but her parents were important bene-factors to the school. Margaret could only envision the chain of events that caused her to be sitting across from Miss Cromwell. Hillie would have run home to her mother; her mother would have stormed into Miss Cromwell's office; together they would have come up with some kind of punishment that would both demonize Margaret and victimize Hillie. Something that would have Hillie come out on top—again.

"Have you been consorting with Alice Fitzgerald?" Miss Cromwell asked.

"What?"

"Are you her friend?"

"I suppose. She's new to our school and I wanted to make her feel welcome."

"And that is the reason you embarrassed poor Ms. Dansbury? To pro-tect your friend?"

Margaret didn't want to drag Alice into this. She knew that Alice was already despised by most of the teachers—who followed Miss Cromwell's lead.

"Not at all."

"So this was on your own accord?"

"I suppose so."

"You suppose so?"

Margaret was beginning to get angry at the line of questioning and Miss Cromwell's tone.

"Well, I was provoked."

"You were provoked?"

"Yes, Hillie Dansbury provoked me."

"How did she provoke you?"

"By being Hillie Dansbury."

The response was altogether sarcastic and Margaret almost giggled at the response. Miss Cromwell, however, was not impressed. She simply stared at Margaret with frozen and frigid brown eyes. Most girls couldn't bear to look her in the eye; even Margaret was mostly demure in her presence. To Miss Cromwell's surprise, this time Margaret stared right back at her.

Miss Cromwell had spotted this same look in Margaret's eyes before—a look of defiance and utter confidence that almost scared her.

"It seems as if our little visits each Saturday aren't enough to curb your willful behavior. Perhaps we need something a little more stringent as a form of guidance?"

Margaret said nothing to this. She had expected to be punished. In fact, she had it in her mind that Miss Cromwell would give her a good whacking across the knuckles with a ruler.

Miss Cromwell had other ideas.

"I think you need to learn something about responsibility, Margaret. Something that will teach you about the feelings of others."

"I think I understand the feelings of others. Hillie Dansbury is the one who needs a lesson in empathy."

"Quiet!" Miss Cromwell shouted in a demonstration that went against her normally composed nature.

Margaret stared at Miss Cromwell but did not shrink from her outburst. She actually enjoyed the fact that she had gotten Miss Cromwell to lose her composure.

Miss Cromwell remained silent for a couple of moments before continuing.

"You will carry a chicken with you at all times. To every classroom, hallway break, lunch, even to gym. You will carry this chicken with you at all times for the entire year."

"Excuse me?" Margaret dared to ask, in total disbelief.

At that moment the door opened and her assistant brought in a full-grown chicken in a wire cage with a leather handle on top.

"This is your chicken. If anything unfortunate should happen to it, you will be expelled from this school. Is that understood?"

The chicken was placed on Margaret's lap. It clucked twice and stared at Margaret.

Margaret was speechless. She just looked at the chicken who continued to stare back at her and cluck. Miss Cromwell seemed to smirk at the scene in front of her.

"Do you have any questions regarding this assignment Margaret?"

"No, ma'am."

"Good. Then you are dismissed."

Margaret took the chicken and walked out of the office as the assistant closed the door behind her. She was befuddled by the events that had unfolded. She was expecting a one-week suspension or a racking of her knuckles.

Never in a million years did she expect to babysit a full-grown chicken.

Walking to her mathematics class, the chicken seemed to be in good spirits and clucked happily. Walking into the classroom, the entire class fell silent. Even the instructor, Miss Bale, stopped speaking mid-sentence.

Everyone stared at Margaret and her chicken.

"Miss Owen, what is that?"

"It's a chicken, ma'am."

"I can see it's a chicken. What is it doing in my class?"

"A form of punishment, I suppose. I'm to keep the chicken with me at all times when at the school."

"Who asked you to do this, Miss Owen?"

"Miss Cromwell."

The class began to giggle and laugh at Margaret's expense. The girls whispered to one another in hushed tones and pointed at the chicken.

"Very well. You may sit down, Margaret."

Margaret took a seat in her normal place and all eyes were on her. A girl she had known since they were both five, Julie Morrow, stared and laughed at Margaret.

"Shut up."

"So are you the Chicken Lady? Is that to be tomorrow's lunch?"

"You know very well this isn't my idea."

The other girls continued to giggle until Miss Bale settled them down and got back to the day's lesson.

After school was even worse. Margaret carried the chicken to her locker and was subjected to snickers and stares and laughter. Gossip travels fast in school hallways—in no time, Margaret's creative form of punishment was common knowledge.

Reaching her locker, Margaret was aghast to discover that someone had put graffiti on it in black ink. Over her entire locker, in block letters, were the words "Chicken Lady." Opening the locker, Margaret found that it had been stuffed with chicken feathers. The feathers poured out of her locker into the hallway. The girls around her laughed even harder, and some began making clucking sounds of their own.

It wasn't just the laughter that Margaret noticed—something was different—the way the girls looked at her and kept their distance. Nobody came to her defense. Girls she had known for as long as she could remember passed her in the hallway and snickered at her.

It had taken Hillie Dansbury just three hours to completely ruin her, and her reputation. The chicken wasn't just a form of punishment; it was a form of humiliation. It was a device designed to take Margaret out of her social stratosphere and reduce her to the dregs of her class.

Evidently Mrs. Dansbury and Miss Cromwell understood the dynamics of a young girls' school all too well.

"A chicken?" Alice asked.

Margaret took a breath. She was in no mood to see Alice right now. She had been the cause of this entire debacle. Margaret didn't feel especially noble at the moment. In fact, part of her just wanted for things to go back the way they were.

"I don't want to talk about it," Margaret tersely answered.

"Margaret...I just wanted to say thank you for everything. Nobody in this school has ever been friends with me, much less stood up for me."

Alice's voice was quivering. Just listening to it, Margaret felt guilty for being short with Alice. Then she looked at her...Alice's hair was green!

"What happened to your hair?" Margaret asked, eyebrows raised.

"Some of the girls held me down in the washroom and poured green dye on my hair. I guess it's because I'm Irish."

Margaret stared at her hair—a ghastly mixture of green glop and Alice's beautiful natural auburn hair. Margaret could see the streaks of tears on Alice's cheeks where she had been crying.

"Oh Alice, I'm so sorry. People can be so cruel," Margaret said and hugged her friend hard, longing to let her know she wasn't alone.

"Perhaps we could use some of my dye to turn your chicken green? I've never seen a green chicken.

Margaret managed to laugh at this little joke.

"C'mon, let's see if we can get you cleaned up a bit."

Margaret washed Alice's hair in the washroom with soap from the dispenser. She washed it five times until her hair wasn't really green, but more auburn with a hint of lime.

"It's the best I can do on such short notice. When you get home, pour some baking soda and lemon over it. That should do the trick."

"A chicken?" Louise Owen shrieked.

"I know," Margaret answered. She had been looking forward to her mother's response, as she knew she would be outraged at the punishment. No doubt she would march right down to her school and give Miss Cromwell a good piece of her mind.

"Margaret, what did you do?"

"I dropped some food on Hillie Dansbury's head. She was deserving of it, I can tell you that."

"What?"

Louise Owen sat down to consider the consequences. She was intimately familiar with the Dansbury family. In fact, she considered Hillie's mother to be one of her better friends. The Dansbury family held quite a bit of pull within their social circle; no doubt that included the actions of their children.

"Oh, Margaret," she sighed.

"What is it, Mother? I thought you'd be on my side."

"I am on your side, but you know how the Dansburys are. By tonight, everyone in the city will know of your punishment."

"That's all you can think about? What the Dansburys will say?"

"No, but it's just that you've been getting in so much trouble lately. I just don't understand…"

"I came to the defense of my friend!"

"Margaret, can you just go to your room?"

Margaret marched upstairs, her cheeks flushed red. She purposely stomped on the stairs hard and slammed her bedroom door behind her. Once she was in the safe confines of her room, she jumped face first on her bed and started sobbing. She hugged a stuffed bear named "Quigly" she'd had since she was four years old. The bear was brown and matted and over the years had become streaked from Margaret's tears. The bear had been her constant companion and her solace whenever she was upset.

She cried hard into Quigly's stomach and held him tight against her body. She felt so alone at that moment and just wanted everything to be back to normal. She wanted her father back and she wanted her friends. She wanted to enjoy going to school and to be "normal." Since she'd returned from Morocco, she just felt so messed up inside. Like the earth was moving beneath her and she constantly had to move and dance to keep solid ground beneath her.

After ten minutes she fell into a deep sleep. She awoke three hours later, realizing it was dark outside. She went to the door and found a tray with a plate of food covered with a cloth. The dinner was still warm and Margaret found herself to be most hungry. Her mother had brought her fish and chips with peas—one of her favorite dishes. She dipped the fried fish in lemon sauce and munched delightedly on the delicate flavor. Later that night she would go into her mother's room to snuggle with her and spend the night in her bed.

The Mamba stared into the sand playing with a necklace made of black beads. The beads helped him think, and he moved them effortlessly between his thumb and index finger. He'd been in this position for almost an hour. Jawad and the rest of the troops sat behind him not making a sound.

Finally, the Mamba spoke.

"We know a villager is supplying information to Malik and his tribe. I want you to find ten people from this village and tell them we are looking for a boy believed to be loyal to Malik's tribe. We will provide the description of Jawad. Then, Jawad will visit each villager. Whoever warns Jawad that we are after him is the informant."

Jawad looked at the Mamba and the other troops.

"Why me, Sire?"

"Because you are a boy and they will be less suspicious."

Jawad nodded his head, as he understood the plan completely.

He would be the one to find the informant and get in even deeper with the Mamba.

"We've got to stop Hillie Dansbury," Margaret told Alice at lunch the following week. The two ate alone, apart from the rest of the students, ignoring the giggles and stares pointed their way.

Over the past week, Hillie and her minions had engaged in a campaign of terror against Margaret and Alice. They stuffed garbage in their lockers, threw a spider down poor Alice's shirt in English class, and poured water all over Margaret and her chicken while Margaret was making a visit to the loo. This was on top of the constant snide remarks, comments, and looks they each suffered through all day long.

Alice nibbled on a cold bit of roast beef and nodded her head.

"From my friend Tariq in Morocco," Margaret began, "I learned that no matter what it takes, always get even with your aggressor. Never be a victim."

"What are we going to do?" Alice asked.

"We're going to give Hillie a surprise she'll never forget, and then we're going to take over this school."

"How are we going to do that?"

"Lean in and I'll tell you."

As Margaret explained her plan to Alice, Alice's mouth suddenly burst into a wide smile and she started giggling.

That day at lunch, Margaret and Alice finalized their plan, a counter-attack to Hillie Dansbury and her friends. They decided to launch the plan the following day.

CHAPTER
— 8 —

THE RAGE OF NASSER AL HABASH

I and the public know
What all schoolchildren learn,
Those to whom evil is done
Do evil in return.
—WH Auden

The Mamba was not always known as such. That was just a moniker he would earn much later in his life.

He was born Nasser Al Habash, and was a sickly boy when he was young. So sick, the village doctor didn't expect him to live long. His father, a drunk, hated him for being weak and frail and wanted nothing to do with him.

Nasser didn't have any friends at all growing up, with the exception of one—his mother. He would come home from school each day, typically having been beaten up by the other boys, and she would console him and hug him and tell him not to worry. This coddling only made his father more furious and more abusive, because he was ashamed to have a weak son.

This continued for years.

When he was thirteen, not much had changed in his life. He was still small. He was still bullied. His mother was still his best friend. His father was still a drunk.

However, he had developed an arch-enemy: a boy named Ahmed, whose sole purpose in life was to make Nasser's existence pure torture. Each day he waited for Nasser before and after school, calling him names and punching him. It made Ahmed feel powerful to humiliate Nasser.

Nobody did anything to stop this abuse. The teachers merely looked the other way. The village elders simply thought Nasser was weak and needed to toughen up. Other parents secretly liked watching their boys beat on Nasser. Nobody came to his defense.

So, anger and hatred began to grow inside him. Nasser disliked everyone, and didn't trust anyone but his mother. He couldn't play with the other children, so he spent all of his time alone, away from others and isolated. He withdrew into himself.

Ahmed and his gang of friends lived for torturing Nasser. One day, Ahmed decided to really get Nasser, so he got some of the boys to hold Nasser down while the others poured flour and molasses all over his body. He struggled to get free, but they held him down until every inch of his body was covered in the sticky substance. As usual, no one came to his rescue. Instead, everyone in the school laughed at him, even the girls and some of the teachers.

He went home crying to the comfort of his mother. Looking at him, she started crying as well, realizing how tortured her son had become.

The molasses did not come off easily. It had to be pulled off, which took off skin and hair. It was excruciatingly painful and took almost three days before all the sticky substance was finally removed. In the process, Nasser lost all his hair, as well as his eyebrows. Patches of skin were gone, leaving red sores and welts.

Nasser's father took no pity on the boy. He scolded him for being so weak and stupid.

One morning, Nasser heard his father yelling at his mother.

"That boy is so worthless, I do not want him in my house!" he yelled.

"He is your son, you cannot cast him out!" she pleaded.

"His is a shame on me and my name. I want him gone by sundown," his father yelled.

Nasser heard his father storm out of the house and the tears of his mother. Coming out of his bedroom, he spotted her crying, with her face buried in her arms at the kitchen table.

"Do I really have to leave, Mother?" he whispered to her.

Looking up, she hadn't known Nasser had heard any of the conversation. Tears in her eyes, she hugged her son tightly and held him close.

"I am sorry my son, it is your father's wishes," she told him.

"But why? I love you and just want to be with you. I have nowhere else to go," he pleaded.

She cried more but understood it was fruitless to go against her husband. His word was law in the household. If he wanted Nasser to leave, then Nasser would leave.

His mother packed a bag for him. Although she loved her son terribly, she also felt it might be best for him to leave the village before he could be tortured any more by the other children.

She did not have any relatives to send him to. There was only one option.

About three miles out of town, a contingent of soldiers was camped out and had pitched tents as a makeshift village.

There was one tent larger than the rest, colored burgundy and gold. As she approached it, two soldiers stopped her.

"I wish to see Ali Tamzali," she said.

"For what purpose?"

"I offer him my son," she said. The soldiers eyed the frail and sickly Nasser, who stared back at them with big sad eyes.

The soldiers laughed.

"Woman, do not waste our time. Your boy is a weakling for all to see," they scoffed.

"He will be an excellent servant to you all. Please, I have no choice. My husband will not have him in our house," she pleaded.

"Do not bother us with your worries. Now, leave before we get impatient," one said.

She fell to her knees, pleading with the soldier. She began crying and held his legs.

"Please, please, I have no other choice," she cried.

The soldier, startled by such a response, was about to pry himself free of her grasp when a voice came from behind them.

"What is the name of your son?" the voice asked.

"Nasser," came her reply.

Ali Tamzali, the future Caid, emerged from his tent. He was handsome, a little more than thirty, and held the stature of a nobleman.

Walking next to the soldiers, who immediately came to attention, he studied Nasser.

Nasser was so small and sickly, yet there was something about him that caught his attention. The boy was hiding something, deep down, a rage that could be harnessed and controlled. Ali Tamzali understood that a lost boy without a cause was easily manipulated. He could be turned into a soldier—his kind of soldier.

"Okay, come with us," ordered Ali Tamzali.

The soldiers, startled by the response, quickly gathered young Nasser, who was still in shock.

"Oh bless you, Sire. Bless you for taking my young son. He will serve you well," his mother said and kissed the feet of Ali Tamzali.

As the soldiers led Nasser away, he looked back to see his mother, still on her knees, wailing, and waving goodbye to her only son.

That was the last time young Nasser would ever see his mother.

Nasser went with Ali Tamzali to live and learn the ways of war and being a soldier. Over the years, he spent most of the time by himself, studying the Art of War and practicing in the way of combat. He would spend hours and hours feeding arrows through his bow until his fingers bled and his muscles ached so much he could scarcely hold the bow up to this shoulder. He became a master marksman and swordsman and won every contest in his regiment. His hours, days, weeks, and years were spent becoming the best soldier in the Caid's army.

The Caid's generals taught Nasser the tactics and strategies necessary to defeat any enemy. Nasser had a keen and strategic mind and could outthink most of those generals by the time he was seventeen.

These years of training transformed a weak and sickly child into a tall, muscled, and athletic young man. He became the Caid's personal dog of war.

All the while, behind the scenes, the Caid was pulling his strings like a puppet master pulling a marionette. He formed a close and personal bond with young Nasser, acting as the father Nasser never had. He encouraged him but also punished him. He withheld praise, only to have young Nasser pant like a hungry puppy to get back into his good graces. The Caid poisoned Nasser's mind with the idea that the Caid's army was his only family and his allegiance to it must be blind and complete.

By his eighteenth birthday, Nasser was given his own squad. He terrorized the countryside and all of the inhabitants of their territory. His reputation grew and eventually a nickname was bestowed on him—The Black Mamba—named after the deadliest snake in the world.

Nasser continued to hold a rage within him forged from the days of being bullied and then abandoned by his mother and father. He took his rage and anger out on all he encountered. He trusted no one. He loved no one. His hatred knew no bounds.

He had been bullied all his life, yet he had turned into the biggest bully of all.

He hated all of humanity.

CHAPTER
— 9 —

THE ROAD TO CHAOUEN

Malik awoke the following morning, rolled over, and felt a piece of paper drop next to him. Sleep in his eyes, he grabbed the paper and lazily read it.

In a moment he jumped up, threw on his clothes, and hurried outside. He immediately went to the boys' tent but all three of them, and their belongings, were gone. Only Aji meowed and purred, and rubbed his body against Malik's leg.

He read the note again.

> Malik,
>
> We heard you and Sanaa discuss the French general in Chaouen. We are going to spy on this general and get all the information for the tribe. Do not worry! We are warriors now and we will make you proud.
>
> Sincerely,
> Tariq, Fez, and Aseem

Sanaa heard the commotion and came to him.

"What is it?"

"The boys have gone to Chaouen to look for the French general. Apparently they overheard us."

"What?"

"I know. I think they have too big a head start for us to catch them."

Malik walked around, angry and more than frustrated with his tutelage.

"Do they understand the danger they are in?" Sanaa asked, already knowing the answer.

"Of course not, they are boys. If the Caid's soldiers find them, there will be no rescuing them. The Caid is looking for blood, and he's looking to make an example of them."

Malik wanted to scream and shout, and wring each boy's neck. How could they be so stupid, so foolhardy?

They were doing exactly what the Caid was hoping they would do. They had made a mistake.

Chaouen is a town nestled in a valley of the Rif Mountains in Morocco. Formed in 1471 as a military fortress, it is renowned because most of its buildings are a light blue color, giving it a magical feeling, as if living in a town in the clouds. The light was especially mesmerizing at dusk, and most said it was unlike any other town in the world.

"I have heard the entire town is blue?" Tariq said, clearly happy to be on the road with his two best friends.

"I know for a fact there are powerful gypsies and witches there," Fez answered.

"It is where Moulay Ali Ben Moussa Ben Rached El Alami defeated the Portuguese. He is one of the most famous warriors in Morocco!" Aseem exclaimed gladly.

"I'll bet in five hundred years, people will say, 'this is where Fez, Aseem, and Tariq, the most famous Moroccan warriors ever, walked the road to Chaouen,'" Fez said, and his friends laughed with him.

Coming up a mountain pass, they could see Chaouen for the first time in the valley below. It was true! The walls were painted an exquisite blue. Even though the town only held about fifteen or twenty thousand people, it seemed enormous to Fez and Aseem. Tariq, of course, had grown up on the streets of Tangier, so it didn't seem that big to him.

Mouths open and eyes wide, the three boys walked the path that led to the city.

"We must be very careful. The Caid has his troops everywhere and we are still wanted!" Aseem explained.

"Yes, we will blend in with the crowd. Don't draw attention to ourselves, and stick together," Fez agreed.

Tariq didn't say anything. This very subject had weighed heavy on his mind. He had heard the Caid had a price on their heads, but he wasn't sure what that meant. The three of them looked like every other boy in Morocco, and without photographs, how would the troops know them? Still, his days as an orphan on the streets of Tangier taught him to be cautious.

"Have you heard from Zijuan lately?" Fez asked.

"Not for a few months. She was supposed to visit us, but she had something to do at the orphanage and got word to us that she wouldn't be coming. I miss her terribly. I like it in the mountains with all of you, but I do miss her and I even miss that stupid orphanage," Tariq answered.

"You will see her soon. She is like your mother! I am sure she is thinking of you," Aseem answered, bringing a smile to Tariq's face.

"You never hear anything from your family, do you Aseem?" Tariq asked.

"No. Never have. They think I am a slave, or dead. Perhaps one day I can visit them," Aseem answered.

"One day we will defeat the Caid and news of your exploits will reach your family—and even all the way to Tangier!" Fez laughed.

"Maybe all the way to England and Margaret will hear of us," Tariq replied and all the boys smiled at that thought.

"I wonder if she is doing well. She was like an older sister to me. I am sure she is quite happy in England back with her family and friends," Aseem answered.

"I am sure she misses us. I hope we will see her again," Tariq said.

All three boys nodded and continued walking. It had been hard on them when Margaret left them, as they had grown into a kind of family. Without her, there was always something missing.

The boys walked for a bit longer, all thinking about what it meant to be a spy.

"Do we need disguises?" Fez asked.

The boys thought about this for a moment.

"Yes, we must find clothes that look like city clothes so we don't stick out," Tariq said.

"How do we get those?" Aseem asked.

"We take them, but leave a donation so it's not stealing," Fez answered.

"What kind of donation? We don't have any money," Aseem replied, ensuring that strict laws of Karma were being followed.

"I will leave my bow and some arrows...those are certainly worth some rags for clothes," Fez concluded.

The three boys, happy with their plan, continued on their journey.

Before too long they entered the city of Chaouen.

Fez and Aseem were awestruck by the many sights, smells, and sounds of a modern city. Aseem was mesmerized by a fire eater who placed flaming swords in his mouth. Fez stood amazed by a modern watchmaker and the mechanization of his equipment. For a couple of hours, the boys wandered the streets, taking in the sights and blending into the crowds. As expected, there were dozens and dozens of orphans around the city streets. So far, none of them bothered the three boys, simply eyeing them suspiciously.

Tariq spied some clotheslines on the outskirts of some apartments. Making sure that nobody was watching, he made a mad dash and collected enough clothes for the three of them and hoped they were the right size. In return, he left Fez's bow and some arrows with three rocks stacked on top as a tribute. The boys quickly changed into their new clothes and walked along the streets exploring the many nooks and crannies of the town.

All the while, the boys were making a map of the city in their heads. They were doing their best to remember every street, alleyway, and police post. Although they looked like normal street urchins, they were, in fact, gathering intelligence.

It was no accident they ended up outside the Caid's outpost.

It was a rectangular building, one story, with a wall about seven feet high completely surrounding the perimeter. An iron gate enclosed the front, with two guards as sentries. A couple of oak trees provided needed shade, and a few of their branches hung over the easternmost wall.

The three boys acted like street urchins, begging for coins, making a nuisance of themselves, all the while studying the defenses of the compound. After forty-five minutes, they congregated in the shadows of a nearby alley.

"I think I have figured out a way to get in," Tariq started.

"The tree?" Fez asked and smiled.

"Yes, I think I can scale the tree and get over the wall. I just don't know about the security inside the compound...I think it will be easy enough to get on top of the roof and then, hopefully, drop down somewhere. The roof is completely unpatrolled and the sentries will not be able to see it from the ground," Tariq continued.

"We don't even know if the French general is in the compound. We've been here for hours and haven't seen anyone come or go," Fez reminded him.

This was true. They had been watching the compound for hours and not one person had entered or left. It was entirely possible the compound was completely empty.

"I am going into the compound and once inside, I will wait and see. I think we will need a bit of luck," Tariq explained.

"What about us? Why do you get to have all the fun?" Aseem questioned, obviously not happy with being left out of the plans.

"Because, in case I'm captured, you two will have to free me! And, you have to set the diversion!" Tariq reasoned.

"Diversion?" Aseem questioned.

"An excellent tactical idea. Yes, we need something to distract all the guards. We also need to see what kind of security they have," Fez agreed.

"What kind of diversion?" Aseem asked.

"I have just the thing. Tariq, go over by the tree with the long limb hanging over, and wait for my signal." said Fez.

"What signal?" asked Tariq.

"Don't worry, you'll know. Aseem and I will wait for you just around the corner at that street stand with the dead goat outside. We will have an eye on the gates from that distance, but we will be hidden from the guards," Fez continued, completely confident in his plans.

"Got it. If for some reason I am lost, meet me at that fountain we saw—the one with the fish swimming," Tariq asked.

"Yes, the one with the koi," Fez corrected him.

"Okay, hopefully this works!"

"The pack always defeats the lone wolf!" Aseem said and all three of them put their hands together and repeated the phrase.

Tariq made his way over to the easternmost side, looking inconspicuous and trying his best to hide in the shadows. He felt his heart pounding in his chest and his breathing started to shorten. He waited for five minutes and was starting to worry when he heard it. The unmistakable sound of gunfire, or, in this case—firecrackers!

"That's it! That's brilliant!" Tariq thought to himself, scaled the wall, nimbly grabbed the overhanging branch, and threw himself up onto the limb. Quickly, he slid along the branch to the other side of the wall and then dropped down in a shadow.

The inside of the compound was chaotic. About a dozen guards ran to the front gate and quickly into the street. There was a courtyard just in front of Tariq leading to the building. He quickly ran across it. Tariq saw a barely open window, about five feet above the ground. He ran and just as he was lifting himself up by his fingertips, he heard something!

Two guards were walking back towards him. Frantically, he pushed himself up with his right hand, and with his left pushed upward on the window. It was stuck! He tried harder, using his shoulder, pushing with all his might. Finally it gave and opened up about a foot.

Tariq could hear their footsteps, and knew any second they would be onto him. He pushed his toes against the wall, skipping like a hamster on a treadmill, until finally he was able to push his feet up and slide his body through the barely open window. Landing with a thump on the other side, he slid against the wall and hoped the guards hadn't heard him.

The guards' voices could be heard just outside the window.

"Probably nothing, just some kids lighting off firecrackers. Good to have some excitement, it's so boring around here," one of the voices said.

"Yeah, about time something happened. Let's go have a smoke over there," the other answered.

Tariq lay against the plaster wall, breathing very heavily and thanking God he was safe.

After a few moments he composed himself and looked around. He was in a room; he figured it was some kind of storage room, as he saw a broom, a mop, and stacks of rags. Quietly, he went to the door, opened it, and looked around.

The hallway went about thirty feet in either direction and then disappeared around a corner. He decided to go left, tiptoeing along the wall, until he came to the corner. Peering around, he saw another long hallway with a couple of doors on both sides.

He would have to move quickly! He would be totally exposed in the open hallway. If someone happened to walk down, he would be found for sure and trapped.

He went to the first door, put his head to it, and heard nothing.

Then, he went to the next door, put his head to it, and heard nothing.

He crisscrossed the hallway, put his head to the next door, and this time he heard muffled talking inside. He couldn't make out the words, but it sounded like there were a few people in the room.

He would have to take his chances.

He made his way back across the hall, opened the first door, and looked in. The room was completely dark. Closing the door behind him, he would have to sit and wait for an opportunity—an opportunity that would come twenty minutes later.

The door across from him opened and three official-looking men walked down the hallway past the room where Tariq was hiding.

"Well, I don't know where he is. He should be here by now. Let's grab some tea and hopefully he'll be here soon," a voice said.

Could they be talking about the French general? Tariq didn't know, but he was about to need a bit of luck. Making sure the coast was clear on either side, he made his way back across the hallway, opened the door where the men had been talking—just far enough to ensure that nobody was inside—and then made his way in.

It was a very large conference room with a big wooden table about twelve feet long in the middle. Each side had four chairs, with two at the head of the table. The room was elegant, featuring a detailed mural of the Caid's kasbah with scenes of the surrounding hills and mountains. On all four walls there were candles and, in the center of the table, a cluster of candles casting light across the entire room.

But where should he hide?

That's when Tariq saw the wardrobe on the right hand side. The large cabinet was on four legs and about thirteen inches off the floor. Without a second to lose, he climbed underneath, contorting his body into such a difficult angle that he wondered if he would ever be able to untangle himself. His face was crammed between the floor and bottom of the wardrobe. He brought his knees up to his chest, trying to make his body as small as possible but making it a little difficult to breathe.

He scooted back to the wall so he couldn't be seen by anyone at the table.

Now, he had to wait.

He waited for half an hour. He was starting to fall asleep when the door opened back up and he heard the voices again.

With a new voice.

A French voice.

"Please have a seat, General. We have some nice tea and baklava coming for you right now."

"Thank you, I will just have tea. Now, let's skip the pleasantries and get down to business as I have to be back in Tangier."

"Of course, General. The Caid sends his apologies for not meeting you in person. His son was just killed in a vicious attack by some rebel filth and he is attending to the funeral."

"I heard of the atrocity," said the General. "Please give him my sincere apologies."

"Of course, General. In his absence, I am permitted to speak on behalf of the Caid."

"Very well, what is your proposition?"

"If the rumors are true of an impending French invasion, you will have your hands full with the Sultan's troops. It will be easy enough to win the cities, but the countryside is another matter. These deserts and mountains are ruled by local tribes. They will be very difficult to defeat and control, as this is their natural habitat. Your planes and tanks will do no good against guerrilla fighters. Just ask the English how they fared against the Americans in their War of Independence."

Just then, Tariq felt something in his stomach. Oh my goodness, he had to go to the bathroom! He felt himself having to pee and tried to think of anything to take his mind off his full bladder.

"What are you proposing?" the General asked.

"The Caid will pledge his allegiance to France. We will align ourselves with you and control the tribes and the countryside as we do for the Sultan. We will establish French law and fly the French flag."

Tariq heard silence for a few moments and tried to take his mind off his increasingly painful bladder. He had to grit his teeth; the pain was becoming unbearable.

"And your Caid will take direct orders from Paris?" asked the General.

"Of course!"

"And collect taxes on behalf of France?"

"We already collect taxes on behalf of the Sultan. We will simply pay France instead of him."

"Very interesting, what do you ask for in return?"

"Arms and troops are all we ask for, General. We need ammunition to defeat these desert rats. If we had modern guns, it would be no problem to control the countryside. These tribes already fear the Sultan. If we have the most modern weapons, they will never consider going against France."

Tariq heard another moment of silence, then more shuffling. He started to count sheep until his head was dizzy. He thought of the desert, which made him think of dryness, which made him think of rain, which only made his bladder worse!

"I will need an agreement drafted, pledging your allegiance to France. I will need something else, as well."

"What is it, General?"

"A French garrison to work with the Caid to ensure he works on the side of France."

"The Caid anticipated this and, I assure you, it will not be a problem. We have drafted an agreement with the proposed terms and treaty."

The general took the agreement, quickly looked it over, and placed it in his briefcase.

"Well then, I am impressed. I will return to Paris in four days' time and will present your proposal to my superiors. I imagine they will want to move quickly if the terms are agreeable. In the meantime, you know how to reach me."

"Of course, General!"

Tariq heard standing up and shuffling and some pleasant goodbyes, more shuffling of feet, until finally everyone had left the room.

Worming his way out of his contorted position, he thought about relieving himself right there on the floor but thought better of it. He started to run out of the room when…his left foot had fallen asleep and was numb!

"Blast! Can anything else go wrong?" he thought to himself.

Dragging his left foot behind him, he managed to get to the door. He made sure no one was outside the room, crossed the hallway, stumbled back down to the storage room, dragged himself through the window and landed hard on the ground. Picking himself up, he immediately began to relieve himself. It was taking forever!

That's when he heard the two guards again!

Couldn't this hurry up? It was taking so long and there was nothing he could do to pee faster. He was worried and hurried and trying everything to go faster but nothing would when…the guards came around the corner and saw him.

"Hey there, what are you doing?" one of them asked.

Tariq coolly looked at them and replied.

"I'm peeing. What does it look like I'm doing?"

"Are you supposed to be here?" the other asked.

"Of course, I'm the new tea boy. I was just taking a break."

"Tea boy?"

"Yes, I was just hired. Would you like some tea? I make a delicious mint tea and would be happy to bring some to you. My name is Mahesh; please let me know if you need anything."

The guards, both confused, looked at one another, shrugged, and continued to walk.

"Yes, yes, bring us some tea. We'll be over at the east gate."

"Yes, Sire, I will bring it right over. I'll bring over some warm and delicious baklava as well."

The guards ignored Tariq and continued to walk their beat.

He couldn't very well go out the way he came in as the two guards would now be standing directly next to the tree. He started to go the other way but that led to the main entrance and many more guards. He wasn't sure what to do until he heard another voice.

"What tea boy? I don't know of any tea boy," the voice said.

"He's over here. He was going to fetch us some mint tea and baklava," one of the other guards answered.

Tariq would be pinched for sure. He looked up and saw that the walls of the compound were actually brick and had little grooves. Months of scaling walls in the mountains had made him somewhat of an expert at rock climbing. So, up the wall he went, placing his fingers in the grooves of the bricks, making his way up until he was close enough to swing his way onto the roof.

"Where is he?" the voice asked.

"I don't know—he was just here. I guess he went to the kitchen."

"All right, if you see him again, come get me. I'd like some tea and baklava as well!"

Tariq breathed a sigh of relief. He was now on the roof of the compound. On his hands and knees, he began crawling across the roof to the other side where, hopefully, there might be a way to escape. The roof felt very steady and he didn't think twice about putting weight on it until, that is, he came to a section with loose terra cotta tiles. They weren't constructed properly and very unstable.

There had been recent rains, which made them even weaker.

This section of the roof was way too fragile to hold any weight.

And Tariq was weight.

Suddenly, he felt himself falling through the air, screaming as he fell, before landing on someone below. Plaster and broken tiles fell on top of him. Dust spilled out everywhere. He looked up to a roomful of guards, some of whom were standing up in awe; others sat playing cards, staring at both Tariq and the fat corporal directly beneath him.

They stared at one another for a second until one of the guards yelled, "Get him!"

Tariq got to his feet as quickly as he could, ran out of the building, and was just behind the French general's car, which was exiting the main entrance. The gates were open for the general, with the Caid's guards at either side in a salute. As the car passed through the gates and turned right, Tariq sprinted out of the compound, completely covered in dust, his face and body as white as a sheet, running as fast as he could down the street.

Being chased by six guards.

Aseem and Fez, who were playing a game of dice with some other street urchins, looked up just as Tariq went screaming by them, covered in white dust with half a dozen guards in hot pursuit.

Looking at one another, they dropped the dice and took off after Tariq and the guards.

"We need to distract the guards!" Aseem yelled.

"How?" Fez replied.

"I don't know!"

Tariq looked back and saw the guards only fifteen feet behind him. He cut through a market square, and then ran through a vegetable cart, causing cabbage, carrots and lettuce to erupt everywhere to the curses of the cart owner. This slowed the guards down a little, as they had to jump over the cart; one guard slipped on a carrot while another banged his knee on the cart.

Darting between more carts, he ran through a restaurant, hitting a waiter, causing him to drop a plate of food on the table of customers in front of him. Tariq ran on through the dining room, into the kitchen, and out through the back door.

Now he was being chased by the guards, the cart owner, and the restaurant owner.

Every manner of profanity was being hurled at Tariq as he sprinted through the market.

Running even faster, he noticed a beautiful building with its huge doors wide open. Hurdling over a fence, he dashed up the front stairs into the building. He soon realized he had entered a mosque, as he ran right into a wedding ceremony, complete with hundreds of patrons. Everyone was dancing and singing and thoroughly enjoying the wedding reception. As Tariq darted through all the people, putting some time between him and his pursuers, he looked back over his shoulder and—wham! He ran straight into something, or someone.

Lying on the ground, a little dizzy, he looked up at the most obese, ugly woman with makeup and cake smeared across her face. Apparently Tariq had run into her and knocked her down! In the process, he had also knocked the piece of cake she was eating all over her face and dress. Judging by her elaborate attire, this could only be the bride! She yelled at Tariq, the fat on her arms wiggling up and down like Jell-O as she berated him.

Quickly standing up, he noticed a sheepish-looking man standing next to the bride in complete amazement. This could only be the groom! His wife continued to yell louder and louder, until everyone in the dance hall had stopped to stare at the scene unfolding in front of them.

Standing up, Tariq did a double-take of the bride and groom, and bowed slightly to the groom.

"My condolences, sir!" he said, before running off through the hall.

This only infuriated the bride even further.

Out the dance hall he went, now being pursued by the police, the cart owner, the restaurant owner, some wedding patrons, and the bride who was shouting above all else, trying to run in wedding attire with cake still plastered all over her face and body.

Tariq noticed a flight of stairs leading up to some apartments on his right. Sprinting up the stairs and onto the rooftop, there was a five foot leap to the next apartment building. Tariq made the leap, but landed awkwardly in some clothes hanging from a line. A pair of trousers covered his eyes and he went crashing to the floor, taking down the entire line of clothes in the process. Picking himself up, the posse was hot on his trail and about to make the leap. He threw the trousers off his face and leaped to the next building.

And then to the next.

He continued to run across the rooftops, crashing over furniture and clotheslines, with everyone in pursuit jumping from rooftop to rooftop behind him, except for the bride, who stood at the farthest rooftop hurling profanities at Tariq.

He finally came to an edge where it was too far to leap to the next rooftop. To his left, he saw some stairs, which he ran down, leading him to a door to his left. Without thinking, he opened the door and ran straight into someone's apartment.

A nice family was sitting down to dinner when Tariq ran through their living room, looked at the meal and smiled, before running through to an open window. Looking out, he saw a tree branch only a foot away. Quickly, he leaped onto the branch and made his way down the tree, almost four stories to the ground below.

Seconds later, the guards, the cart owner, the restaurant owner, and half the wedding party came running through the same living room, pardoning themselves to the family of four eating dinner. The family pointed to the window, but the party decided that taking the stairs was more prudent than following Tariq down the tree.

Running outside, Tariq knew he had to lose his captors. He doubted he could outrun them for much longer, as there were just too many of them. He had to find a hiding spot!

He didn't know which direction to run and he began to panic.

That's when he saw them—red hand prints along a wall in an alleyway!

Then, in his head, he heard the unmistakable voice of his friend, Aji.

"This way, Tariq," the voice commanded.

Tariq immediately tore down the alleyway, following the red hand prints.

Turning a corner, he saw a wagon harnessed to a horse, and the door was slightly ajar in the rear. Without a moment to waste he dove in the back of the wagon and closed the door behind him. The interior was a mass of boxes, shelves, and even a bed. Above, there was a cabinet on either side. Quickly, Tariq made his way up, opened a cabinet, and squeezed inside. It wasn't too bad a fit, especially after squeezing under that coat closet; at least here he was able to stretch out. He had to move some clothes and such to the front, which actually made for a nice pillow.

He felt his heart racing and prayed that nobody saw him enter the wagon. From inside the cabinet, all he could hear was his breath. After a few seconds, he heard the muffled sounds of the posse running and shouting past him. He waited and, after few more moments, he heard their voices again. Obviously they were searching for him. He continued to hear their voices when, amazingly, he heard the door lock behind him and the wagon started to move.

It looked like he was safe from the posse, but now he was in a wagon headed to somewhere. Where?

He had no idea.

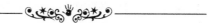

Margaret and Alice sat outside the Dansbury residence. It was a plush house, complete with ten bedrooms and a half-acre English garden out the back. It was a Victorian home, barely ten years old, with indoor plumbing and electric light fixtures. The Dansburys had spared no expense in designing the house with the latest technology and fixtures.

Today, of all days, the house was especially made up and fit to order. It was Hillie's fifteenth birthday, and her mother went overboard in decorating the house with vases of fresh flowers, ribbons, balloons, and intricately cut paper garlands. Six long tables, each covered with English linen and dressed with the finest china and cutlery, sat arranged in the backyard awaiting the sixty party guests. At the far end of these tables was a circular table made of fine Italian marble. Atop this beautiful table sat a five-layer white birthday cake with fresh strawberries dotted on the edge of each layer. Below the table was a velvet rug on which guests could lay their presents for Hillie. The Dansburys had already laid a dozen gifts under the table.

Margaret and Alice, of course, had not been invited to the party. This wasn't a tragedy to Alice, because she'd never been invited to anything of Hillie's, but for Margaret it was a different story. This was the first birthday of Hillie's that Margaret had ever missed. Even when she was an infant, their respective mothers had celebrated their daughters' birthdays together.

Margaret might have felt bad about what they were about to do, except that Hillie and her clique had increased their attacks against Margaret and Alice over the last couple of weeks. They spread vicious gossip about the two of them, at one point initiating a rumor that Alice had spent time in a mental institution prior to arriving at their school. Both of them had been called "little smellies," because Hillie insisted their breath reeked of garlic and fish. This couldn't be further from the truth as both girls took excellent care of their dental hygiene. This just went along with all the other jokes, snickers, and glaring faces that Margaret and Alice were subjected to every day.

But they were about to get even.

Two weeks ago Margaret had drafted a document entitled "Operation Mayhem," in which she and Alice would conduct a series of attacks against any and all aggressors. Hillie and Miss Cromwell were at the top of the list.

Margaret had decided, once and for all, that she wasn't going to be a victim—to any of these people. She had to fight back, but fight back in an intelligent manner.

Nobody could know that she and Alice were behind these attacks. They must remain safely anonymous to ensure that no further harm came to either of their families.

The two girls sat hidden safely behind shrubbery at the rear of the Dansbury home outside the servants' entrance, which led directly to the kitchen where all the food and drinks were being prepared. This hiding place was a good vantage point, but still twenty feet from the entrance— they had a lot of ground to cover quickly without being seen. They only hoped that an opportune moment would present itself. Otherwise the mission would need to be aborted.

Margaret disguised herself with a cap and oval glasses in the event anyone spotted her. Alice wore a hat and scarf to cover her red hair and face as much as possible.

In the front, guests started to arrive, while the kitchen servants went about carrying out platters of tea cakes, imported cheeses, crackers, fruits, cookies, and even some Russian caviar for the adults.

A giant paned glass window allowed the girls to see the comings and goings of the kitchen staff. Margaret stared at the twelve pots on the counter that had just been put out by a staff member. Undoubtedly they were for the tea that was about to be served. The English loved their tea; they swore by it, and would drink two or three servings each at a party like this. Undoubtedly, the Dansburys would serve the finest tea in England, and were sure to serve it early, just so Mrs. Dansbury could hear the compliments about her "lovely tea selection."

At last the kitchen was empty; Alice and Margaret sprang into action. Quickly, they moved to the entrance. Finally, they were inside the kitchen, looking over the tops of the tea pots. Each pot had a silver tea leaf holder inside, patiently waiting for the water to boil so the leaves could steep before being served to the guests.

Alice and Margaret each produced a bottle of "Needles Extra-Strength Laxative" and proceeded to pour several tablespoons in each pot.

"Hurry," Alice urged, as she finished pouring into the last pot.

"I think I hear someone coming!" Margaret whispered.

Footsteps could be heard coming down the hallway, the wood creaking with each step. Mrs. Dansbury swung open the kitchen door and stared at the empty kitchen. The tea pots stood like good little soldiers on the table, awaiting the hot water.

"For goodness' sake," she exclaimed, clearly irritated with the staff, and proceeded to pour boiling water in each tea pot, quickly putting the lid on each so the tea would stay hot.

A staff maid by the name of Imelda entered the kitchen soon thereafter, to the scorn of Mrs. Dansbury.

"Imelda, I wanted the tea served first, prior to the appetizers. Please bring these out in two minutes time and begin serving our guests," she ordered.

"Yes, ma'am," Imelda obediently answered.

Mrs. Dansbury stood, hovering, as Imelda hurriedly prepared the tea pots on a circular tray and began to bring them outside. Mrs. Dansbury ensured there was a cup of cream and sugar for every tea pot, arranged on tiny doilies for a proper presentation.

Alice and Margaret lay hidden in a low, extra-wide platter cupboard, just by Mrs. Dansbury's ankles. The cupboard was closed, but they could hear her voice and the movements outside. Both of them were completely scrunched together in the cupboard, trying not to make a noise.

"Wait Imelda, don't use that tray, there's one down here that's more presentable," Mrs. Dansbury instructed and was about to open the cupboard door where Alice and Margaret were hiding. Mrs. Danbury's fingers were only inches away from the handle! Alice and Margaret held their breath, certain they would be discovered.

"Wait ma'am, I moved that really nice tray to the pantry. I'll go get it," Imelda interrupted, just as Mrs. Dansbury grabbed the cupboard's handle.

"Very well, please be quick about it," she said, pulling her hand away and going back to the tea arrangement. Margaret and Alice couldn't see one another, but they both had relief on their faces.

Imelda didn't take long at all. Mrs. Dansbury went about arranging the new tray for perfect presentation, and then went outside to her guests, followed by Imelda with the massive tray on her shoulder.

"Let's get out of here!" Margaret whispered to Alice.

"I'm with you."

The two girls squirmed and wiggled out of their tight compartment, ran out of the kitchen and back to the hidden confines of the shrubbery. Looking back as they ran, they made certain they were not spotted. After several moments, catching their breath in the bushes, they backtracked and ran out into the residential street. Running down a block and then cutting over, they made their way down an alley to a tall tree. They scrambled up the tree, each finally resting on a limb protected by leaves and branches. From their perch, they were completely hidden and could easily watch the Dansbury party.

Down below, Hillie's birthday party was in full swing. Most of the guests had arrived and stood around the grounds eating biscuits and, of course, drinking their tea. Margaret knew that Hillie and all her friends were drinking tea because they were trying to be so "grown-up." These girls had even started drinking it during breaks at school, sitting around a cafeteria table, pretending to be adults. It was just one more activity that Margaret and Alice had been excluded from.

"Just wait," Margaret whispered, a sly grin on her face. Alice smiled back at her.

Neither girl had ever done anything like this. They knew it was bad, they knew they could get in trouble for it and yet, somehow, it felt so good. It felt so good to fire back at their tormenters, to not feel like such a victim or an outcast.

To feel strong.

The two girls hung on the limb when, suddenly, an elderly woman shrieked "Oh my goodness!" and went running to the house.

Margaret and Alice looked at each other, started giggling, put their hands over their mouths to stop from laughing, and continued to watch the party.

There was a distinctive murmur, as the guests could scarcely guess at what had caused the woman's unexplained behavior. Soon, they went back to what they were doing, continuing to eat and drink and be merry.

After a few moments, Alice and Margaret noticed a couple of guests hold their stomach and begin running for the house. This didn't go unnoticed by the other guests, and soon the murmur of the party was a quiet hum as the guests were trying to surmise why people kept running to the house.

Three more guests excused themselves and quickly went inside the house. By this time, the remaining guests were nervously looking at one another and hardly anyone was saying a word.

Then Margaret saw it. Hillie Dansbury's face! Hillie doubled over, grabbed her stomach, and ran to the house, followed by two other girls.

Guests dashed back out of the house—no doubt because all the lavatories were occupied—and ran to the trees on either side of the house. Guests came running out the front door and down the block. They ran to other houses on the street, knocking on doors, begging to use the facilities.

The scene was complete and utter chaos.

Margaret and Alice continued to giggle and finally they climbed down from the tree and began laughing hysterically. Both fell to the ground and Alice laughed so hard she snorted, making both girls laugh even harder.

"It's not true, Alice," Margaret finally managed to say.

"What isn't?"

"Revenge isn't a dish best served cold. It's a dish best served with a laxative."

At this, both girls began rolling on the ground, laughing so hard they were crying at the same time.

The following Monday, Margaret and Alice ate lunch together as usual. Hillie and her clan came in, but none of them looked remotely chipper or happy. They all looked miserable. Hillie merely sat with her back to a wall, not eating and not saying a word. In fact, none of the girls said a word.

"Should we go say something to her?" Alice asked.

"No, she mustn't have a clue it was us. Besides, we still have Miss Cromwell on our list."

Alice smiled at this.

Aseem and Fez had become split off from Tariq. The Caid's soldiers were everywhere looking for him, so the two boys had to keep a low profile and keep up the façade that they were regular orphans. For hours they scoured the city streets but could not find Tariq. Awakening at daybreak, they continued to search the streets and stood watching outside the compound, but there was no sign of him.

At just past noon the next day, the gate opened and a group of the Caid's guards came through. One of them was at the head of the group, looking more important than the rest.

Fez recognized him instantly.

"We must hide—now!" he whispered to Aseem.

The two of them pretended to scrounge for garbage as the group passed them. Fez ensured that his face was hidden from the group. After they passed, Aseem looked puzzled at Fez.

"What was that about?" Aseem asked.

Fez's skin had gone white and his pupils were dilated with fear.

"The man at the head of that group. He is from my tribe. He is the man who betrayed my family to the Caid. His name is Nur," Fez explained, a solemn sound in his voice.

Aseem looked at Nur as he passed down the street. He was young and had very long hair down to his shoulders. Aseem could just make out his face, which was narrow and shaped like that of a bird.

"He is the man who killed your family? I thought you said it was Zahir."

"It was Nur who caused their deaths by being an informant against us. He helped Zahir to trap my family, and our entire tribe, resulting in their massacre."

Fez began to cry, and Aseem held and comforted him. Tears rolled down Fez's cheeks, and he buried his face in his hands. All the memories and feelings of that fateful day came rushing back to him. He sobbed for another five minutes, while Aseem simply held him and told him everything would be okay.

"The last thing my father said to me was to avenge them. He meant Nur. He meant I must kill Nur!"

"Yes, you must, and I will help you," Aseem replied softly.

"You will?" Fez stammered.

"Yes, we will avenge your family and then find Tariq. That is what we do. We look out for one another, right?"

Fez stopped crying and dried his tears on his dirty shirt sleeve.

"First, let's try to find Tariq, and then we'll come up with a plan for Nur. Malik will worry about us," Fez suggested, deep in thought.

"Malik will be fine. We have important matters right here."

Fez gathered his thoughts for a moment before speaking again.

"Tariq is not in the jail, or we would have heard something. The Caid's guards do not appear to have him. We even checked the funeral homes and he is nowhere to be found. So, he must be hiding somewhere."

Just then, a voice came from behind the boys. They had been so pre-occupied they had completely forgotten about their surroundings.

"Say, aren't you the two boys who escaped from the Caid's kasbah?" the voice asked.

Aseem and Fez froze with fear.

They had been discovered.

Malik paced apprehensively in his tent. He had not slept for days and was constantly worried throughout the day.

Where were the boys?

He had heard nothing.

"Do not worry Malik, I'm sure they are fine," Sanaa said, coming into his tent.

"I wish I could share your optimism," he replied mournfully.

"Those three have a knack for survival. I'm sure we would have heard if something had happened to them. I have heard nothing from my spies about boys being captured in Chaouen. Besides, ours is a tough life. Boys must grow into men at an early age. They were ready. And they are probably our best opportunity to learn of the Caid's plan. Please, do not let this trouble you. The boys wanted to go," Sanaa tried to explain.

Normally, she didn't believe in such pleasantries. However, she had known Malik for most of her life, and she had never seen him so troubled.

"I suppose so," he said, but not entirely convinced.

"I have, however, received word that a shipment is being sent to the Caid in two days' time. Let's prepare a party to intercept it. It will give you something to think about besides the boys," she offered.

Malik nodded in agreement.

"Okay, let's discuss the route and make preparations."

CHAPTER
— *10* —

A MOST INTERESTING COURTSHIP

Years Ago

Zijuan walked up the city street with little Sanaa behind her, now seven years old. Zijuan had become a surrogate mother to Sanaa since rescuing her from the slave market in China. The trip from Shanghai to Morocco had been uneventful, and Captain Basil had been a complete gentleman. Zijuan had done her best to return all the children to their homes—that is, all the children who had homes. These efforts had taken her the better part of three weeks and Sanaa was the last of them.

That wasn't an accident.

Sanaa was undoubtedly Zijuan's favorite. Zijuan saw fierceness in her that reminded her of herself. Sanaa was so quiet and studious and never raised a fuss or complained. She had taken to following Zijuan wherever she went like a lost puppy, and Zijuan found that she enjoyed the company. In fact, she nicknamed Sanaa "Little Shadow," as she was always at her side.

It had taken days for Zijuan to finally discover the whereabouts of Sanaa's home. She discovered that little girls have poor memories and no sense of direction. After asking more than a dozen people, she finally procured the proper address. Fortunately she had learned enough Arabic over three months to make simple conversation and had a rudimentary grasp of the language.

The house was two stories tall, nice but not opulent, with a little garden out front. It was obviously a house of the middle class. As she knocked on the wooden door, Zijuan felt a sense of dread, as she realized this would be the last time that she spent time with little Sanaa who, oddly, didn't seem excited about seeing her home. Zijuan had expected the girl to be beside herself with joy at the prospect of seeing her parents and brothers and sisters for the first time in months, but Sanaa simply stood at Zijuan's side, holding her hand, a blank expression on her face.

"Yes," an old woman said, answering the door. She was obviously a servant and appeared to be in her sixties. She looked at Zijuan and then, seeing Sanaa, burst into tears and hugged her, bringing her up into her chest.

Zijuan stepped back, allowing the woman to hug and kiss Sanaa and hold her tightly.

There was a commotion in the house, other voices were heard, and soon a large, burly man stepped outside. Seeing Sanaa, the look on his face went from one of fierceness to one of astonishment.

Yet, he didn't go to her.

Soon, a woman of about thirty came to the door, saw little Sanaa, let out a shriek, and started to go to Sanaa. But the burly man stopped her.

A young boy and girl then came to the door, each surprised to see little Sanaa, but both were held back by the man from hugging or even going to her.

Zijuan didn't understand.

The old woman continued to hold and console Sanaa. The man stepped back inside with the family and closed the door.

The old woman looked behind her at the closed door. Immediately her outlook towards Sanaa took a turn for the worse. She was still crying, but her tears seemed to be from sorrow now rather than happiness. She hugged Sanaa, but in a way that seemed to say she'd never see her again.

Zijuan continued to wait, not wanting to disturb the family. She waited for five minutes, until finally the burly man opened the door, stepped out, and immediately closed it behind him.

He came right to Zijuan.

"How did you find my daughter?" he asked in a most unfriendly voice. He had an overgrown brown moustache and his breath reeked of garlic.

"I rescued her from a slave market. I have traveled a long time over a great distance to bring her back to you," Zijuan tried to explain.

The man took in this information, rubbed his right hand on his chin, and seemed to be thinking.

Finally, he spoke to Zijuan.

"My daughter has shamed my family. I cannot welcome her back in this home. She is your problem now."

Zijuan had to take a step backwards to absorb this news. Was her father really telling her that he did not want her?

"You are her father?" she asked.

"Yes!"

"My Arabic is very bad. Do I understand that you do not want her?"

"That is correct. She has shamed my name and will not be welcome in this house. Now and forever!"

"But she is your daughter!"

The man was beginning to become angry and Zijuan could see this might end badly.

"She is your daughter now. My wife and children are forbidden from seeing her again, or from ever speaking her name again."

"But she is just a child, how could she shame you? She was the one who was kidnapped!"

The man became angry at this line of questioning from a woman. How dare a slight and skinny woman question his authority? Stepping forward, he was about to hit Zijuan when, suddenly, her demeanor changed. She matched his ferocity and stood her ground.

She knew she could break his back within a few seconds.

The standoff continued for only five seconds until the man, finally understanding that Zijuan would not back down, stormed off, grabbed his wailing servant and closed the door behind them.

Zijuan and Sanaa were alone.

Zijuan almost broke into tears herself. How could a father ever cast his seven-year-old daughter out into the world?

"Come Sanaa, you are mine now," Zijuan whispered to her, taking her hand and leading her away from the house. They walked quickly out of town. Sanaa never said a word, simply walked behind Zijuan.

Outside of town, there were still about twelve children who did not have homes. They had set up a makeshift camp, where they waited for Zijuan to return. The orphans were surprised to see Sanaa still with her, but secretly glad. Sanaa would join the ranks of those with no home.

Zijuan did not have a plan. She hadn't enjoyed what little city life she had experienced in Morocco and felt the children would be much more vulnerable to the underworld and the temptations of modern life if she stayed in the city. She decided they would be better off in the country, yet she knew nothing of how to survive in the Moroccan mountains. She purchased a map from a merchant to get an idea of some trails leading into the Rif Mountains.

Securing a basic cart and the bare necessities of food and clothing, she and the children headed out on a dirt trail into the countryside.

For four days they traveled, finally reaching the base of the mountains and heading up into a mountain pass. It was spring, so mornings and evenings were still quite cold, but the days were warmed by the sun. Zijuan did an admirable job setting traps for rabbits and squirrels and shooting the occasional dove. Still, being unfamiliar with the countryside was a real disadvantage, and hunting went much more slowly than she would have liked.

On the fifth day, she decided to set up camp in a protected area next to a stream. There was an abundance of trees to protect the children from the elements and a bit of an overhang from a cliff that served as a natural shelter. Zijuan had them foraging for branches to stockpile for a fire. They put down rugs and put up tents for homes. Zijuan assigned some of the children to fish detail, knowing there would be plenty of brook trout for the taking. With the rest, she went on a hike to look for fruits or berries.

They walked for a couple of miles without seeing much, until they came upon a dry area. There they found a tree with yellow fruit spilled on the ground. Zijuan picked up one of the fruits, was about to bite into it, when a voice came up from behind them.

"No, no!" the voice yelled.

Zijuan dropped the fruit on the ground, stunned that they had been followed.

A man dressed in a brown robe came running from behind them. He had a slight black beard dotted with gray whiskers, and his skin was bronzed, with wrinkles at the cheekbones. His face was very thin.

"No, no!" he continued to yell and point at the ground.

"Thank you," Zijuan said and bowed slightly.

"You speak Arabic?" the man asked.

"A little, I am still learning."

The man studied Zijuan; it was the first time he had ever seen an Asian person, man or woman. He looked around at the children and seemed confused by the situation. Zijuan could see he was a kind man with a ready smile.

"Who are these children?" he finally asked.

Zijuan explained the entire situation, from her discovery and rescue of the children in China to their return trip to Morocco. Zijuan explained that these children were orphans she had saved from slavery. The man listened intently, his facial expressions showing more and more surprise with each twist of the story. He learned there were even more children, back at the camp fishing and gathering.

After Zijuan was finished, he nodded his head, thought for a few seconds, and then spoke.

"Come, you will join our people. We will teach you the ways of the mountains."

"No, that is too generous, I could not impose on you like that," Zijuan argued.

"It is Allah's will that I met you on this trail. It is Allah's will—you were brought to me for a reason. We will take you in—and the children too—as if they were our own. Are we not all one people in your God's eyes?" the man asked, kindly.

Zijuan could see the compassion in the man's eyes and decided, on the spot, to trust him. Besides, she still didn't quite know what she was going to do in the countryside or how she would care for the children.

Quickly they returned to camp and packed up, and made their way deeper into the mountains. Zijuan learned that the man's name was Armestan and he was part of the Gzennaya tribe. He was very high up in their chief council and his opinion held much weight within his tribe.

After two days, they came upon an encampment with about a hundred people. It was morning, and the camp was just waking when some of them saw Armestan and came to welcome him. Amazed at seeing Zijuan and the children, some of the people wanted to touch Zijuan's face because it was so different from their own.

Soon, the entire tribe surrounded the group and there was much laughing and welcoming. Zijuan and the children were shown to various tents, which were constructed in a manner of minutes, and told to stow their belongings inside. Zijuan was quickly shuffled to the various chieftains and presented with all manner of presents and gifts. Every face was warm and generous and completely selfless.

There was no reservation that Zijuan and the children would join their tribe. Children, and especially women, were held in very high esteem within their tribe. The story of Zijuan's journey quickly made it around the tribe and she turned into a kind of celebrity. Zijuan proved to be a valuable addition, and was instantly considered the best fighter in all the tribe. In fact, the males would seek her counsel on fighting skills. Soon she would be training the entire tribe to fight.

This went on for three years without incident.

One day, Armestan appeared again with a boy of about ten. He was dressed very differently than the rest of the children. His clothes were from the finest tailors and he seemed to be of noble blood.

Armestan quickly explained the situation. He had found the boy wandering in the desert. His father had cast him out of the house for performing poorly in a horse race, saying that the boy had disgraced his name and his family.

The other children were curious about this boy. They gathered around him, staring at his dirty face, which was streaked with dry tears.

"His name is Malik," Armestan explained.

Sanaa listened to the story and stared at Malik. They were the same age and she could see the loss and hurt on his face. His story reminded her so much of her own.

There was something else extraordinary about this boy.

He was beautiful. His features were soft and delicate, and his face was narrow and handsome. Sanaa had never thought of boys in romantic terms before that moment, but, for Malik, she felt something.

Malik did not see Sanaa staring at him. He did not really see anyone. One moment he was playing in his father's magnificent house, and now he was joining a mountain tribe who lived in the dirt. He didn't understand why any of this was happening to him.

Soon, he was shuffled off to a tent where he joined an outdoor classroom with the other children. The class was held under a massive oak tree where a teacher explained the differences in the various plants—which ones were edible and which ones were poisonous. Then, a different teacher began teaching the basics of tracking and the entire classroom went on a hunt to track a deer. That night, they all sat up and were given lessons on celestial tracking by the stars.

All the while, Sanaa stared at him, but couldn't summon the courage to actually speak with him.

After a week, Malik still hadn't really spoken to anyone. Some of the other boys were beginning to pick on him a bit and labeled him a rich boy. A few of the bigger ones were teasing him when he decided he'd had enough and hit one in the mouth, knocking him to the dirt.

The boy, who was quite a bit bigger than Malik, gathered himself and realized he had blood coming from his lip. Enraged, he tackled Malik.

Three other boys joined in on the scrum, tackling and kicking Malik.

Sanaa, seeing what was happening, jumped into action and kicked one boy in the shin, sending him off screaming. Grabbing another boy by the neck, she flipped him over her shoulder where he landed hard on the ground.

The other boys, afraid of Sanaa, quickly backed off and ran away.

"Thank you," Malik said, dusting himself off.

It was the first time they had spoken.

"You could have taken one of them, but four was not fair," Sanaa replied.

"Not too many for you! Where did you learn to fight like that?"

Sanaa blushed with embarrassment at his compliment. Zijuan had secretly given Sanaa private lessons and she had become the best fighter of all the children. In fact, she was such a fierce fighter the other children were all petrified of her—even at ten years old!

"My name is Malik," he said, and extended his hand to hers.

"I am Sanaa," she whispered, thoroughly embarrassed to be talking to him.

The two shook hands and Sanaa could hardly contain herself at his soft touch. If she was infatuated with Malik before, now it had turned into a full-blown crush.

Still, she was only ten.

The two became best friends and did absolutely everything together. They hunted, trapped, built campfires, and played game after game together. Since both were loners, they really didn't have too many other friends within the tribe. They simply liked each other's company that much.

After five years, Sanaa still had strong feelings for Malik, but she didn't know how to express them to him. They were, after all, best friends and she didn't want to jeopardize their friendship. There were whispers among the other children that they were a couple, but nobody dared say anything to their faces. They had become, without a doubt, the best fighters in the entire tribe.

In fact, none of the boys would fight with Sanaa, so she was always forced to fight Malik in the village games. Their competitions became more and more intense, as both were so competitive.

At one of the games, they were pitted against one another in a game that required both agility and fighting ability. A log was placed about ten feet off the ground. Malik and Sanaa started at opposite ends, each with a three foot long stick. The object was to knock the other off and the winner would be declared tribe champion.

These public games were taken quite seriously by the tribe and everyone both attended and participated in them. To do well was to gain stature within the tribe and a position of leadership.

Sanaa gingerly walked across the log, her footing secure, watching Malik's every move. She expected him to rush at her in an effort to throw her off-balance.

Malik, for his part, started out a bit timid on the log. He considered rushing Sanaa, but thought it better to be conservative. He tiptoed across the log, stick in hand, preparing for attack. He was much more aggressive than Sanaa and typically attacked first, whereas Sanaa was more of a counterpuncher, who would parry attacks before launching her own offensive.

The two were now only a few feet apart. Malik did something sneaky, bringing his stick down and swinging for Sanaa's ankles. Sanaa, unprepared for such an attack, couldn't get her stick down and had to jump two feet in the air, bringing her knees to her chest, just missing the stick beneath her feet. She landed hard on the log and barely missed falling.

Malik, seeing that she was off balance, immediately launched another attack, this time at her face.

Trying to maintain her balance, she backed up a foot while maneuvering her stick so Malik's stick was blocked and deflected to one side.

The crowd gasped with appreciation.

Sanaa quickly regained her footing and parried with the butt of her stick at Malik's nose. He just managed to move his head away in time.

She quickly brought the stick overhead in three quick successions, driving him backwards, and making him play defense as he was forced to block her blows.

Understanding that each attack must be met with an equal counterattack of aggression, she would not allow Malik to bully her.

This back-and-forth set of attacks went on for a full minute of constant action. The two combatants never stopped moving and never stopped attacking. Their moves were a whirlwind of activity, and the audible snap of their sticks was like two woodpeckers destroying a tree.

The crowd erupted with applause and cheered. Usually the matches lasted just a few seconds; this was turning into an epic battle. At one point Malik brought his stick full force against Sanaa's upper arm and almost knocked her off the log. She somehow managed to maintain her balance and launch a counterattack.

Then, Malik made a mistake.

He got too close to Sanaa.

Stick-fighting was meant to be fought at a distance. However, in his haste, he was within a foot of Sanaa.

Seeing his mistake, Sanaa distracted him by doing a three sixty with her stick overhead. Malik was so focused on the stick he forgot that he was within kicking range.

Sanaa quickly stepped back and launched a perfect side kick, outstretching her leg and landing her heel perfectly on Malik's jaw.

The kick was powerful enough that it drove Malik backwards, forcing him to lose his balance. He landed hard on his backside, and then fell off the log completely.

Sanaa had won!

Again the crowd erupted in applause, as this was one of the best battles they had witnessed in some time. Malik continued to lie on the ground, his jaw sore and blood pouring from his lips. The fall had knocked the wind out of him, and he was gasping for air.

He had been beaten, but worse, he felt humiliated.

Sanaa, a little embarrassed by all the adulation, leaped off the log to help Malik. She could see he was in some amount of pain.

"Are you okay?" she asked.

"Fine," he answered tersely.

"Great match, I thought you had me," she said, trying to make him feel a bit better.

"Good match," he mumbled, and then walked away.

Sanaa could clearly see he was disappointed and decided to let him be alone. Soon she was surrounded by the tribe's people who placed a wreath around her neck and took turns congratulating her.

Later that night, she went to Malik's tent to find him. She was happy at winning the match, but the way she felt about him and their friendship was much more important than some stupid competition. She found him in his tent, lying against a pillow, looking upset.

"Good match, eh?" she said, trying to make polite conversation.

He didn't say anything.

"Malik, what did you want me to do? Throw the match? You know that I'm a good fighter because we practice all the time…"

"That's different," he interrupted her.

"Why?"

"Because then it's just us. This was in front of the entire tribe."

"So, because it was in front of the tribe, that's what is upsetting you?"

"You wouldn't understand because you're a girl."

"What does that have to do with it?" Sanaa asked, obviously quite bothered by Malik's tone.

"I'm expected to be the best warrior in the tribe. I'm going to be the one fighting in wars."

"So will I!" Sanaa said, defiantly.

Malik stared straight ahead, his pride still very wounded.

"I don't think we should spend so much time together, Sanaa," he finally said.

"What?"

"I...I need other friends. I think we should spend time apart."

This wounded Sanaa more than anything else. What had she done that was so awful? She had competed and beaten him fairly. Why was Malik acting like this?

"Why? You are my best friend, Malik!"

"People think we are boyfriend and girlfriend, that's why."

Sanaa started to cry because she wanted Malik for a boyfriend. It's what she had always wanted.

She couldn't say anything. He had purposely tried to hurt her, and he had accomplished his objective. Staring into space, he ignored her tears.

"Fine," she said, and stormed out.

Sanaa went to a faraway brook and broke down, crying harder than she had ever cried in her short life. It felt as if her guts had been ripped out of her body. All the pain of her father's rejection came to the surface. All those emotions she kept deep down inside of her came up and she was sick, vomiting her food until there was nothing left. She couldn't vomit or cry any longer.

She sat on a log for half an hour until a strong feeling came over her.

She decided right then that she would never allow anyone to hurt her again. She had opened her heart to Malik and he stomped on it. If the world was this cruel, then she would fiercely protect herself.

At that moment, she decided to dedicate her life to becoming the best assassin in Morocco. She would be the best warrior in the tribe—all to spite Malik.

Never again would she allow Malik to see her feelings for him. In fact, she decided at that moment that she had been a stupid little girl for having a crush on some dumb boy.

Collecting herself, she walked back to her tent and slept for twelve hours. The next day, as usual, she went off to training. Malik was waiting for her, and wanted to apologize for his outburst. He felt horrible about the things he said and didn't sleep all night.

The truth was, he wanted Sanaa for his girlfriend and shared her feelings.

He began to apologize to her when she cut him off.

"You don't want me as a friend? Fine, we are not friends. I will be your comrade-in-arms and nothing more," she said and walked off.

She ignored him the rest of the day, the week, the month. Each time he tried to apologize, or talk to her, she walked away. She never even made eye contact with him.

This continued for months until eventually Malik gave up. They would be acquaintances and fight alongside one another, but she never gave him any kind of warmth or emotion.

In fact, she didn't show any warmth or emotion to anyone in the tribe. She simply trained all the time and became such a fierce fighter that most of the boys wouldn't even spar with her because she never fought at anything less than one hundred percent.

Neither she nor Malik wanted to speak of that incident again.

CHAPTER
— II —

SETTING A TRAP

After just one day, the Caid received his answer from the French—it seems they had anticipated his arrangement.

They had agreed to all of his terms. In a day's time, the French would send two hundred troops, currently stationed at a fort outside of Tangier, along with a convoy of rifles and ammunition. They had even agreed to send him money to pay his troops. Caid Ali Tamzali looked over the agreement with a sinister grin on his face.

It had all worked according to his plan.

He was now allied with a vastly powerful army, one that would help him defeat his enemies once and for all.

Miss Cromwell sat at her desk as she did each and every day after school. Obviously fastidious, she kept her office overly neat. Not a speck of dirt could be found. She demanded order in her life, and any kind of mess was seen as unacceptable. She used this time to fill out evaluations of others. The biblical verse "judge not, for ye shall be judged" meant little to her—judging others was her favorite pastime. She wanted to control others and constantly searched for ways to do so, always looking for little weaknesses in their character or lives.

As she sat at her desk, putting notes in yet another journal, she thought she heard something in the room, like the sound of a cupboard being opened. Looking around, she saw nothing and continued with her work.

After a few moments she was sure that she heard buzzing. Yes, she was positive she heard a buzzing sound, and then the buzzing grew louder and louder. Standing up, she looked around and that's when she spied them—bees! Not just one, but ten, then twenty, until finally a swarm of bees surrounded her. She swatted at them furiously.

That's when they began to sting her.

Throwing her hands up and screaming, Miss Cromwell started to run out of the room when her ankle caught on a leg of the desk, tripping her to the ground. This just upset the bees even more. The stings hurt and began to burn. She tried to stand up, but couldn't manage with her twisted ankle. In agony, she dragged herself to her hands while the bees continued to sting her. There were dozens of them, and they were more disturbed now that her fall had crushed some of their brethren. She screamed for help, but nobody heard her.

Still trying to stand, she grabbed a side of the desk and finally made it to her feet. The bees had stung her face and already the skin was starting to swell around her eyes.

In one urgent motion, dragging her swollen ankle, she made it to the door, opened the door, and slammed it behind her. A couple of bees made it out with her, but most were still in her room—trapped!

Slumping against the door, she felt her face swelling from the dozens of stings. After a few moments she gained the strength to limp out of the school to safety. A nearby teacher heard her screams and came running to her side. The teacher, a humble woman by the name of Allison Singleton, escorted her to the hospital, where they immediately attended to her sprained ankle and her very swollen face. The bees had turned her face into a big marshmallow! She would miss almost a week of school recovering.

Outside, Alice and Margaret knelt next to a ventilation shaft. A small crate-like box sat next to them, where they had kept the bees until they released them into the shaft that led directly to Miss Cromwell's office. They giggled with delight as they heard her scream and fall. After a couple of seconds, they took the box and ran off the school grounds, careful to conceal their route and identities.

It would have been perfect, except that a police detective heard what happened and made some inquiries. It turned out that two school girls had purchased two hundred bees from a local beekeeper just the day before. These two girls attended the local academy. It wasn't long before the detective made his way to Alice's house and then to Margaret's house.

After a brief inquiry, both girls confessed to the crime.

Margaret's mother was horrified. She sat Margaret down after the detective had left.

"Do you know what you have done?" Louise Owen screamed at her daughter.

Margaret sat in an overstuffed chair and she seemed to diminish in size. She was no longer the confident and rebellious teenager, but a scared little girl who knew she'd made a huge mistake.

"You've been expelled. Expelled! The only reason the detective didn't charge you with a crime is because you're a minor! That poor woman will be in the hospital for another week!"

"So what? I'm glad she's in the hospital! You don't know what she's like! She's evil, pure evil, and she got what she deserved!" Margaret yelled back.

Without thinking, Louise Owen brought her hand back and slapped Margaret hard across the face. They both were stunned at the action as neither Louise nor her husband had ever hit their children.

Margaret didn't say anything; she simply felt the sting of the slap, and tears began to run down her face.

"Margaret, I know you don't like her, but this is no way to go about getting even. You could have killed her!"

"I know. I'm sorry," Margaret whispered.

"I don't know what I'm going to do. You can't go back to that school now, and I doubt any other public school in London will have you."

Margaret sat there and began to realize the gravity of her situation. Not that she minded being expelled—she had grown to hate her school and dread each and every day she spent there. However, she never intended to put this much stress on her mother.

Dreyfuss had been docked in the Galite Islands for a day when a mysterious letter was presented to him from someone in Lanzarote. Opening the letter, he quickly read it and then had to re-read it. The letter was from Cortez—alias Sharif Al Montaro—explaining he was on the *Angelina Rouge* and reporting that they would be docked at Ile d'Yeu in a week's time.

"First mate, prepare the crew, we depart for Ile d'Yeu. I do believe we have Basil and Charles Owen finally trapped!" Dreyfuss ordered.

The crew was frenzied with preparations, and the British ship soon departed, full steam ahead for Ile d'Yeu.

Dreyfuss sat in the cockpit reading the letter and wondering if it was real. So many times he was sure he had the *Angelina Rouge* in his grasp, only to be outwitted by Captain Basil and Charles Owen. He was taking a chance on a simple letter, but the fact it was from Montaro meant he had to take this gamble. If anyone could capture the *Rouge*, it was Montaro.

Dreyfuss desperately wanted to arrive at Ile d'Yeu before the *Rouge* so he could ambush her and blow her out of the water.

The Mamba stared at the man in front of him. He was known to be a spy for Malik, and the Mamba had gotten to him a week earlier. His plan to use Jawad as bait had worked to perfection. It had only taken ten minutes of torture for the man to finally relent.

"And you gave them the information I specified?" the Mamba asked.

"Yes," the man sheepishly answered.

"What did you say?"

"That a shipment of arms was due in three days' time on the northernmost route."

"Good. You are sure it got back to Malik?" the Mamba asked.

"Yes, I have never failed them before," the man stammered.

"Excellent. Well, we shall have a surprise for Malik when he ambushes that shipment," the Mamba answered, not smiling and not amused by the man and his weakness.

He was a poor villager who had helped Malik and the rebellion. Over the months, he had provided valuable information on the Caïd's movements and troops.

"Are you going to kill me?" the man asked.

"Kill you? No, why would I kill you? You are now a spy for me. And, I want you to continue to spy for Malik and give me exact accounts of the information you provide to him."

The Mamba then threw the man a bag of coins—more money than the poor villager could have made in a year.

"Thank you, Sire," the man stammered and stumbled out of the Mamba's tent.

The Mamba was not stupid. He knew the only way to catch Malik was through the use of spies and intelligence. That was something the Caid had not figured out for himself. It didn't matter how many thousands of troops the Caid commanded or how modern their machines, he would never catch Malik and the rebels through force. They were too smart and too slippery in their mountains.

The Mamba would catch them utilizing cunning strategy.

Tariq was trapped! The cabinet in the wagon had locked him in. Rather than banging and shouting to get let out, he had simply relented and fallen asleep. It was actually quite comfortable and the spare clothes made a nice bed and pillow.

He had slept all through the night and into the morning.

He awoke when the wagon stopped and he heard rumbling around the cabin. A voice grumbled outside. Tariq lay listening when, suddenly, the cabinet door opened up and a man, looking very tired, stared into Tariq's eyes.

"Ahhhhhhh!" the man yelled.

"Ahhhhhhh!" Tariq yelled back.

Tariq fell out of the cabinet onto his stomach. He tried to make a run for it but the man grabbed him by his shirt.

"Who the heck are you?" the man yelled in strongly-accented Arabic.

"The Caid's men are chasing me. I needed a hiding place! I meant you no harm," Tariq replied quickly.

"All that fuss back in town was about you?" the man questioned

"Yes, I suppose."

The man, continuing to hold Tariq's shirt, stared at him up and down.

"Well, anyone who is an enemy of the Caid is a friend of mine. What did you do?" the man asked, letting go of Tariq's shirt.

"I am his sworn enemy," Tariq answered.

"That makes two of us. His troops keep hassling me and demanding payment every darn mile. That's why I travel at night. I'd rather worry about bandits than the Caid's soldiers."

Tariq liked this man!

He was about thirty years old with brown skin, and wore a type of cowboy hat with one side folded up. He wore a brown jacket, a button-down tan shirt, and thick, tan trousers. His brown boots were weathered and dusty. A talisman hung from his neck.

He looked like one of the American cowboys that Zijuan had described in her bedtime stories at the orphanage. She intrigued all the boys with stories of Doc Holliday and Wild Bill Hickok and even showed them some illustrations.

The man studied Tariq and nodded. A slight grin appeared on his face.

"My name is Tariq. I did not mean to startle you."

"Name is Jack. My friends call me Melbourne Jack."

"You're American?"

"No, Australian, mate."

"Australia?"

"You've never heard of Australia?"

"No, where is it?"

Melbourne Jack relaxed a bit and began to make preparations for a pot of coffee.

"A site a long way from this place, mate. Big, hot, and full of sand, that's Australia. At least, that's how I remember it."

"What are you doing in Morocco?"

Melbourne Jack smiled at this line of questioning. He'd come up with a variety of answers for inquiring minds regarding his whereabouts in Morocco. Sometimes he'd say he was on a religious pilgrimage. Other times he might say he was looking to purchase the famous Moroccan rugs, although he had finally stopped using that one because everyone and their cousin was a rug maker.

"On a bit of a walkabout," he replied casually before jumping on his wagon.

"What is a walkabout?" Tariq asked.

"You don't know what a walkabout is?"

"No."

"Well, a walkabout is like being an explorer, I reckon—seeing a place just because you're interested in seeing it, without a purpose."

Tariq thought about that for a second.

"So you're just riding around?"

"Pretty much, yeah, that's the point," Jack replied, and began to exit the cabin.

"You're welcome to breakfast. I understand you probably don't eat pork, but I've got some nice eggs and a bit of lentils."

Tariq was famished!

"Yes, please, I will help you prepare. That is very kind of you," Tariq replied excitedly, exiting the wagon, and began gathering sticks for a fire. He was accustomed to working hard for Malik and wanted to make himself useful.

The two made breakfast together. Melbourne Jack had a bit of a sixth sense about people, and he recognized the goodness in Tariq.

"So what's your plan?" he asked.

Tariq shrugged his shoulders and continued to hungrily shovel lentils into his mouth.

"To make my way back to Chaouen and find my friends."

"Look mate, Chaouen is swarming with the Caid's troops. Besides, it's at least a fifteen mile walk, and if the bandits don't get you, you'll look like a tasty treat for a jaguar."

Tariq hadn't thought about any of this.

"I must make it to my friends—they will be worried about me," Tariq replied solemnly.

Jack studied Tariq and scratched his head, thinking of a solution.

"You live in Chaouen?" he asked.

"No, my tribe is in the Rif Mountains."

"Well, I'm heading that way myself. I could give you a lift and then you could make your way back to your family. I'm sure your friends will head home after a while."

Tariq lifted his head at this thought.

"Really? You could give me a ride? That would be very nice of you."

"Just help me out a bit. It's only a couple of days' journey and then we'll have you back with your family. No worries mate!"

Tariq smiled at this thought. Besides, he instantly liked Jack and it would be much better to travel with him by wagon than to walk back by himself. He felt bad about leaving Fez and Aseem, but they would head home sooner or later and he would be reunited with them in just a few days.

"Okay, thank you Melbourne Jack!" Tariq smiled and the two shook hands.

"Where are we going?" Tariq continued as they picked up their dishes and packed the wagon. After ten minutes, they were up and rolling. The horse lazily began walking at the sound of Jack's voice. Tariq sat up on the coach seat with Jack.

"Up here a ways, further into the valley. No sense going into the desert. Looks like there might be a storm coming our way and it's a nasty business getting caught in a desert storm."

Tariq felt a sense of adventure. Yes, he was away from his friends, but by nature he was restless and enjoyed seeing new things. He looked up at the valley on either side of them and noticed the swallows chasing tiny moths. The air smelled fresh with pine; he took in deep breaths and allowed his body and mind to relax. The day rolled on with Tariq taking in the landscape. He talked with Jack about his days in the orphanage, and being sold as a slave, and finally of his time living with Malik. Jack smiled at the boy's stories and couldn't decide if they were fact or fiction because they were so amazing.

In the late afternoon, Tariq fell asleep against Jack's shoulder as the sun was starting to go down. Melbourne Jack stared at the sleeping boy and smiled. He was happy to have the boy on board with him. But something else stirred inside of him, a deep need to somehow help Tariq.

"Where are we?" Tariq asked. He awoke laid out on a fine rug. About fifteen feet away, a fire roared. Melbourne Jack sat next to the fire, preparing something on a stick with his dagger.

"Not sure where we are. Looked like a nice place to stop for the night."

"What is that?"

"Oh this critter? A rabbit happened along. Make a tasty dinner, he will. Not too gamey, with a good bit of fat on him. Must be easy living for a hare in these parts."

Tariq stood up and walked next to Melbourne Jack. He could see the skinless rabbit on the outline of a long straight branch, prepared to enter the fire. He also spotted what looked like a bent stick next to Jack.

"What is that thing?" Tariq asked.

Jack looked down and retrieved the object and held it in his hand.

"This, mate, is a boomerang. It's how I killed this little critter. You've never seen a boomerang?"

Tariq shook his head.

"Let me show you how it works. You see that little bit of a branch over there on the top of that shrub?" Jack asked and pointed at a branch approximately one hundred feet away.

"Yes."

"Watch this!"

Jack put a leather glove on his right hand, took a few steps back, and flung the boomerang overhand. The boomerang made a large circle, hit the branch square, knocking it off the shrub, continued its circle, and returned right to Jack, who easily grabbed it with his gloved hand.

"Wow!" Tariq yelled.

Jack smiled at the appreciation.

"You want to try?"

"Sure!"

Jack took off the glove, put it on Tariq's hand, and then gave him a short lesson on how to throw a boomerang.

"First, find the wind and make sure it's blowing against the left side of your face. Then, you must have the face of the boomerang facing up—good! Next, throw it overhand, with just a flick of the wrist. It doesn't take much effort for a short distance. Place your four fingers on the bottom and your thumb on the top like that."

Jack showed Tariq the proper motion and held his hand in place.

"Okay, let it rip!"

Tariq took a few steps backwards and then threw the boomerang as instructed. It went straight and then landed fifty feet away.

"You know what they call a boomerang that doesn't come back, mate?" Jack asked.

"What?"

"A stick!"

Tariq shot him a skeptical look.

"Okay, you go find it and keep practicing. It takes lots of work to get good with one of these. It took me years of practice."

Tariq did as he was told, found the boomerang, and then kept throwing it into the night, guided back by the light of the campfire.

Jack went about preparing dinner and after a while called Tariq over.

"Would you do the honors, mate? I've got a couple of other things to do before supper. Just keep him about a foot or so above the flames," Melbourne Jack asked, handing the branch to Tariq.

"Sure!"

Tariq handled the task expertly, keeping the rabbit just above the fire. He had roasted many things and understood to turn the rabbit continually so it was cooked on all sides. It was also important not to get too close to the flames as that would burn it and roast off all the fat.

Melbourne Jack went inside his wagon and soon had a kettle and a large canteen in his hands. He sat back down next to Tariq and went about preparing a small stove next to the fire, placing rocks in a square and building a small fire within the rocks using embers from the big fire. Next, he placed the kettle on the small fire and dumped the water from the canteen into the kettle. Finally, he slowly rolled a cigarette, placed it in his mouth, and lit it with an ember from the fire.

Tariq watched Jack move. He was very deliberate and slow in his movements, without a care in the world. Tariq also noticed a chain around Jack's neck, with some rocks and beads at the end.

"What is that?" he asked, pointing to the necklace.

"Well, my mother back in Australia was an aborigine. I spent most of my childhood in the bush with her people. This is a kind of good luck charm."

"What is an aborigine?"

"They were the original inhabitants of Australia, much like your Berbers in these mountains. Great hunters and they could live out in the wild for months at a time."

"What happened to them?"

"Well, the English government decided they needed a place to send all their criminals and unwanted. So, they chose Australia. Once that happened, it went awful for the aborigines."

"Why?"

"I don't know why. The English say they wanted to civilize Australia, but I don't really see how slaughtering hundreds of thousands of people could be considered civilized."

"Your people were slaughtered?"

"Like lambs at a feast."

Tariq nodded in acknowledgement.

"So that necklace is a good luck charm?"

"Yes, it is supposed to keep bad luck away from me."

"Does it work?"

"It's worked so far."

"So, you're just traveling through our country with no purpose at all?" Tariq asked.

Melbourne Jack shifted at this line of questioning. He knew he liked Tariq, he just didn't know if he could trust him.

"Actually, I'm looking for treasure."

"Treasure?"

Melbourne Jack had, in fact, not told even one person about his treasure hunt in twelve years. It was something he kept very, very secret. However, a sense told him to discuss it with Tariq and Tariq would somehow be important in his quest. He had learned long ago to trust his sixth sense.

So, Melbourne Jack went to his wagon, looked for a few things, threw some things aside, and came back to the fire with a folded cloth. He carefully unfolded the cloth and showed it to Tariq. On the cloth was a map.

"This is a map of this region. You can see the mountain range here, and over here is the ocean. I think the treasure is right here," he said pointing to a large tower on the map.

Tariq studied the map inquisitively. It was a very old map and was torn in three pieces. He was quite taken by it.

"So what's this treasure about?"

"Oh, it's something very special. I've been searching for it for years. This is actually the third map I've had—each one seems to lead to another. I hope this is finally the spot!"

Tariq had never seen the language on the map, either. It looked like Arabic, but was different enough that he couldn't make it out.

"How did you come into possession of the map?"

Melbourne Jack smiled at this question.

"Ah, let's just say I took it off someone's hands."

"Do you think you're close to finding it?"

"I have no idea, my friend. I think I'm in the right valley, but it's difficult to tell by this map. There are dozens of valleys around here that could be this one. It looks like an opening to a lion's head in front of this cave."

Tariq studied the map a bit more and saw the lion's head in front of the cave. In the cave were four symbols—a cross, a circle, a picture of the moon, and finally, a sign of death.

"What do these symbols mean?"

"Not sure, never seen those before."

Tariq looked at the map and became more and more fascinated by it. He started to daydream of fantastic treasure and bounty. The many symbols on the map intrigued him. Then, he saw something that was familiar.

"I know this place. This tower, it is just outside our mountain range."

Jack stared at Tariq in amazement.

"You know where this is?"

"Yes, I think so."

"Tariq! That is where the treasure is supposedly buried. I might be reading the map wrong, but I'm pretty sure that's it."

Tariq smiled and continued to stare at the map.

"Can I come with you?" he asked.

"You?"

"Yes, I will help you find this place. I only require a small bit of the treasure for my friends."

Jack smiled at this.

"It's not that kind of treasure, Tariq. It's more of an artifact. But, if you help me find it, I'll be sure to help out your people."

Tariq thought about this for a minute.

"I think it will be good if I am with you. It will look better if you have a local boy at your side."

"Okay, partner! First we eat. Then let's go find this treasure!"

Tariq was happy with this idea. He liked Melbourne Jack. He was funny and easygoing.

And he was on a great adventure!

ONE FROM THE
STOLEN GENERATION

The aborigines were the native people of Australia. They usually had dark brown skin and most had big, inquisitive eyes and lots of bushy brown hair. For thousands of years they lived off the land; they were very basic people. They respected the land and all that it provided for their people. They were peaceful by nature, known for their happiness and warmth.

In 1786, London was overcrowded and crime-ridden. The English prisons were filled to capacity, and rancid conditions existed in every inch of the prisons. The English had been relocating many of their criminals to the United States for years. But, after the War of Independence, that policy was stopped.

The English needed a new place to send all their criminals.

About fifteen years prior, Captain Cook, an English naval captain, had been sailing in the South Pacific and discovered a massive continent—later to be called Australia.

Captain Cook thought Australia would make a perfect spot for the English to begin exporting all their criminals, thieves, prostitutes, and otherwise unwanted members of society. So in 1786, the first English criminals were sent to Australia, which began a mass exodus of unwanted from England to Australia.

At first, the aborigines welcomed their guests to their new land and tried to befriend them. Soon, however, the aborigines learned that the English, and these criminals, were not there to be friendly—they were there to conquer.

Gangs of English criminals prowled the Australian countryside, looking for aborigines to slaughter. In addition, the English inadvertently brought with them ordinary diseases that killed off many of the aborigines. Their immune systems just weren't prepared.

It got much worse for the aboriginal people over the decades.

Gold was discovered in Australia in the mid-nineteenth century. Millions of English settlers descended on Australia to search for gold. These settlers saw the aborigines as a threat, yet beneath them. So, the English developed a policy of removing aboriginal children from their homes and placing them in the care of English couples, or the church, in order to "civilize" them.

This became known as the "stolen generation" of children who were taken from their parents.

Melbourne Jack was only six years old when he was stolen from his parents in 1888.

His tribe was living in the Australian outback when a garrison of English soldiers and merchants surrounded them. The English soldiers began taking all the children from their homes and forcing them into a wagon. Jack's name wasn't even Jack back then. It was Amaroo, which means "a beautiful place" in the native language.

His mother and grandmother screamed and his father sat crying in the sand as Jack was carried away by two British soldiers and placed in a wagon, along with the other children from his tribe.

It would be the last time he ever saw his family.

The caravan carrying all the stolen children traveled for two days before coming to a stopping place. A svelte man, wearing a tailored linen suit, studied all the children as they were lined up outside his tent.

"This one will do," he said and pointed at Jack.

Quickly, Jack was removed from the caravan and stood silently as all his friends disappeared from his sight. He was left standing next to the distinguished man in the suit.

"What's your name?" the man asked.

"Amaroo," came the whispered reply.

"What? That's no name. From now on your name is Jack, that's a much better name. My name is Foster Crowe; you can simply call me Mister Crowe. I run this circus and you are our new stable boy. It will be your job to water and clean up after all the animals in your circus, you understand?"

Amaroo, now Jack, stared at the man in disbelief. He was much too young to really understand what was happening. Quickly, he was shuffled to meet a young lady with long, auburn hair and a dirty calico dress.

"This here is Jack. He's your new stable boy," Crowe said, and walked away.

Jack stared up at the girl, completely paralyzed.

"Well, hello there Jack, my name is Amanda. You'll be helping me take care of the animals, isn't that exciting?"

Jack continued to stare, as though in shock, at his new situation.

"Well, I imagine you've had quite a scare. Let's get you fed and washed, and then I'll start showing you your new home and job."

Amanda was quite a pleasant and loving girl and took Jack by the hand to her tent. There she gave him a nice dinner of rabbit stew and biscuits, and then made sure he had a proper bath and new clothes.

"Where are you from?" she asked, only to have Jack remain silent, still in complete shock regarding his new lot in life.

She continued to pepper him with questions and he continued to remain silent. Finally, she relented and just sat in silence while he ate his dinner. He was a very cute little boy; he had problems using the silverware and eventually just used his hands to shovel in his meal. His long and curly brown hair hung over his eyes and his cheeks were oversized, making him look like a guinea pig with long, shaggy brown hair. He was thoroughly pleased with the food and kept licking his fingers, enjoying the juices from the stew.

"What's that around your neck?" she asked, touching the talisman around his neck. His grandmother had placed it there just as he was being taken by the British troops.

"It's quite beautiful isn't it? You must take care of that," Amanda said, smiling at the little boy. Her nature and touch were extremely gentle, and her face was young and soft, with brown freckles across her nose. She was only sixteen, but had a mature and worldly presence about her.

Jack began to relax.

"Okay, come now, let me introduce you to your new friends!" she said, taking him by the hand, and leading him out of her tent and down to a series of cages and tents. Jack was in wonderment of it all, walking through the assortment of tents on the way to the wild animals. The tents were all sorts of bright colors, and a wide variety of circus performers walked about, practicing their many skills.

There were jugglers, flame-throwers, and a man walking on six-foot wooden stilts. Two clowns juggled knives back and forth, and a really short little man practiced every manner of somersault. A tightrope walker walked on a wire strung between two poles, and an acrobat practiced walking on his hands over a bed of hot coals.

Walking to the first cage, there was an immense tiger lying on a bed of straw, content and sleeping.

"That is Matu; do not worry about him, you are much too young to feed him. Come, I'll show you your first pets."

They walked to the next cage, where looking up at Amanda and Jack was an adult zebra! He nodded his head and looked at Jack with an inquisitive look.

"This is Ciqa. He's very tame and very friendly. Look, here, feed him some carrots," Amanda instructed and placed the vegetables gently in Jack's hands.

Jack carefully placed the food up to the cage bars, and Ciqa began gently eating and shaking his head in appreciation.

"Zebras are naturally very aggressive, and it took us three years to tame Ciqa. As far as we know, he is the only zebra that has ever been tamed so much that he can be ridden. It is quite an amazing feat!" Amanda explained.

Ciqa continued to stare at Jack and shake his head.

"Ah, see, he likes you. Come; let's see the rest of the animals."

Amanda introduced Jack to Bora, the elephant, as well as a pack of trained monkeys. There was Ila the koala bear and Asi the lion. They even had a toucan named Frank and a parrot named Sam!

Amanda showed Jack how to water them, feed them, and clean their cages. Then she showed him how to talk to them and treat them gently and stroke their fur. She talked to them softly and all the animals purred with affection.

"Most circuses are very mean to their animals," said Amanda. "Foster would never allow that. He seems like a hard man, but actually, he's very nice. It's difficult to run a circus like this, but he treats everyone very fairly."

Jack, still wide-eyed, followed Amanda everywhere like a little puppy dog. He was introduced to Majesto the Magician and Frida the Fortune Teller. He met all the work hands and everyone greeted him with a hearty hello and a smile.

But Amanda was his favorite.

Each night, after doing his chores, he would snuggle up in her bed and she would read him bedtime stories and sing lullabies to him. It reminded him of times when his grandmother would sing to him under the stars.

The years passed and Jack grew into his role in Crowe's Magical and Mystical Circus of Wonder. He looked at the circus as his family and got along well with everyone, learning their tricks and trade.

There was something about this circus that was different from every other circus. The acts were different and the people were different. Rather than acts like a bearded lady or strong man, Crowe's seemed to be real.

For instance, Majesto had an act whereby he could read minds and even have people talk to their dead relatives. Frida consistently predicted future events, such as an earthquake that shook the ground. One time she advised travelers to avoid a valley that was eventually consumed by locusts and was amazingly accurate with the weather. Her predictions often guided the circus on which direction to take, which towns to visit, and which to leave.

The animals were different, as well. They didn't even really require a trainer. Amanda simply whispered in their ears and they did exactly as she instructed. She never used a whip to beat them, always just a kind word.

Jack began to work with a knife thrower by the name of Hermes. At first, Jack could barely get a knife to stick in a piece of wood. After much practice, he could throw four knives at once and hit four different targets square on.

That's when it got interesting.

One day, Hermes placed a blindfold around Jack's eyes and gave him instructions.

"Do not try to see the targets, and do not think of yourself as blind. Instead, feel the targets. Be part of them. Close your eyes and relax."

Jack did as he was instructed and, after Jack appeared relaxed, Hermes continued.

"Take one knife and feel it going into its target. Do not aim! Let it come to you, and when it does, throw it."

Jack relaxed, breathed, and threw the knife.

It missed the target completely.

"That is okay. We will continue to work on it. Try it again," Hermes instructed.

Over time, Jack learned to relax and reach a kind of meditative state. He got so good he could hit a balloon flying in the air while blindfolded. He could throw six knives at once and have each one find their target.

Then, he took things a bit further and became an artist with a boomerang.

Boomerangs were better than knives because they could come back to him. He practiced for hours and hours, throwing them at just the right angle so they could knock a thimble off of a barrel and return right to his hand.

It got so he could throw four boomerangs at four different targets, hitting them all and sending all four boomerangs right back to him.

He got so good he could hit a scattering mouse from fifty yards away.

At last, Foster gave him his own show!

Performing in front of packed tents, he dazzled the crowd, hitting a wide variety of complex targets. For his signature trick, would strike the cigarette out of an audience member's mouth while blindfolded.

None of it was trickery.

It had taken Jack years to develop his knife and boomerang throwing skills and it involved no magic at all for him to perform. All of it was the result of hard work, as well as his special ability to relax and feel his targets.

Next, Foster had an idea that was sure to be a big hit among the audiences. One day, he took Jack away from the tents, about three miles away, to a field with a massive balloon! The balloon was huge!

"What is that?" Jack asked.

"That, my friend, is a hot air balloon—the newest thing in air travel. And, you and I are going to captain it!" Foster said, smiling a big toothy grin.

"Really?" Jack asked.

"Just you wait and see!"

The hot air balloon was colored red, orange, and yellow and was fully inflated. A worker had secured it to the ground and it sat in the field, waiting for Foster and Jack. Stepping into the wicker basket, Foster let go of the ropes. Soon the balloon was rising into the sky.

"Yeah hah! Have you ever seen something so beautiful?" Foster yelled.

Hot air balloons had been around for a hundred years and were all the rage in Europe. The publication of Jules Verne's novel, *Around the World in 80 Days*, had increased the popularity of hot air ballooning in Europe, and it was now catching on in Australia.

The two sailed higher and higher until they were just over the circus. Everyone had come out to see the balloon, and Foster safely commanded her down to the ground as everyone in the circus ran around and yelped and screamed at the newest addition.

"Hi everyone! Meet our newest Hot Air Balloon Captain— Melbourne Jack!" Foster roared, and everyone clapped and hollered.

"Melbourne Jack?" Jack asked.

"It has a better ring to it than just Jack," Foster explained with a wink.

Jack was only fifteen, but Foster put him in charge of the balloon. Each day he practiced for eight to ten hours—powering it up, controlling it, bringing it down to earth and back up again. He practiced circling around targets and even picking up targets. He got so good he could bring it down within a foot of the ground, pick up a person into the wicker basket, and then launch it back up. He could turn the balloon in any direction he desired by rocking the basket back and forth.

That's when Foster explained his newest routine to him.

"Melbourne Jack—I just love the ring of that—you are going to be our newest attraction. You are going to perform amazing stunts in your balloon, and combine them with your knife and boomerang throwing skills. It will be like nothing the public has ever seen before."

Foster went over and over the routine with Jack for months until it was perfected. Jack would come out of the sky into the center of the packed arena. He would involve willing spectators by plucking them from the ground, circling around, and returning them safely back down. Other times Jack would jump out of the balloon, run alongside it throwing knives at targets, only to jump back in and power it up, narrowly missing the screaming and ducking audience members.

The crowd would watch in awe as Jack launched his boomerang from a hundred feet in the air, hitting a target only three feet off the ground. Every time, the boomerang circled right back up to Jack in his balloon.

Melbourne Jack's best trick, however, was hanging by a rope, upside down by his ankles, as the balloon was about twenty feet above the ground. Throwing his knives, he would hit the apple off a spectator's head and then climb back up in the basket.

Everyone in the circus was impressed.

Amanda really was, more than anyone else.

She had continued to be like a mother to him through the years. Their bond had grown close and she protected and coddled him. She couldn't believe how he had developed his routines and become an integral part of the circus. He was turning into such a brave man before her eyes.

One night, she decided to tell him a secret she'd been withholding ever since his arrival as a child.

"Jack, this circus isn't all that it appears to be," she started.

"How do you mean?"

She sighed and sat down next to him as he continued to read *20,000 Leagues Under the Sea*.

"There's more to us than meets the eye. That day when you were chosen by Foster was no accident. He knew you were a special boy."

"How?" Jack asked.

"It's difficult to explain how. You see, while we enjoy entertaining and putting on show, there's a much deeper purpose to our existence. We are what you call a balancing act."

"A balancing act?"

"The world is changing all around us. Machines are taking over the hands of man. Industry is taking over for God. It is a very difficult time, but also a very exciting time."

"So what do you do?"

"We can never forget that we are part of a natural order. Everything in this world, and the next, is connected. There is good and evil everywhere. We keep order."

Jack sat up, obviously thoroughly confused by the conversation.

"How so?"

"By fighting against darkness. By keeping people in tune with their more natural selves."

"Can you give me an example? Because I'm quite confused."

Amanda thought for a moment before continuing.

"I've taught you that every action has a consequence. For instance, if you steal from me, the natural law means that something bad will happen to you. You might have something stolen from you. Likewise, if you value money above love and friendship, you will never truly attain happiness, as the pursuit of money is a superficial pursuit. We are entering an age where people are honoring material things above spirituality, morality, and love. It is a very dangerous time for mankind."

Jack continued to think for a moment.

"So how does me flying a balloon and throwing knives help the balance?" he asked somewhat sarcastically.

Amanda laughed at this.

"It doesn't, not really. But, it does do something else."

"What?"

"It prepares you for being a warrior," she said very seriously.

"A warrior?"

"Yes, that's what you've been doing all these years. We've been training you without you really knowing you were being trained."

"Training for what?"

"It's no accident that the world is turning to machines and forgetting the natural order of things. There is a force, a very dark force, behind such a movement. This force is responsible for the genocide committed against your people, the aborigines. It destroyed people who were naturally in tune with the ways of the world, people who valued love, respect, and family above all else. They had little use for material things. Your people weren't above the natural order of things—they were in tune with it."

Jack thought about this for a long time, and it was starting to make sense to him.

"And I've been trained to fight against this force? It is some kind of evil king I must destroy?"

"No, it doesn't work like that. It's like this—this dark force is like a poison that can enter a man's heart and destroy it. It can take a perfectly good person and turn them evil. How this happens is through anger, mistreatment, jealousy, and even guilt. So, although an evil king as you put it is, indeed, evil, it is the poison in his heart that must be cleaned out. Every person can be good, or evil."

"I think I understand."

"This battle, it occurs in the physical world and in the spiritual one. There are evil spirits and guardian angels walking among us. The evil spirits try to enter our hearts and pollute our souls while guardian angels seek to protect us."

"So I've been training to fight this evil?"

"Exactly! Soon, Foster is going to ask you to go on a quest."

"A quest?"

"Yes, all in good time. You will understand," Amanda said and kissed him goodnight.

Jack continued to perform his routines as usual over the coming months. He and Amanda didn't speak again of the true purpose of the circus, but he did begin to notice things he hadn't really noticed before.

For instance, Amanda would walk the animals at night, even the tiger, without a leash. He had never thought this odd before. The animals just walked beside her as if going for a Sunday stroll. And although many circuses were known for hucksters and conmen, this circus never robbed anybody. In fact, Foster's acts were whimsical and fun, not at all strange or weird.

He noticed that children especially loved their circus and flocked to all of the acts. The parents seemed to get caught up in the excitement as well, and Jack often witnessed a change in normally placid individuals— they would become giddy and animated.

One day, as Jack was walking behind the main tent, he noticed a small opening in Majesto's tent. He saw Majesto sitting on the floor on a rug, his legs crossed and eyes closed. He seemed to be chanting.

Jack stood in front of him, awestruck by the odd scene, when suddenly Majesto opened his eyes.

"Hello Jack," he smiled.

"Hello."

"Wondering what I'm doing?"

"Yes."

"I'm transferring subliminal messages to our many friends in the crowd."

"What's a subliminal message?"

"It's a message that's like a whisper in your ear. You're not even sure you heard it; it might have just been the wind. However, our brains are very acute, so they pick up on it."

"What messages?"

"Oh, things like, 'respect your fellow man,' 'do unto others as you would have them do unto you,' 'treat all animals and the earth with respect,' those sorts of things."

"Really?"

"Yes, ever wonder why people are so happy at this circus?"

"Well, yes, I was just thinking about that."

"This is one of the reasons. I'm secretly whispering positive thoughts to them that only their brains can receive. It's like a dog that can hear a high-pitched whistle."

"But how?"

Majesto smiled at this.

"Let's just say that I have my ways. I understand Amanda discussed our little secret with you. Good. Has Foster talked to you yet?"

"No."

"Don't worry, he will," Majesto said, and then smiled, closed his eyes, and went back to transferring subliminal messages.

Jack walked away, thoroughly perplexed by the conversation.

Two days later, Foster came to Jack's tent. Foster, who hadn't seemed to age a day since Jack had known him, sat across from Jack, looking him deep in the eyes.

"So, it would seem you now have a good idea of the true purpose of this circus," he started, staring at Jack as if sizing him up and down.

"Yes," Jack nodded in obedience.

"And what are your thoughts on the subject?"

"I think I understand about the good and evil forces. I'm still not sure how we fight the evil force."

Foster sat back in his chair and studied Jack some more. The air smelled of jasmine and pine; undoubtedly Amanda had lit some incense in this room. She was always doting on Jack, ensuring his room smelled nice and his clothes were cleaned and pressed.

"Think of it more like a positive and negative force. If a person is constantly exposed to positive experiences, the way they perceive the world will be positive. If they are exposed to negative forces, the way they perceive the world will be negative. The forces work behind the scenes."

"So, how do we fight this negative force?" Jack asked.

"Oh, there are many, many battlefronts—too numerous to discuss each one. But some are physical battlefronts, supernatural battlefronts, battles of minds and hearts, and political and religious battles."

"Foster, I have a question," Jack stammered. He was still very nervous in Foster's presence.

"Yes?"

"Why did you change my name? Why was I taken from my parents?"

Foster sighed heavily as he knew this conversation was long overdue. At seventeen, Jack was at the age when boys turned into men and began to question themselves.

"The British authorities forcibly removed you from your parents. They gave you to us. But, that isn't the entire story. I had been watching you for some time and knew you would come to us."

"Watching me?"

"Well, yes. I felt your presence, let's just say that. When the Brits came that day, I knew immediately that you would join us. I changed your name to protect you."

"Protect me?"

"Yes, in a way. I had to give you an entirely new identity. See, our little circus is protected from the forces of evil. It's almost like we're invisible. Changing your name was just a little something to help hide us."

Jack nodded, as this made perfect sense to him.

"Now, I have a quest for you," Foster continued and leaned forward.

"What quest?"

"There are artifacts in history which serve a great purpose. Artifacts which serve as a map for humankind, intended to keep us on our path. Some of these artifacts have been lost and others have been destroyed. We are guardians of some of these artifacts, and there is one in particular I want you to find," Foster said, reaching into his coat pocket and pulling out a map.

Foster unfurled the map on a small table, and placed a stone on each corner so the map was spread out flat.

"This map represents the path to that artifact: Alexander the Great's personal diary."

"Alexander the Great? But why him?" Jack asked.

"Because there is no figure in history more divisive than Alexander the Great. Either he was a force for good or a force for evil; we still can't be certain. His diaries may tell of the tactics he used, and his influences. If we come to understand these, we may better understand him."

"And this map will lead me to it?"

"Yes! But it will be very dangerous. The forces of evil will sense your quest and try to stop you, but the forces of good will seek you out as well."

Jack studied the map. It was so very old and interesting.

"When do I leave?"

Foster smiled—Jack was, indeed, turning into the man Foster had hoped he would become.

"You leave next week, after your eighteenth birthday. It will be a very difficult journey and may take you years to complete. This journey will give you many clues that will lead to more clues. But this is not an easy endeavor. Do not give in or give up. Nothing that is worth accomplishing ever comes easily."

Jack departed the day after his eighteenth birthday.

Over ten years later, he would find Tariq hiding in the back of his wagon.

CHAPTER
— 13 —

FEZ SEEKS AN OLD FRIEND

Malik and Sanaa led an expedition to an overpass that was still covered in snow, pines sticking up from the ground, their branches bare. Malik ordered half the troops on one side and half on the other side. He then spread them out, about ten feet apart, and had everyone lie prone. His men were excited, but nervous at the same time. They had been through this drill countless times before, and instinctively knew how to behave. Once lying prone on the ground, the troops didn't move a muscle. They remained perfectly still and focused.

The intelligence Malik had was that an arms shipment would be traveling through this pass en route to the Caid's kasbah.

Sanaa was positioned on the ridge opposite him, her bow poised and ready to strike. She felt excited, yet calm in the moment of danger.

For half an hour they waited, until Malik could make out the faint sound of horses. He looked up and saw one of his falcons circling overhead, flying in a pattern that seemed strange to Malik. Usually, the falcon would make two figure eights to signal an oncoming convoy, but this time the bird was flying erratically, diving and bobbing in patterns that didn't mean anything to Malik.

It was as if the bird was trying to warn Malik of something but he didn't know how to communicate it.

Malik continued to switch between watching the bird and the road. Something wasn't right!

"This does not feel right; something is very, very wrong," he whispered to one of his men.

The rebel looked at him with worry. What was Malik talking about?

Malik spied Sanaa on the opposite ridge and pointed up to the bird, still flying frantically in the air and making erratic gestures. Sanaa looked at Malik with a confused look on her face and then seemed to understand.

Malik felt his throat tighten and his pulse beat in his heart. His hands became sweaty and his vision dizzy.

"We go!" he whispered.

"Malik, they are just around the bend!" answered one of his men.

"I don't care, we go now!" Malik said, gave some hand gestures, and then started running down the ridge to their horses.

Sanaa, on the other side, saw what Malik was doing and issued the same orders. Both groups were now running away from the convoy when the first arrow pierced the back of a rebel just to Malik's left.

Then another.

Then another.

The forest was alive with bullets and arrows being shot at them from all sides. Quickly mounting their horses, the group, now half their original number, twisted and zagged through the forest trees in an effort to escape their pursuers.

They had been ambushed!

Malik and Sanaa were out in front as bullets continued to ricochet off trees. They ducked and swung their horses wildly in an effort to confuse their pursuers.

Behind them, the Mamba and his soldiers were in full pursuit, fanned out in a formation to cover all areas of escape, and riding at a full gallop.

The ambush had almost gone completely as planned, except the rebels were somehow alerted to their presence a little sooner than he had liked.

Aiming his rifle, the Mamba took a bead on a rebel, steadied his breath, and pulled the trigger.

The man fell from his horse—dead!

Now there were only a few rebels left, up ahead about fifty yards, trying desperately to evade the Mamba's troops.

Another shot rang out and another rebel flew to the ground.

Through the forest they rode. There were only two left now, and they were better riders than the rest. Several times the Mamba almost hit a tree trying to match their maneuvers.

Up a hill, and then down a dangerously steep embankment, his soldiers followed their prey. The embankment was so steep that their horses sat down on their rumps and slid most of the way. A couple of the soldiers' horses stopped abruptly and flipped their riders.

No matter, they had these rebels!

Up ahead, Sanaa and Malik rode frantically, not sure if they were the only two left of their raiding party. They could feel their pursuers closing in on them. Urging their horses faster, Malik tried frantically to think of an escape route...

Ahead they faced a mountain and ridge wall. They wouldn't have any escape route.

They would be trapped.

Fez and Aseem slowly turned around. They expected to see a rifle pointed at their heads, courtesy of the Caid's soldiers.

Instead, they were met with a smiling face. Doing a double take, they instantly recognized the face in front of them.

"Habib!" Fez said excitedly.

"At your service," Habib smiled and even bowed a little.

"How did you escape from the Caid?" Aseem asked.

"Tariq freed all of us when he rescued you. Didn't he tell you? We have been hiding in cities and enjoying our freedom."

Habib was a smaller boy, skinny, with a dark complexion and very short, kinky black hair. He was known as a bit of a mischief-maker and played practical jokes constantly on boys in the Caid's dungeon. That said, he was a very good guy.

His dress was that of a street urchin, meaning, raggedy clothes and dirt caked on his face.

"So, all of you are here?" Fez asked.

"No, some of the boys went to other cities and a few returned to their families. It was tough at first in Chaouen. There was a gang of boys who ruled the city. But, soon, we drove them out and now we rule the city!" he explained quite proudly.

Aseem was so glad to see Habib. They had become good friends in the Caid's dungeon, and Habib had cared for him when he was beaten and scheduled for death. Each day, Habib had brought him extra rations of water and food and told him that everything would be fine.

"Where is Tariq?" Habib asked.

"We don't know," said Fez.

"He came here with us but we have lost him," Aseem explained.

Habib was elated by this news.

"Tariq is here! That is so exciting. He is like a legend to us street boys. Without him, we would probably all be dead by now."

"So you'll help us find him?" Fez asked.

"Of course! Come, let's have a look around."

Habib led Fez and Aseem back into the city streets. They walked among the merchants and food carts and were ignored by pretty much everyone. Once in a while, a merchant would curse at them and shoo them away.

As the boys crossed the street from the city jail, they saw a homeless man lying in the street, a bottle of wine in his hands. Technically, it was illegal to drink any form of liquor in Chaouen; however, that law was rarely enforced.

The homeless man was covered in even more dirt than Habib. His bottom lip was large and swollen from getting hit by one of the Caid's guards. He smelled of fish and sweat; long, greasy hair hung over his eyes.

"This is Timin. He was a bookmaker who was beaten and imprisoned by the Caid's troops and thrown into a dungeon for fifteen years. He lost his family and now he seeks them, but cannot find them. So, he must drink to forget his sorrow," Habib explained.

Timin, still a relatively young man, looked at Habib and then at Fez and Aseem.

"I drink because I want to drink, and my sorrow is my own. What brings you, Habib?" Timin asked.

"Any news of a boy imprisoned by the Caid's troops?" Habib asked.

Timin shook his head. He was a very friendly fellow who was on good terms with Habib and the rest of the street urchins.

"None for the past few days, other than the usual beatings by the guards. Is this about all that excitement the other day?"

"No, um, we were just wondering," Fez hurriedly answered.

"Ha! You're a bad liar my friend. So, it is about all that excitement. The Caid's men are none too happy about being embarrassed like that. I heard it was quite a commotion! You three should be careful; the guards are beating any urchins they see in hopes of beating the right one."

Habib, Fez, and Aseem all nodded at this news.

"Yes, I got a good clip yesterday, but I just thought it was the normal stuff from those donkeys," Habib explained.

Timin sat up and took more of an interest in Fez and Aseem.

"I haven't seen you two before, you're not from around here. You look like city rats, but there's something different about you."

Fez looked at Aseem, and Aseem tried to answer convincingly.

"No, we're from Marrakesh. We're here on a religious pilgrimage."

Timin started laughing and then coughing because he was laughing so hard.

"My friend, it is obvious you're not from the streets. An urchin who traveled all this way from Marrakesh on a religious pilgrimage? You might as well have told me you were a genie that came from a lamp. But, I like the two of you. Go and get me some lunch and we will discuss what you are doing in Chaouen."

Habib nodded to Aseem and Fez, and right away they left Timin in search of food.

"How can he help us, Habib?" Aseem asked.

"He may look like an average beggar, but Timin is actually very smart and a sworn enemy of the Caid. The Caid took his family from him and he has sworn his vengeance. He knows everyone in the underworld and has many contacts and allies."

Habib stopped at the entrance to a shopping bazaar and spotted a food cart selling lamb and beef shawarmas. The moist pieces of meat, wrapped in pita bread, smothered in tomatoes and a spicy white sauce smelled absolutely amazing.

"Okay, that is our lunch!" Habib announced.

Fez looked at the stand. His stomach roared in anticipation. They had eaten only some scraps since their entry into Chaouen.

"I don't have any money, Habib," he said mournfully.

"Money! Who has money? We're going to steal it!"

"I cannot do this, Habib. I cannot steal something that is not mine." said Fez.

Habib looked at him in complete disbelief.

"Why not?"

"My father would not approve. Although he is dead, I know he watches over me."

Habib nodded. He could appreciate Fez's honor code.

"How about you?" he asked, looking at Aseem.

"I cannot steal either, Habib—nothing against you, it is just our way."

Habib stood in front of them, putting his hands on his waist, almost like a teacher lecturing some students.

"Listen you two. This isn't like life in the mountains. Living in the city is very hard and our survival depends on our ability to steal. It is a way of life. Nobody will give us a job. Nobody will allow us in their schools. Society tosses us aside, so how are we supposed to live? I don't like stealing either, but what choice do I have?"

Fez and Aseem considered this for a moment before Fez answered.

"I understand, Habib, but that man, he is just an innocent merchant trying to feed his family. That food costs him a lot of money. He is not the Caid or his men, who are our true enemy. He is just a father trying to get by, just like you or me."

Habib stared at the merchant, a man who looked like he might have a wife and children at home. He seemed happy, and smiling, but a look of worry was about him.

"I don't believe this! Fine, what is your idea? How do we get lunch if we're not going to steal it?"

"What if we stole it from the Caid's soldiers?" Aseem asked.

"What do you say to that?" Habib asked Fez.

"Well, I think that would be okay, considering the Caid's soldiers are our enemy and they steal from everyone else."

"Good, because two of them are over on that wall just sitting down to lunch," Aseem explained, pointing at two soldiers who had taken their meal from another merchant. Gobs of lamb, duck, and rice sat piled high on a plate, steaming hot.

"Okay, here's the plan," Aseem began whispering the plan to Habib and Fez. The two of them giggled and smiled at the plan, and then all three went off in their respective positions.

Moments later, Fez and Habib began running down the street with handfuls of sawdust in their hands. Just as they reached the two guards, the boys threw the sawdust directly in their eyes, blinding them, and continued to run down the street as fast as they could. The guards, blinded, jumped up and tried to run after the two, but they bumped into a cart of clothes and both fell down.

Within moments, their vision had cleared but Fez and Habib were nowhere to be seen. The entire court erupted in applause at the two urchins who had gotten the better of the two guards. Nobody liked the Caid.

Wiping dirt from their shirts, they went back to their lunch.

It was gone!

Aseem had been waiting behind a statue and at just the right moment, snagged the plate, running in the opposite direction until he was safely out of sight.

The plan had worked to perfection. Fez and Habib had run by them so fast, the soldiers hadn't gotten a good look at the two, and then they'd been blinded. The boys had been clever, and would not be identified as the culprits.

Moments later, the three sat with Timin, munching on the meat and savoring the juices and moist rice. The lamb was especially delicious, so soft it could have been cut with a spoon.

"Okay, down to business. What do you boys want with the Caid?" Timin asked.

Fez looked at him apprehensively. Could he trust this man?

"Do not worry, my little friend. I am a sworn enemy of the Caid and his soldiers. I would never betray your trust," said Timin, smiling.

Fez decided it would be safe to trust him. He would, however, leave out the part about the French general, as that was very sensitive information.

"There is a man called Nur who is responsible for massacring my people and my family. He was once part of our tribe, but he betrayed my father to a man named Zahir," Fez explained.

Timin stared at Fez, his mouth open in disbelief at what he had heard. "Did you say Zahir?"

"Yes."

The man sat back and tears started running down his cheeks, streaking the dirt on his face.

"Zahir is the name of the boy who betrayed me all those years ago. I have sought him out, but I have never found him. I heard he joined the Caid's army."

Fez felt bad for the man, who sat sobbing into his hands.

"If it is the same person, then, yes, he was the Caid's head of security until…"

"Until what?"

"Our friend Tariq tricked him into betting everything he owned on a camel race. Zahir lost everything and ran away from the Caid in disgrace. I do not know of his whereabouts."

Timin smiled a bit at this news.

"This Tariq sounds like quite a character. So, how can I help you?"

"I must take vengeance on Nur. He is responsible for my family being murdered. I cannot leave Chaouen until he is dead."

Timin stared at Fez and immediately understood how serious Fez was about his mission. He saw the emotion in Fez's eyes and heard the conviction in his voice.

"All right, then, let us plan this nasty piece of business and you will have your revenge."

That night, Aseem, Fez, and Habib stood in the shadows outside the compound. Like bats hanging from a tree, they were hardly noticeable.

About eleven o'clock, the compound doors opened and Nur walked out by himself. It wasn't surprising. Only the lowly guards slept in the compound. The higher-level officers had their own quarters in the city.

The moon was almost full, providing plenty of light as Nur walked quickly through the alleys and streets of Chaouen, completely oblivious to the three shadows following him. All three boys had cloaks over their faces to conceal their identities. It wouldn't have mattered anyhow, at such a distance away, Nur wouldn't have recognized them.

Fez didn't want to take any chances.

Nur continued to walk, consumed with some other matter, when he came to the gate of his house. It was quite a big house, with three stories and a large courtyard in front. A servant opened the gate for him and he disappeared inside.

"We can't get in through the gate. Let's look at the room," Aseem said.

The three boys made their way up to the rooftop of an adjoining building that looked right into Nur's house, but there was absolutely no way to jump to his roof from that distance.

There was, however, a rope line to the apartment next to Nur's that might hold their weight. It was fortuitous that the rope was installed by the city for a recent festival and was designed to hold a heavy banner. The city workers neglected to cut the rope when the festival was over. Fez tested the rope—it seemed solid enough.

"We should come back tomorrow," Aseem told him.

"No, we don't know if he'll even be here tomorrow. We have to go now!" Fez answered.

"Fez, we don't know what kinds of weapons he has or if he has guards. We don't even know how we're going to kill him."

"I don't care. I will not let him escape. He murdered my family!" Fez cried and Aseem could see the hurt in his face.

Aseem knew he had no choice.

"Okay then, we go. I have a knife. Perhaps that will be enough."

Fez smiled, appreciating his friend's loyalty.

"Habib, stay here on lookout, Fez and I are going in," Aseem ordered.

Habib simply nodded his head. His nerves were getting the better of him. Killing an officer of the Caid was serious business.

Fez went to the rope and tested its strength again. He grabbed onto it upside down so his back was to the street and his belly was pointed to the sky. Swinging both ankles around the top of the rope, he began pulling himself with his hands one over the other until he was slowly shimmying across the gap. The rope proved durable; Fez made his way over the dark street, lit only by lanterns from apartment windows, until he arrived at the rooftop of the opposite building. Aseem did the same and soon both boys were on the rooftop next to Nur's house. Like two cats, they leaped a modest three-foot gully and landed on Nur's rooftop. They spotted a window on the east side, slightly open. It looked like it led to a hallway that wouldn't be watched. Climbing down, using the grooves in the bricks as finger holds, Fez opened the window a bit more with his left foot and gently dragged himself into the house.

Aseem followed him and closed the window behind them.

They were in!

The hallway was very dark and was covered with a rug. Staying close to the walls, they made their way down the hallway on their hands and knees. At the end of the hallway, a staircase led down to the next level, illuminated by a couple of candles hanging from the wall. Fez and Aseem heard some talking downstairs. They saw a door just to their right.

All of a sudden, they heard someone coming up the stairs. Making their way backwards, they hid in the shadows behind a pillar. The footsteps grew louder until someone was at the top of the stairs.

It was Nur!

He opened up the door on the right and went in, gently closing it behind him.

"Those must be his quarters," Fez whispered.

"Yes, let us wait awhile for him to get to sleep and then we will go in after him."

The two boys waited for thirty minutes and then slowly made their way across the hallway.

Fez opened the door as gently and quietly as possible. Aseem followed behind him with his knife drawn.

Gingerly they entered the room and closed the door behind them. Peeking inside, the door opened up into yet another hallway and then a huge room—likely Nur's bedroom. It was completely dark, but the boys' eyesight had adjusted well enough that they could make out any shapes in the darkness.

Fez began to tremble. All the memories of his family being slaughtered suddenly came back to haunt him. He started to hyperventilate. Standing up, he made his way along a wall. Aseem could see the fear in his eyes—even in the darkness! Aseem grabbed his friend's shoulder, as if to tell him that everything would be okay. Fez looked back at and smiled; he appreciated the gesture and felt his breathing start to calm.

Then, out of nowhere, someone had lit a torch!

In a moment, Nur was standing in front of them brandishing a sword.

"So, little Fez, it looks like I haven't quite finished the job. You've come to join your parents!" Nur sneered.

The steel of the sword glistened in the torchlight and Nur looked ready to pounce.

Murder in his eyes.

CHAPTER
— *14* —

NAPOLEON BONAPARTE SLEPT HERE!

That morning, there was a nice eight-knot breeze, the oceans were calm, and even the outline of distant land could be seen. Charles was up early, not having slept much of the night. He watched the sun come up over the horizon as he took the helm.

By his account, the land must be France. They had made it!

He had the crew pull in the main to catch a bit more wind. With any luck, they could touch shore by noon and have their lunch in France.

Basil came up to the deck, sleep still in his eyes, sipping a cup of mint tea. Immediately he saw land and a smile came to his face.

"Ah, a sight for sore eyes. That must be France, eh?"

"Yes, I believe so."

"It will be good to get our feet on land. I think we'll be safe on French soil. I wouldn't mind something other than fish and grog for dinner," Basil said, hitting Charles hard on the shoulder with his palm and laughing a hearty laugh.

They sailed through the day and anchored at mid-afternoon. Captain Basil, Charles, and a small contingent of crewmembers rowed a tender to shore, managing the crashing waves and finally touching sand. Dragging the boat to shore, Charles felt his legs wobbling beneath him. At one point he almost fell down.

"Hard to get used to walking on land after so long at sea," Charles said and laughed.

The crew of six walked up the beach and looked like a bunch of drunkards, swaying back and forth, trying to find their balance.

The beach was actually made of small pebbles that made way for jagged rocks of solid granite. Directly in front of the group were sprawling hills and cliffs made of solid rock. It was a desolate place, with just a few trees scattered about the beach. The rock was mostly gray with a mix of deep red clay in some areas.

The group began an exploratory mission, climbing up the rocks and into the mainland. Charles had a crewmate place markers every two hundred feet so they could find their way back. That didn't look to be a challenge; it was mostly flatland devoid of trees. Still, always better to be safe than sorry, Charles had learned, and he insisted on leaving a trail.

The group walked for more than an hour, trudging along, going upwards; they slipped on the rock every now and then, but were making good progress. It wasn't so hot that day, and a good layer of clouds provided plenty of shade and protection. As they continued to walk on a narrow trail between two ridges, Charles noticed a footprint. Tracking over rock is not only difficult, many times it is impossible. However, this footprint was in an area of clay and rock, so it could easily be outlined and traced.

"Looks like we're not alone. This can't be more than a few hours old," Charles offered.

"Well, I'm sure this beach is inhabited and there is a village to be found close to here. Let's press on and hopefully we can find lodging before nightfall," Basil replied.

They followed the trail for another half hour. It narrowed to the point where they had to walk single file as the walls rose up fifty feet on either side. The sun was beginning to set, casting obtrusive shadows along the walls, made even more eerie by the echoes from their footsteps.

Passing around a bend, they came to a wooden ladder going up the right side of the cavern.

"Charles, let's climb up. It's probably nothing, but you and I might as well get a closer look," Basil asked.

"After you, always age before beauty," Charles joked.

"No, I think it goes brains before beauty," answered Captain Basil.

They both smiled and began climbing up the wooden ladder. The wood was held in place by metal bolts, and the ladder was quite sturdy. It went up twenty feet, then thirty, and then almost to the top of the wall, ending at a small cave entrance. After lighting a torch, the two crawled in the cave. Instantly, it was moist and pitch dark. Soon they were able to stand and walk downwards. The torch illuminated about three feet in front of them, but after that it was a black abyss. Drops of water splashed on the ground and their feet sloshed through puddles of water and mud. This went on for about two hundred yards until they came to a long tunnel with a wall at the end. Charles pointed the torch down and, at his feet, saw an illuminated tombstone. Charles held the torch to read the words on the gravestone.

"What does it say?" Basil asked.

"You won't believe it," Charles replied.

"What is it?"

"It says this is the grave of Napoleon Bonaparte!"

Basil bent down and stared at the writing on the stone. Sure enough, in deep letters carved on the stone, were the following words:

"Here lies Napoleon Bonaparte, the greatest leader France has ever known."

Basil and Charles stood up and looked at one another. Could it be true? Was this really the resting place of *the* Napoleon Bonaparte?

The both looked for any other wording or hints, but there was nothing, just a humble grave in the back of a dark cavern.

"We should get back to the crew," Charles said and Basil agreed.

Making their way back proved faster than the initial journey, and they were soon peeking out of the cave entrance. Only, the crewmates they had left behind were no longer alone.

They were on their knees, hands behind their backs, with masked gunmen pointing revolvers at their heads. Directly opposite Basil and Charles were half a dozen more gunmen with rifles pointed at their chests.

The gunmen all wore brown riding pants tucked into high black boots. Each had on an identical white shirt and an oversized red belt with a massive round buckle made of gold. Red handkerchiefs covered the entire lower part of their faces, masking their identities.

The apparent leader, standing to the side of the crew, yelled up to Basil and Charles in French.

"Come down and your friends will not be killed."

Basil and Charles, realizing they were outnumbered and outgunned, dutifully made their way down the ladder until they were standing face to face with the leader. His handkerchief now hung around his neck so his face was fully visible. He looked to be about forty and handsome, with about four days' growth on his chin, evidence of a black beard speckled with gray.

"We're not your enemies, we're simply lost," Charles replied in French.

"Anglais?" the man asked.

"Yes."

The leader looked at this group and sized them up and down.

"What are you doing here? What were you doing up there?" he demanded of Charles.

"Simply trying to find a village for the night."

"And what did you find up there?"

"Apparently that's the grave of Napoleon Bonaparte, but I don't believe it for a second," Charles replied with a hint of disdain.

The man laughed and said something in French to his comrades, Charles didn't hear what it was but it must have been a joke, because they all started laughing.

"You don't believe? Why not?"

"Because Napoleon died in exile in the South Atlantic in 1821. Everyone knows that."

"That is what Napoleon wanted everyone to think. The truth is, he led a resistance force on this very island until 1829. It was kept quiet by the French authorities because they couldn't have anyone believe that he was still alive and remained a threat."

"And how do you know this?" Charles asked.

"Because my great-grandfather fought with him, as did the great-grandfathers of many of the men with me."

Charles looked at the men. They had the look of soldiers—weathered and hard. Their eyes were serious and focused intently on him.

"So what are you doing now?"

"We honor the legacy of Napoleon and fight for the glory of France."

Charles and Basil looked at one another. They found themselves in a predicament without any easy answers. They were surrounded and outgunned, that much was for sure. What they were not sure of was whether these men were friend or foe.

"Why are you here?" the leader asked.

"We're finding our way to Spain, and France is a nice stopping point," Charles replied.

The leader stepped up to Charles and studied him.

"You are not French, where are you from?"

"England."

"And the others?"

"Morocco mostly, but some are from other parts of Africa."

"Morocco!" the leader replied, obviously excited by this.

"Yes, mostly, why?"

"Oh, Morocco is very good. They fight the current French government as we do."

Basil asked Charles what the leader had said and Charles translated. Basil and the leader nodded to one another.

"Well then, I welcome you to the Ile d'Yeu and the country of France."

"Which part of Yeu would this be?"

"You have reached the Pointe du Chatelet, which is more deserted than the rest of the island. Most inhabitants don't come around here for fear of bandits."

"Which would be you?"

"Of course!" laughed the leader.

"Well, Monsieur Bandit, my name is Charles Owen—and this is Captain Basil."

"My name is Henri. It seems that you are both enemies of the French government?"

"We are enemies of tyranny in whatever form it shows itself."

"That is a good answer. While my friends and I fight in the memory of Napoleon, at heart, we are anarchists."

"Anarchists?"

"We distrust all government and believe in the free will of the people."

Charles, secretly, didn't understand this philosophy. Believing in the will of Napoleon and calling yourself an anarchist was like saying you're a vegetarian while eating a hunk of steak. Napoleon, being a dictator—a benevolent dictator, but a dictator nonetheless—would have hated the idea of anarchy. Still, these men had them cornered and outgunned, so it seemed best to go along.

"Interesting point of view. Well, what should we do now? You have us surrounded and outgunned."

"We can fight, and many of us would die, or we can show you our camp and have a party to celebrate our new friendship."

"I'll take the party," Charles said and both he and Henri smiled.

"I thought you would."

Henri nodded to his men. On his signal, each put down his rifle, came over and individually hugged each crewmember of the *Angelina Rouge*. Their smiles were warm and honest and they were genuinely glad to be with their newfound friends.

"What is going on?" Basil whispered to Charles.

"I have no idea, but these Frenchmen are a bit strange," Charles replied, and they both looked at one another with dumbfounded expressions. Henri and his band of anarchists led the crew through some mountain passes, down along an ocean ridge, and finally to an encampment about two miles away. The camp was comprised of a series of brightly covered tents, about twenty in all, with barrels of wine and food, drums, and donkeys. Bunches of grapes hung from stretched rope, and weaponry was strewn about. The middle of the camp featured an enormous fire pit.

The camp inhabitants eyed the newcomers with a bit of suspicion. Henri went over to a beautiful woman with long brown hair hanging down to her waist and talked with her for a few moments. The conversation was quite animated, and eventually the woman went off in a huff.

Henri returned to the crew.

"That was my wife. She thinks I'm crazy for bringing you back to our camp and thinks you are all French spies. You're not spies, are you?"

"Uh, no, definitely not," Charles replied sheepishly.

"Excellent, that is what I thought. Now, we will prepare a feast!"

An intelligence officer this man was not.

More of Henri's people slowly appeared and greeted the crew. Some of the crew spoke French, as was common in Morocco, and got along quite well with everyone in the camp. These people were more like gypsies than French revolutionaries, and everyone wore bright, attractive clothing. Within an hour a pig had been slaughtered and strung up to roast over a roaring fire. Henri and his men produced a series of guitars and drums and began singing the most beautiful French folks songs. Jugs of both white and red wine were passed around and before long everyone was singing and dancing and laughing with one another.

Back at the *Angelina Rouge*, Cortez waited apprehensively on the deck. His instructions at this point were to wait, that Dreyfuss would eventually show up, but Cortez wasn't sure when or how he might arrive. He hoped Dreyfuss would show up before Charles and Basil returned. That would make taking the ship quite simple.

Then, in the distance, Cortez thought he saw the outline of a large ship in the fog. He was sure he saw a brief glimpse of a large gun on the deck. It could very well be Dreyfuss stalking the *Rouge*.

Cortez felt the palms of his hands become sweaty as he scanned the fog, but the ghost ship had disappeared.

The village was home to a simple Berber clan. For centuries they had made their living in the Rif Mountains. They had gone to war with the Caid, the Sultan, and dozens of other invaders and warlords. It came as no surprise one morning when a scout sent word that troops were descending on their tiny village.

But this was different.

This attack wasn't just a few dozen troops, as was the custom, but over two hundred French Legionnaires, accompanied by fifty of the Caid's usual troops.

The Legionnaires were dressed in blue uniforms with white sashes down their chests. Rifles with long bayonets hung over their shoulders and the troops marched in unison, looking quite impressive in the Moroccan countryside.

Even the Caid's soldiers possessed new uniforms and rifles.

At the head of the delegation was none other than Caid Ali Tamzali.

"Get everyone in your village out here!" the Caid yelled at the tribal chieftain.

The chieftain gathered about sixty people in all and lined them up in front of the Caid. Only about ten men were older than twenty years old. The rest were children, women, and elderly people.

The Caid nodded to one of his sergeants. The man stepped forward and read off a scroll:

> These are the laws of the land. Disobedience will mean death.
>
> No person shall be out after nightfall.
>
> No person shall carry a sword or gun of any kind.
>
> Schools are not permitted.
>
> Taxes will increase by 20% starting with the full moon.
>
> Any person caught speaking against the Caid or his army will be met with death.
>
> On his twelfth birthday, every boy will be required to join the Caid's army and swear allegiance for a minimum of four years.

The soldier finished reading and stepped back into the rank and file. The Caid nodded again and quickly the French troops sprang into action. They gathered every boy who looked between twelve and eighteen and forced them to join them, about thirteen boys in all.

The fact was, some of the boys were as young as ten. Mothers screamed and wailed and fathers wanted to kill the Caid, but they all knew that to take a stand against him would mean instant death.

The Caid nodded to his troops again. The soldiers immediately ransacked the entire village and in a matter of minutes had collected every knife and gun that belonged to the villagers. They took anything of value as a form of taxation, including blankets, horses, lamps, even pots and pans. Then, a group of soldiers took torches and lit what looked to be the school aflame. The tent slowly began to burn and was soon engulfed in flames.

"I will have a tax collector return each and every week to collect taxes and ensure that all laws are being followed," the Caid said, and without another word, trotted off with his troops and his new collection of boy soldiers.

This was just the first village. The Caid planned on doing the exact same thing to every village in his region.

Nobody would dare defy him with the French troops and new rifles at his disposal.

Tariq and Melbourne Jack stood at the base of a rock tower. It's difficult to describe exactly what they were looking at. It had taken them four days and four nights to finally reach it, and they now stood looking up at a tall tower, completely flat on all four sides going straight up about five hundred feet in the air. The tower was made of hard, reddish rock and was slippery on the surface.

"You think this is the place?" Tariq asked.

"Must be, it's right here on the map. I can't imagine anything else like this. The coordinates point right to this spot," Jack answered.

The map was encoded, and it had taken Jack almost two years to finally decipher the code. He figured out that the numbers in certain areas were longitude and latitude marking the exact spot of certain clues. The only problem was the map was incomplete. They needed to gather these clues first, in order to learn the exact coordinates of the next spot on the map. Most of the time, the clue was simply some numbers written on a rag and placed in an old bottle. Jack didn't know if this was the spot of the treasure, or simply another clue.

Tariq walked over to the wall and felt the surface—it was almost completely smooth.

"How are we going to climb all the way up there? It is smooth like glass."

"I thought of that my friend. In fact, the last clue said something cryptic about being able to fly like an eagle. I can't fly like an eagle, but I do have the next best thing."

Jack went to his wagon, opened up a floor board, and began pulling out a lot of cloth, some kind of steel contraption, and a large bag of tools.

"What is this?"

"In one of my former lives, I used to fly hot air balloons. When I saw that picture on the map, and the clue about flying like an eagle, I figured I'd need a way to get to the top. Since I'm not much of a rock climber, I came up with this idea."

"What idea?

"I'm going to float to the top of that bugger in my own personalized hot air balloon," Jack said, with a wide grin.

He began unrolling the material and tying ropes to the end, ensuring the ropes were very straight and untangled. He tied the silver contraption near the bottom of the cloth and returned to the wagon for yet another bag full of thin metal pylons.

"This is my own design. My balloons have a wicker basket for a cockpit, which would have been all hell to drag around the Sahara. I designed a lightweight metal basket that could be easily assembled just about anywhere."

Tariq watched with fascination as Jack went about constructing his own personal balloon basket. The vertical pylons attached to smaller pylons at the base to make a floor. Then, he completed the basket by securing it with rope that acted as a safety barrier at the top of the pylons and in the center.

"Safe as can be," he said, still grinning.

He made one last trip back to the wagon and emerged with three steel canisters, each the size of an oversized football.

"I've got the propane to power up and I'm good to go!"

Tariq stood back and watched as Jack first hooked up the basket and then connected the propane to the burner. He worked at a furious rate, dripping in sweat, a whirlwind of activity as he assembled the balloon in under an hour.

Finally, he placed some steel spikes in both front pockets and looped a small hammer through the back of his pants.

"Okay, she's ready to launch. I tested this baby once in Cyprus, and it worked out reasonably well. I'm just going to float up there, have a look-see, and get right back down. I've got her secured to the ground with those spikes. When I tell you, undo the spikes and I'll go up."

Tariq nodded his head in anticipation. He didn't notice that Jack's voice had gotten more and more animated and louder and his movements more pronounced—he was obviously nervous, perhaps even frightened.

"Okay then, let's get this baby going!" said Jack.

He stepped into the basket and pulled the string attached to the burner. Soon hot gas spilled from the burner into the balloon above. The balloon began to rise and fill and after a few moments it lifted Jack off the ground. Quickly, he was about six feet in the air.

"Go ahead and pull the spikes!" Jack yelled down to Tariq.

Tariq quickly pulled all the spikes out of the ground as instructed while Jack controlled the balloon's altitude, keeping it just off the ground. Once the spikes were out, he pulled hard and the burner whistled with appreciation. The balloon began to rise higher and higher until it was a hundred feet off the ground. It was only about half the size of a normal balloon, or envelope as it is called, and a little more round, in order to give it more stability. The sides were the color of a hodgepodge rainbow, since Jack had to make it from material gathered from other hot air balloons.

Tariq stood stupefied on the ground. Never in his entire life had he seen something like this.

As the balloon sailed upward, Jack felt his palms become sweaty and had a bit of a lump in his stomach. Watching Tariq becoming smaller and smaller below him, Jack realized that if the balloon now failed he would plummet to his death. He tried not to think negative thoughts and focused on commanding the balloon. His fingers pulled at the burners with the touch of a surgeon. He had to be careful to not give the balloon too much heat, otherwise it would overshoot the landing and he'd float away and have to start over—a costly error that would take him the greater part of another day. He hoped he'd calculated the correct wind speed to

push him right to the top. His speed was a little greater than he'd anticipated, and he started to rise faster than he'd wanted. His position was
good now, but if he didn't slow down, soon he would pass the side of the
tower and within seconds would be beyond the tower, completely out of
position, and would have to bring the balloon down and start over.

With only seconds to act, he powered down and the balloon crash
landed on the surface of the tower. The basket skidded in the sand for
twenty feet, at which point Jack hopped out and ran alongside it, holding
it with a rope. Just a few feet from the edge, he stopped it and went about
securing it with a series of spikes. Deflated completely, the envelope
of the balloon fluttered harmlessly to the ground just as Jack finished
securing it.

Satisfied the balloon was secure, he went back over to the edge,
drenched in sweat and breathing heavily. He waved down to Tariq, who
quickly waved back.

He scanned the top of the tower; there wasn't much to look at from
his perspective. The top was, for the most part, completely barren with
the exception of a few shrubs and one small scrub oak almost directly in
the middle of the tower's top. After walking around the top for a good
twenty minutes, he couldn't find anything that might be a clue or some
kind of secret opening. Sitting down in the dirt, he crossed his legs and
tried to understand what could be meant by the clue. It clearly marked
the top of this tower—he had to be in the right place!

He stared at the small oak tree—that had to be it! A solitary scrub
oak must be the perfect marker.

Going to the small tree, he looked around it and felt it up and down,
but it felt and looked like an ordinary tree. Getting on his hands and
knees, he dusted around the perimeter of the tree until he came to one
spot that seemed to be different from the rest of the area around it. The
ground seemed to be softer in that spot. Jack began digging furiously
with his hands until he had pulled out two feet of dirt.

He hit it! His fingers touched steel!

Digging faster, he felt a steel box about twelve inches square. Within
moments he'd dug all around it and pulled it out of the ground. The box

was copper and completely caked in mud. There was a small chain locked around it, which he quickly busted off with a rock. Opening the box, Jack looked upon the prize he had been seeking for so many years.

The diary of Alexander the Great!

Amazingly, it was in good condition, the pages still strong and durable. The box must have somehow been completely resistant to the elements.

Tucking the diary away in his breast pocket, carefully wrapping it in a rag, he returned the now-empty box to its resting place and buried it.

While walking back to the edge to signal to Tariq, something in the horizon caught his eye. A group of riders headed right for their position—about twenty in all. They were riding fast and hard and spitting up dust in their wake. Quickly, he went to the supply bag and brought out a monocular. Returning to the edge, he aimed the monocular at the riders and adjusted the focus.

It was the Caid's men; he could tell by the colors on their mounts. They had been following their trail and would be on Tariq in moments.

Trying to signal to Tariq below, he pointed at the riders and shouted to him. Tariq shrugged his shoulders—he didn't understand!

Jack had no way of signaling to Tariq. He didn't know if he'd been spotted by the advancing riders. The balloon was most likely out of sight, and he doubted they would have spotted him from that distance.

He couldn't get to Tariq in time. And, if he tried, he would surely be spotted by the riders and captured.

Jack had no choice—he would allow the riders to capture Tariq and make his getaway by night. It would be impossible for the riders to capture him during the night, or even during the day unless his balloon failed.

Jack felt a wave of melancholy come over him. It should have been the best day of his life, but he felt sick leaving Tariq to the Caid's soldiers. He just didn't have a choice. The diary was much too important, much too vital to risk falling into the wrong hands.

Walking back to the balloon, he sat beside it, waiting for the sun to set in about three hours so he could make his escape.

Tariq would be on his own.

Nur lunged with his sword aimed at Fez's face. It was only inches from finding its mark when Aseem leaped up and parried it with his knife. The sword was blocked, but the force was so great it knocked the knife to the ground.

Without thinking, Aseem launched himself and, with his left fist, punched Nur hard in the throat, knocking him backwards.

Nur staggered a little and then swung wildly at Aseem, who ducked and narrowly avoided the steel above his head. Aseem continued to back away, trying to keep a safe distance between himself and Nur's blade.

Frustrated, Nur stepped forward as Aseem stepped backwards. They were in the bedroom now and Aseem felt the bed frame at his heel—he was cornered and would have nowhere else to move! Nur lunged at him, and without thinking Aseem threw up a blanket and sheet that were crumpled on the bed, covering Nur's face and blinding him just as he brought his sword down.

Quickly, Aseem went for Nur's knees, issuing a side kick taught to him by Malik. It didn't have the accuracy he had hoped for, but the force put Nur on his knees. Nur finally knocked the sheets and blanket off of him and could see again. Standing up and circling backwards, he cornered Aseem against two walls with no means of escape.

Nur was breathing heavily, with knees bent, as he gripped the sword tightly and lunged forward to slash at Aseem. Seeing that Aseem was trapped, Fez grabbed a bottle of olive oil from a nearby shelf and threw it on the floor in front of Nur.

Suddenly, Nur felt himself flying upwards, his feet lifting in front of his face, his body entirely off the ground.

Before he knew what happened, his head slammed onto the floor—unconscious!

Aseem gently walked towards him. Nur's head was in a strange position and he wasn't moving. He nudged Nur with his right foot but nothing happened.

"I think he's dead," Aseem said.

Fez walked over and pushed Nur on the shoulders. No movement.

Quickly, Aseem placed a candle just underneath Nur's nostrils to see if the flame moved.

It did not.

Nur was dead – a freak accident more than anything else.

Aseem grabbed Fez and they bolted from the room. Some of the servants were walking up the stairs, calling for their master and receiving no response in return.

Jumping across the rooftop, they made their way back to the rope and shimmied their way over to the other side. Nur's house was now a mess of activity as lights were turned on and people began to understand what had transpired. A servant opened the gate, ringing a bell and calling out "my master has been murdered...my master has been murdered!"

Habib, waiting for them, urged them to the opposite end of the rooftop, where they jumped down ten feet to another rooftop, ran across it, and then leaped down to the ground. Running through a series of hallways and alleys, they ran and ran until they were on the other side of town.

They had escaped!

On the *Rouge*, the crew was fast asleep with only one guard on watch. That guard happened to be Cortez. He had been waiting for some kind of attack, and hoped it wouldn't be a bombardment, as he would probably be killed in the action. Then, in the distance, he heard it.

The distinctive sound of a steamship engine.

Quickly, he put a white flag with a large X in black chalk and waved it from his rifle. This was the signal he'd been told to give to alert Dreyfuss that he was not to be harmed.

Down below, as the crew slept, it was difficult to hear anything other than waves crashing against the side of the ship. The crew depended on the watchman to alert them of any danger. Aquina, the first mate in charge now that Captain Basil was on land, was sleeping peacefully in his quarters when he felt the cold gun barrel against his forehead.

Cortez waited anxiously for Dreyfuss and the beautiful sight of the Union Jack.

As the ship drew nearer, Cortez felt his heart sink.

The ship wasn't Dreyfuss as he had assumed.

It was a French ship—a French war ship looking for pirates.

Cortez watched as a squad of French soldiers pointed their rifles at his head and cannons were aimed square at the side of the *Rouge*. They were looking for pirates and, evidently, had found their prize.

The *Rouge* was the most-wanted ship in the Mediterranean.

Putting up his hands, he knew he was trapped.

CHAPTER
— *15* —

SAINT CATHERINE OF ALEXANDRIA

"You're going to France and that's the end of it!" Louise Owen yelled at Margaret as she ran down her hallway and shut her door behind her.

They had been arguing like this for three days.

Louise had decided to send Margaret to a boarding school in the south of France near Marseilles. It was a school run by nuns, and more importantly, it was far away from England. Margaret had become so difficult to understand, much less discipline. Louise needed time to breathe.

There was something else, a secret she had wanted to tell her daughter, but could not.

Shortly after her return to England, she had been called to the Foreign Relations office on urgent business. Once there, a man by the name of Monte had sat her down in his office, offered her some tea, and explained some very unfortunate business.

A Lieutenant Dreyfuss had been attacked by Charles Owen and a group of pirates. They had killed several of his men, and burned and massacred an entire village off the African coast.

"That is an impossibility," Louise had coldly answered.

Unfortunately, all the British authorities had to go on was the word of this man Dreyfuss. They also had eyewitness accounts from other British officers confirming the attack.

Louise listened to this news in absolute disbelief. Her Charles? A pirate?

It was unfathomable.

She tried to explain how absurd it all seemed. Charles was a family man and a decorated British officer. Why would he join some pirates?

Monte, to his credit, agreed with her. It all seemed genuinely preposterous.

His superiors had agreed.

Until Charles Owen could be brought in to trial to explain his actions, everyone wanted to keep this very hush-hush. It would be quite an embarrassment to have a British officer messed up with any kind of pirating activities.

So, Louise was merely instructed to report any correspondence with her husband to the British authorities at once. She left the office in a state of absolute shock. She didn't understand any of it—if she could only talk to Charles and get his side of the story.

Then, a couple of days later, a cryptic letter addressed to her arrived from Turkey.

The letter didn't have a return address. Opening it, she immediately recognized Charles's writing; however, the letter was written in code! It was a code he had shown her years ago, something he had devised during the Boer War to prevent enemies from intercepting and interpreting their company's orders. It was a very simple code, but it depended upon knowing a poem. With his soldiers, he had chosen *Gunga Din* by Rudyard Kipling.

The code was a series of numbers that corresponded to a line and letter in the poem. All the recipient had to do was match the numbers to the letters to decipher the code.

The Owen family's code was based on the famous passage, *All the World's a Stage* by William Shakespeare, which he had each family member memorize.

Louise quickly fetched pen and paper and went about deciphering the letter. It took her only thirty minutes. The letter read,

> My Darling,
>
> I miss you and the children terribly. But I must make this brief. After you jumped ship, I was captured by a man named Basil, who is reputed to be a ruthless pirate. He showed me a different story than I'd ever imagined. There is a rogue British Lieutenant by the name of Dreyfuss who is the real pirate. Dreyfuss is massacring entire villages and sinking fishing boats in the name of British commerce. I had to flee with Basil and am now a hunted

man. I pray the British authorities will learn the truth. Please have faith in me, my love.

Your Charles.

Louise couldn't believe what she was reading.

It was true!

Charles had joined forces with a pirate, but the story wasn't what the British authorities had suspected. Louise's first instinct was to tell her children and give the letter to Monte. However, she reconsidered after taking the situation into account.

If it was true, then the British authorities might be trying to protect Dreyfuss and hunt down Charles. If they knew she was knowledgeable about Dreyfuss, then they might try to "hush her up."

She decided to hide the letter and not tell anyone she had heard from her husband—not even the children. They mustn't know any of this, as many of their school friends had parents who were high up in the British government.

But how could she help Charles? Somehow she needed find out who she could—and could not—trust within the government.

Margaret was another story.

She understood Margaret's anger and confusion. She had been extremely close to her father and losing him obviously threw her world into disarray. Being in the stifling British society only complicated the matter. The most important thing for Louise as the adult in that society was to keep a stiff upper lip and continue giving the impression that everything was going along just fine. It was another thing, however, to ask it of a fourteen-year-old girl, for whom such a charade was practically impossible.

She considered showing Margaret the letter, but decided against it. Louise could see Margaret throwing this information into Hillie's face the moment she was taunted. It was just too dangerous.

So, she finally decided to send Margaret to Saint Catherine's boarding school in southern France. That was the end of it, there would be no discussion. It might only be for a semester, but they both needed a break from all this drama.

And Louise needed time to think.

Two weeks later, Margaret stood at the foot of Saint Catherine's School, located on the outskirts of the Cevennes region of southern France. The Cevennes region is so-named for a sprawling mountain range covered with green oak and chestnut trees, rolling hills, and the bones of many ancient castles and abbeys long since abandoned. The rugged terrain was, at one time, inhabited by wolves and bears, but those had been slaughtered from existence long ago. Now, wild boars and mountain goats ruled the rustic hills.

"It will be fine, Margaret. It's just for a little while until things settle down at school," Louise said, trying in vain to reassure her daughter.

Margaret burst into tears and hugged her mother as David stood and watched his sister. Margaret knew she deserved this. She understood completely that her actions could have seriously harmed, or even killed, Miss Cromwell.

The worst of it was that Alice was sent back to Ireland to live with her aunt. So, even if she had stayed in England, she would have had no friends left.

The school compound was quite beautiful, nestled among a group of chestnut trees along a creek bed. It was actually a converted abbey built in the tenth century. A tall green oak tree was at the center of the school grounds. Girls walked to and from the various buildings, all dressed in the traditional school uniform of a gray sweater, white blouse, black skirt, white ankle socks, and black shoes. Some glanced over at Margaret while others ignored her completely.

The main building was located in the center of the compound. The three Owens walked to the main entrance, dropped Margaret's luggage, opened a large wooden door, stepped into a small office, and shut the door behind them. The flooring was a musty, white ceramic tile cut in large, twelve-inch squares. The ceilings were high, with wooden oak beams cut across the middle. A rather large mahogany table with six chairs around it sat to the left. To the right was a small desk with three impressive book shelves filled to the brim with books. In the far corner sat a woodstove with a fire burning inside, keeping the room comfortably warm.

They stood there for five minutes until the door opened behind them and a small, plump woman of about fifty-five entered the room and closed the door behind her. She was dressed in a typical nun's habit and waddled, rather than walked, to the table. She sat and motioned for the others to join her.

"Please, sit down," she spoke in French.

The Owen family sat around her placidly and waited for her to speak.

"So, this must be Margaret. I am Sister Anne. Welcome to Saint Catherine's. I understand that you speak fluent French?'

"Yes, Sister," Margaret answered.

"Excellent, that will make life much easier. Our curriculum is very straightforward: classes from seven to two o'clock each day, afternoon activities, then dinner at six. As a new girl, you will be required to set up dinner each weeknight and brunch each weekend. Every student is required to attend mass on Sunday, as well as play a sport and play a musical instrument. Do you play a sport or musical instrument?"

"Both, Sister. I'm an avid sailor and equestrian, and I play the piano."

"Excellent! A well-rounded education is what we strive for at Saint Catherine's. Do you know anything about Saint Catherine?" Sister Anne asked.

Sister Anne stood from her seat and went about preparing a pot of water for tea on the woodstove. Taking out four teacups with matching saucers, she returned to her seat.

"No, Sister, but I'm eager to learn."

"That's a painting of Catherine behind me on the wall. Catherine was the daughter of King Costus and Queen Sabinella, who ruled Alexandria. Catherine was immensely intelligent and a diligent student of the arts, sciences, and philosophy. At a very young age, she decided she would never marry unless she met someone as intelligent and dignified as she was. The Roman Emperor Maxentius attempted to convert Catherine to his religion by having his greatest scholars and philosophers debate with her. Instead, Catherine converted all of them to Christianity. The emperor was so enraged he had all those great minds put to death and had Catherine beheaded."

Margaret looked at the painting above the desk. It depicted a beautiful woman sitting in a chair, dressed in an elegant red robe with gold sashes, looking to her left with her hand on a wheel. In her hand appeared to be some kind of wand and on her slender head sat a lavender crown.

"Joan of Arc said that Catherine was one of the saints who came to her in her dreams," Sister Anne continued as she went to the whistling pot, grabbed it with a rag, and poured the hot water into a teapot with tea leaves to steep.

"Milk or sugar for anyone?"

"Both for me," Louise answered.

"Both for me, please," Margaret answered.

"Um, both please," David sheepishly answered.

Sister Anne prepared each cup with milk and sugar, and then placed all four cups on a wooden tray, which she brought to the table and set in the center. She strained the tea leaves as she poured the tea, handing each of the Owens a cup before continuing.

"Saint Catherine was a modern woman who was killed for her ideals. She strove for the betterment of both herself and her fellow man and woman. We follow her ideals at this school and expect our students to strive for their own philosophy. We believe in independent thought, debate, and the respect of others. As long as you adhere to this philosophy, I expect you'll enjoy your time here," Sister Anne concluded.

Her tone had turned much more serious. Whereas before she had been quite accommodating and dainty, now Margaret saw she could be a commanding presence.

"Yes Sister, I'll do my best," Margaret answered.

The truth was that Saint Catherine did interest Margaret. She liked everything that Sister Anne was telling her about the school. Sister Anne didn't seem at all like Miss Cromwell. Rather, she seemed like someone Margaret would like to know and learn from as a mentor.

"Excellent! Well, I will show you to your quarters and then have one of the girls provide you with a tour of the premises."

Sister Anne led them out the office and down a path to a small house. It wouldn't be fair to call it a dormitory, because it was the size of a two bedroom house, complete with a tiled, triangle-shaped room. The interior was quite pleasant with wooden floors and five beds, three on one side and two on the other. Each bed was made with a beautiful comforter in light blue, yellow, and green. The room smelled of jasmine. On the far bed, a solitary girl sat cross-legged reading an untitled book.

"Sophie, this is your new roommate from England. Her name is Margaret. I'm sure you'll make her feel comfortable in her new home," Sister Anne requested.

Sophie arose from her sitting position—she might have been the most beautiful girl that Margaret had ever seen. Her face was flawless and her skin was like porcelain. Long, chestnut hair flowed down her back and she carried herself like an Egyptian queen, walking toward Margaret with a regal quality.

"It is a pleasure to meet you, Margaret. I hope you will enjoy your stay here. This is your bed across from mine and this is your dresser for your belongings. You can store your luggage under the bed," she said and kissed Margaret once on each cheek.

"Thank you. Um, this is my mother, Louise Owen, and my brother, David."

"It is a pleasure to meet with you both. I hope your visit to my country has been enjoyable," Sophie said and kissed both of them on the cheek. David blushed with embarrassment at being kissed by such a beautiful girl.

"It has been delightful. Your school is wonderful and I think Margaret will enjoy herself immensely," Louise said.

"Ah, your French is perfect," Sophie exclaimed and everyone laughed.

"Won't you join us for dinner? It should be ready in about half an hour," Sister Anne asked Louise.

"Sadly, David and I must depart or we will miss our return ferry from Marseilles. The school looks wonderful and thank you for accepting Margaret on such short notice," Louise explained.

"Ah, but she is such an accomplished young lady, I'm sure she will fit right in with us. Here, let me escort you to your carriage."

Sister Anne walked Louise, David, and Margaret back to the waiting coachmen. Margaret hugged her mother with tears in her eyes and then gave her little brother a big kiss and hugged him as well. She suddenly missed the safety of her home and the familiarity of her native land. The overwhelming fear of being in a new school in a new country suddenly felt like too much and she broke down and dug her face into her mother's chest like a little girl.

Louise started to cry a bit as well, hugging daughter right back and consoling her by stroking her hair and holding her tightly.

"You just need a little break to figure things out. You've been through so much and I don't think dreary London could hold back such an ambitious girl as yourself," Louise whispered to her and managed to make Margaret giggle a bit.

"I'll do my best, Mother. It won't be like the last school, I promise."

"Okay then, go back and get acquainted," Louise said, releasing their embrace.

"Mother, just one thing."

"What is it?"

"Could you please give word to Alice that I miss her and check in with her parents? They are awfully lonely in London society and I think they could use a friend."

"Given everything that's happened, I might not have many friends left. I'll pay them a visit and write you soon about Alice."

"Thank you!"

Louise and David boarded the carriage and Margaret watched it trot away down the hill. David waved goodbye the entire way, staring back at his sister until they were out of sight.

"Come now dear, let's get you settled in," Sister Anne said to Margaret gently taking her hand, and returning Margaret to her house.

The house was now filled with Sophie and two other girls.

"So, you are from England. You're not a supporter of that tyrant Cromwell or that butcher William the Orange are you?" one of the girls asked Margaret as she entered the room.

"No, I don't think so..." Margaret stammered back, unprepared for the barrage.

"You don't think so, or, you think so? Or, you do not think so?" she replied.

"I don't think so," Margaret replied before sitting on her bed.

The girl across from her was short, almost five inches shorter than Margaret, with red hair and freckles and an athletic build.

"Margaret, this is Inez. She is from Marseilles and comes from a long line of smugglers and pirates. Her great grandfather was beheaded during the French revolution," Sophie explained.

"Oh!"

"Although you are English, I shall treat you with the utmost respect," Inez said proudly.

"Thank you, and I will treat you with respect as well," Margaret answered, unsure of where the conversation was going.

The other girl in the room introduced herself to Margaret.

"My name is Etienne. My parents are from Burgundy and are winemakers. We own a vineyard that has been in our family for over one thousand years. We make the best wine in all of northern France, this I am sure of. Do you want to try some?"

"I suppose so," Margaret answered.

"Excellent, I happen to have a flask right here!" she exclaimed and starting passing a silver flask around the room. It came to Margaret and she took a small sip. It was quite good! She was accustomed to the wine used in their church services, which was watered down and cheap. This was very different and quite tasty.

"It's very good!"

"See, I told you, the best wine in all of northern France."

Etienne was very thin and had a fun and inquisitive face. She had long brunette hair and two buck teeth that stuck out a little when she smiled. Her teeth didn't make her look awkward; rather, they strangely made her look more attractive.

"So, what did you do wrong?" Sophie asked.

"What do you mean?" Margaret asked.

"You must have done something wrong to get sent all the way to France. Besides, Saint Catherine's is different from other boarding schools. The administrators don't care as much about money or status as a lot of other schools. They want a diversified student class."

Margaret didn't know quite what to say to this line of questioning. Should she just be honest with these girls? Or try to feign the truth?

She decided to be honest.

"There was this awful girl, Hillie, in my class. So, at her birthday party, I put laxative in the tea and everyone in the party got the runs. It was a mess. Then, I put bees in my headmaster's office and she had to go to the hospital for a week because of so many stings."

The other girls sat stunned.

"I like this girl; she's not one to be messed with!" Inez shrieked.

"Tell us more!" Sophie begged in anticipation.

"This is a scandal!" Etienne yelled and all three girls surrounded Margaret on her bed.

"Well, there's more to it than that, but I'm not sure you would believe me," Margaret tried to explain.

"Why not? The truth is almost always more interesting than lies," Sophie said.

"Well, here goes. I was vacationing with my family off the coast of Morocco about a year ago when we were attacked by pirates. My father took our boat and diverted the pirates away from us while my mother, my brother and I swam to shore. We made our way to Tangier, where I was kidnapped and sold into slavery to an evil Caid. I met three boys named Tariq, Aseem, and Fez who became my best friends. I was to be made a slave for the Caid's son, but we escaped into the mountains with a rebel group. Tariq and the others attacked the Caid and almost defeated him. Then, we had to move the camp. I was escorted back to Tangier and put on a steamboat for England. I guess I didn't make the transition well because I really became a terror. I'd always been a good student and a good daughter, but I just couldn't be in stuffy British society after all that. I met this girl named Alice and everyone in our school hated us and tried to torture us. That's when I put laxative in Hillie's tea and bees in Miss Cromwell's office."

The three girls lay there, mouths open, and eyes wide in disbelief.

"My goodness what a story!" Sophie yelled.

"Pirates! Slaves! Kidnappings! It's got to be true," Inez said.

"What happened to your father?" Etienne asked.

"I still don't know. I miss him terribly. I pray he's not dead, but nobody has heard from him since the pirates went after him."

Sophie came and put her arm around Margaret.

"You're very brave, Margaret. I will pray for your father tonight," she said and hugged Margaret. The other two girls came and joined in and Margaret felt like she was being squeezed like a sardine in a can!

Soon, all four girls were outside and going to dinner. Margaret had never felt so welcome in all of her life. The other girls were equally as inquisitive and, once word got around of Margaret's exploits, she was a minor celebrity at the dinner table. Different girls peppered her with questions about Tariq, Fez, and Aseem, and especially about Sanaa. She didn't let anyone know that she had actually killed a guard, as that was not something she took pride in accomplishing.

Margaret, after only a day, already felt at home in her new surroundings.

Even a month later, nothing had dampened Margaret's enthusiasm for her new school. The teachers were amazing! They were not abusive or condescending and challenged students to find answers and stretch their imagination and intuition. There was competition, but it was to better oneself, not to put others down.

One day Margaret was called into Sister Anne's office. Had she done something wrong? She didn't think she had broken any rules. In fact, she'd been receiving straight A's since she arrived.

That's when Sister Anne came into the office flanked by a new student. Immediately Margaret stood up and ran and hugged the new girl, embracing her wildly, and holding her tightly.

It was Alice!

Both girls cried and whirled around and hugged one another.

"I can see you two know one another!" Sister Anne said, smiling.

"Oh, what a surprise! How did this happen?" Margaret asked.

"You two can catch up on pleasantries later. Margaret, we'll move Alice into the spare bed in your house. We accepted her on one condition—that you tutor her in French. As she hardly speaks a word, it will be up to you to bring her up to speed. Is that understood?"

"Oh yes, yes, it will be no problem Sister Anne!"

"Then help her with her bags and show her around."

The two girls left the building, dragging Alice's enormous travel trunk behind them.

"What happened? How did you end up here?" Margaret asked.

"I was miserable in my new school and your mother contacted my parents. Apparently they were very impressed with your mother's description of Saint Catherine's and they had no objection to my coming. I just need to learn French!"

"It will be no problem—I'll teach you—and you will love it here! It's the best school ever, and the girls are so nice."

The two girls joined the others and soon Alice was part of the group. Although she didn't speak French, the other girls accepted her and helped her learn her lessons.

For once, Margaret was happy and content. Still, there were unanswered questions that nagged at her. Her father's disappearance was still a mystery and she wouldn't truly be at peace until she knew what had happened to him. She wondered about Fez, Tariq, Sanaa, Malik, and Aseem and hoped they were all safe. She wanted to contact them somehow, but this seemed impossible.

With time, maybe she could learn to accept it.

Malik and Sanaa made their way around a bend and then—nothing! A wall was in front of them, and to their side, a ridge that couldn't possibly be scaled.

They were trapped!

Circling their horses, they waited for the inevitable.

"I do not see an escape, Malik! We are trapped!" Sanaa said.

Malik, circling his horse, frantically looked for an escape route, but there was none. The only way out was the way they came in.

Sanaa began to draw her sword and Malik told her to put it down.

"We cannot fight, Sanaa. Our only hope is to surrender," he said, trying to hide the defeat in his voice from her.

As Sanaa slid the sword back in her scabbard, Malik could, for the first time, see the fear in her eyes.

Within seconds, the Mamba and his soldiers came galloping on them. Quickly, they surrounded Malik and Sanaa.

The Mamba, his bald head glistening with sweat, stared straight into Malik's eyes.

"Is this the one?" he asked Jawad.

Jawad, right next to him, quickly answered.

"Yes, that is Malik—he is their leader! And that is Sanaa, she is their best assassin."

The Mamba let out a little smile.

"Sire, let's kill them and be done with it! We have caught our prey," one of his soldiers said.

"NO! I have plans for these two. A quick death will not do them justice," the Mamba sneered in reply.

Ordering them to dismount, the Mamba's men quickly put Malik and Sanaa down on their knees and tied their hands behind their backs.

"I'm surprised you won't fight me like a man, Mamba," Malik sneered at him.

"But why kill you quickly, when you are so deserving of a slow and painful death?" the Mamba answered, with slight glee in his voice.

A rifle butt to the head of each sent both Malik and Sanaa forward—unconscious. Quickly, each of them was tied to the back of a horse with hands and feet bound.

The Caid's soldiers rode off with their prey.

CHAPTER
— *16* —

OUTMANNED AND OUTGUNNED!

Charles, Basil, and the rest of the crew decided to return to the *Angelina Rouge* the morning after the festivities with the Napoleon anarchists. Henri decided to join them with a few of his men to ensure they found the path back to the water. Also, Basil had agreed to give them a barrel of rum for their hospitality, a gift that Henri readily accepted, and which kept him in the good graces of his wife.

The day was already turning hot. It was about eight miles to the ship and the hike was largely spent in silence. Most of the men had headaches and suffered from a lack of sleep—in no mood for conversation. Flies buzzed around their necks, sipping on their sweat and biting them.

They were almost to the beach when Charles noticed something out of the corner of his eye. Most men would never have noticed it, but his years of military training and combat experience heightened his senses for anything out of the ordinary.

He noticed an extinguished cigarette on the ground around thirty feet ahead and on his right.

Maybe it was nothing, but the spot where it lay would have been the perfect spot for an ambush. They were coming into a narrow enclosure and surrounded by large rocks on either side.

"Wait," he ordered.

The rest of the men stopped, looking at Charles, wondering what he saw that they did not.

"Stay here, I'm going to check on this ridge."

Charles took out a revolver from his waistband and began scaling the hill on his right. He did it very, very slowly, crouching as he walked, scanning for anything out of the ordinary. A couple of pebbles dribbled down the hill from his footsteps, but other than that, he was quiet as a mouse.

Then he saw it!

Someone was behind one of the rocks. He saw a shoe poke out from behind a boulder.

"Ambush!" he yelled and ran backwards.

At once, the hills came alive with French soldiers, popping their heads up from behind boulders, firing at the group and running with bayonets in hand, yelling "Charge!"

Basil, Henri, Charles, and a few others fired back at the group in hasty retreat. Bullets whizzed by their heads as they ran back, trying to put some distance between themselves and their attackers.

They made it about thirty feet.

There was a group of boulders on either side of the trail they could hide behind and return fire. However, beyond the boulders, there was a clearing of about three hundred feet that led to another mountain pass.

There was no possible way they could run through the clearing without being cut down by the soldiers.

To make matters more complicated, two members of their group had been grazed by bullets—one in the arm and the other in the neck. They weren't serious wounds, but they would slow down any kind of escape.

Basil, Charles and Henri hid behind the boulders and occasionally returned fire, while the French soldiers took up positions about forty feet away, firing at the group and pinning them down.

"Hold up firing back at them, we don't have much ammo," Charles ordered.

His group stopped firing and now the only sound was the occasional whistle of a French bullet flying past their heads.

"Any ideas?" Henri asked.

Charles looked around, ascertained the situation, and immediately knew the answer.

"Our only hope is to make it through that clearing. If we can get through, then we can probably lose them in that mountain pass. There will be places to return fire and stop their advance. Unfortunately, I don't think we can make it without being cut to shreds. It's too far."

"We can just wait here, no? Pick them off one by one?" Henri answered.

"No, it will be too easy to flank us. All they need to do is send some soldiers around either bend and we'll be surrounded." "I agree with you Charles, we must try and make it through the clearing," Basil said.

Charles already knew the solution. He must stand there and cover the soldiers while the rest of the group escaped. It was the only answer.

"I'm going to cover you while you make that clearing. I can probably hold off the group for five or ten minutes which should give you enough time to make your exit."

Charles could have asked one of the lowlier guards to provide cover while he and the others made their escape, but that would have been cowardly. As a leader, he expected more of himself, and felt he should make the greatest sacrifice.

Basil looked at this friend. He also knew this was the only possible escape route, and that Charles would most likely die trying to save them.

"You can't hold them off by yourself. I will stay as well."

"Basil, you need to captain your ship and save your crew. I can manage..."

Before he could continue, Basil cut him off.

"My ship is already gone and my crew has been taken prisoner. I will not let you fight them alone Charles. It is my choice."

Charles knew Basil wouldn't take no for an answer, and he secretly appreciated his friend's response.

"We'll each need two weapons and some reserve ammunition. It won't take them long to figure out our strategy and they'll charge if they know there's only two of us."

Henri looked at both of them and answered.

"I will stay as well, I cannot let you two stay alone."

"I appreciate that Henri, but you've got to ensure your family and tribe are kept safe. You've got women and children to look after. You know these mountains better than anyone and can ensure the group's safety," Charles replied.

Henri looked down at the ground because he knew Charles was right. He could lead the group and protect his village. But he hated to leave a fight.

"All right, my friends. You are both brave beyond belief. My people thank you."

Basil and Charles nodded and smiled at him; they both appreciated his honesty and bravery.

Henri passed two loaded pistols to Basil and Charles with some spare ammunition. Basil and Charles set up on either side of the trail behind two boulders—taking the best position to repel a charge by the soldiers.

"On the count of three! One, two, three...*go!*" Charles yelled.

The group ran in the opposite direction while Charles and Basil opened fire at the French troops. The trailhead erupted in a sea of gun smoke as both men fired off several shots at the French so they wouldn't make a charge at them.

The strategy worked.

Henri and the group sprinted in the opposite direction. The French were coming under fire too heavy to attack. One soldier tried to lead a charge, but was quickly cut down by one of Basil's bullets as it ripped through his leg. The man lay screaming in agony, completely exposed, and unable to move due to his shattered leg.

The shooting stopped and all that was heard was the man's groaning.

"Pick your man up and get him some first aid. We will hold our fire," Charles yelled in French.

Basil looked at him as if he was mad, and Charles sternly returned his look. He wasn't going to kill a wounded and helpless soldier.

After a minute, two soldiers sprinted from behind their cover, picked up their fallen comrade, and dragged him back to safety.

The respite gave Basil and Charles an opportunity to reload their weapons.

"Do you think we could make it across the clearing?" Basil asked.

Charles looked at the clearing; it would be an all-out sprint for three hundred feet or more. Only thirty feet separated them from the French soldiers.

"Without cover? I don't know. Undoubtedly they've got long-range rifles and could pick us off like rabbits. The fact they now have a wounded colleague might make a bit of difference, but probably not much."

"I don't think we have much of a choice. If we stay here, we'll either be overrun or captured and I don't like either scenario," said Basil.

Charles looked at the clearing. It was a long distance to cover in such a short amount of time. However, Basil was right; they couldn't stay in their current position for much longer without a charge by the French. In fact, Charles was surprised they hadn't already charged through their line. If he had been their commander, he would have already sent his troops through and overtaken their position.

"On my count of three, fire as many shots as you can and we'll make a run for it."

Charles began counting down; both men braced themselves, looking at the French side, seeing the movement of a few troops, and steadying their guns. That's when they both felt it.

The distinct feel of steel at the back of their heads.

Instinctively, both men dropped their weapons and put their hands up. Looking back, six French soldiers had somehow managed to flank their position.

They were immediately taken prisoner and hauled away.

Tariq was surrounded!

The Caid's soldiers went right to his position and quickly formed a circle around him, their horses stamping, kicking up dust, and huffing through their nostrils.

"Who are you?" the leader asked.

Tariq didn't know what to say. He was taken completely by surprise and had no time to hide or retreat.

So that's why Jack had been trying to warn him.

"Who else is with you?" the leader asked again.

Tariq again said nothing, which aggravated the leader even more. Tariq had learned long ago to keep his mouth shut around any kind of police or military. He knew escape was impossible, so he merely put his hands on his head and dropped to the ground on his knees. He also knew what could happen next.

"I want a perimeter established, and scout the area for tracks. He's just a boy, he can't be here alone," the leader, a rough guard by the name of Aman, ordered the others.

The Caid was scouring the countryside for any and all rebels and anyone of suspicion was to be taken into custody. Aman had a feeling about this boy; something just wasn't right about him. It was the way the boy ignored his questions and refused to provide any answers, like he had been interrogated before, and had been trained on how to behave.

Aman sneered at him and began looking around the area. The wagon would have been too big to handle alone, so he must have had help. In fact, he saw two sets of foot prints all around the wagon but, then, nothing! It was as if the larger set had disappeared into thin air.

"Whose footprints are these?" he asked Tariq.

Tariq said nothing. He continued to stare at the ground with his hands on his head. He had a blank stare about him, as if he was lost in deep thought.

"Where did this person go? Who is he? Who are you?" Aman demanded.

Tariq continued to say nothing.

"Ahhhhhhh!" the sergeant yelled. In anger, he kicked Tariq in the back, knocking him on his stomach. A nasty welt rose up where a shoe had connected with Tariq's skin.

Tariq, for the first time, felt afraid. He had been hit and kicked so many times in his life that he'd lost count. This sergeant kept searching for answers. Did he know about Tariq? Was the Caid now searching for him because he had freed Aseem?

Whatever he did, he must keep his mouth shut and not let anyone know anything about him.

"We are hunting for gold," Tariq finally blurted out.

"Gold?" he asked.

"Yes, my uncle and I."

"Where is your uncle?"

"I do not know. I awoke from a nap and he was gone."

"His footprints disappear into thin air?"

Tariq shrugged his shoulders as if he didn't have the answer.

"Have you found any gold?"

"No, we only just arrived."

"Hmmppphhh."

He did not know what to think of this boy. It was a believable enough story, as there were many gold hunters in this area. Still, he had never seen the boy and the wagon was completely unknown to him. As he was raised in the area, and served as commander for over 100 miles of land, it was his business to know of any travelers and their business.

His soldiers returned and gave him a report on the surrounding area.

"We didn't find any kind of tracks except for the wagon tracks. It looks like there might be one other person, but we can't find a trace of anyone else," reported the lead scout.

"Listen, we camp here for the night. If his uncle does not show, we will take the boy to the Caid's kasbah for questioning."

The soldiers saluted and began preparing camp to set up for the night. They made Tariq collect sticks for a fire and even made him cook dinner for them using Jack's food.

Tariq did as they asked, but secretly he was terrified by their conversation. If he was, indeed, sent back to the Caid's kasbah, then he would be exposed for sure. His mind raced with escape possibilities, but no openings presented themselves. Two guards were strategically placed to prevent any kind of escape. The other issue facing him was where could he go if he did escape? It was still mostly desert for miles surrounding him.

His only hope was Jack.

Through the night he expected Jack to come and save him by knocking out some of the guards—but he never showed. In the early morning, the soldiers broke camp, made breakfast, and the troops mounted their horses.

"Well my little friend, it seems your uncle is nowhere to be found. You are coming with us and any escape attempt will be met with death," the sergeant told him.

As they rode along, the sergeant looked at him and spoke.

"I have a feeling about you, boy. I have a feeling that you are the one the Caid seeks. I have a feeling you are going to bring me much fortune and prestige within the Caid's army."

Tariq's heart sank even lower. He had been hoping he would wind up with everyone else and perhaps just slip away in anonymity. Now? He was suspected, which meant a close eye would be kept on him at all times. Escape would now be close to impossible.

CHAPTER
— *17* —

A PLAN IS MADE

F ez, Aseem, and Habib sat with Timin in an alley under a wooden crate. It was raining now, soaking their hair and shoulders. Fez was still a bit in shock over the nasty business with Nur.

Timin was more than impressed.

"There's definitely more to you than meets the eye, Fez! What you did showed a tremendous amount of courage."

"It was Aseem who saved my life," Fez said, trying to deflect the attention.

Aseem would have none of it.

"What you did was very brave, Fez! You have avenged your family and your tribe. It was a very difficult task. Now, you can sleep well at night and put this behind you," he said, putting his arm around Fez.

Fez looked at him and smiled a bit. It was not in his nature to be a killer, and he was still unsure how he felt about it all. Was he even a killer? True, he had thrown the olive oil, but the death had been more like an accident. On the one hand, he was so happy to finally avenge his family. He could still see the image of his father, with his last breath, telling Fez to avenge them. And he did it! Nur deserved to die, he was sure of that much. Yet, there was still a pit in his stomach he was trying to understand.

"Where will you two go now?" Timin asked. "It won't be safe for you here. The Caid's soldiers will be looking for you."

"We are going back to our tribe. Our work here is finished," Fez answered.

Habib thought about this for a moment.

"We could help you!" he answered excitedly.

"Who?" Aseem asked.

"Timin and the rest of the street boys—we could all help your resistance against the Caid."

"How?"

"By being spies. As I said before, we run these streets, but most of our time is spent doing stupid crimes and harassing other boys. What if we could all spy for you? Keep an eye out on the Caid and his movements? We would be the perfect spies because nobody cares for some stupid street kids. Nobody pays us any mind at all!"

Aseem and Fez both looked at each other, nodding their heads, appreciating the idea.

Timin smiled as well.

"It is a good plan. But, you would need a leader—someone to organize the group and issue missions and orders. You would need a way to communicate with your tribe."

Aseem and Fez thought about this for a minute.

"What about you, Timin?" Habib asked excitedly. "You could organize the group. All the boys respect you and you know everything about Chaouen and Tangier."

"But I don't know anything about spying. What would I do?" Timin asked.

"You know everything about the prisons in Morocco. You could call on your contacts in those areas, Timin," Habib continued.

Timin continued to consider this for a few moments. The rain had finally stopped, and the sun came out from behind the clouds. The boys lifted the makeshift shelter off their heads and sat on some crates, thinking of this new plan.

"It is a very good plan, actually. We could have our own set of codes and ways of communication. The Caid wouldn't be able to do anything without our knowing it!" Fez continued.

Timin stared at the ground, pondering, until finally he spoke.

"The Caid and the Sultan have ruined my entire life. I have no family. No home. I have lost everything because of them. My life is nothing. If I have one opportunity to defeat them, then I must take it. I was wrongly accused of being part of the resistance. Well, now I am part of the resistance! I will help you and I will develop a spy network that will bring down the Caid!"

Timin felt an overwhelming sense of relief at saying this. For so long he had been defeated and beaten down and now he finally had a chance to stand up to those who had wrongly imprisoned him.

"We must have codes that are impossible to break. We must have a way of communicating with one another. And we must have a way to expose double agents," Timin continued, talking out loud, more and more excited by the conversation.

"Well then, how do we get started?" Aseem asked.

"We start with the codes and how we will communicate," said Timin. "The spying part will be easy, as every servant, street urchin, and homeless man is known to me. Everyone who has been abused and tortured and oppressed will want to join the cause. Gathering this intelligence will not be difficult."

He continued to think and gently poked a stick in the ground, making circles in the dirt as he thought about the plan.

"Fez and Aseem, must you depart for your tribe? If you could stay for a week or two, then we could organize this in such a way that it would be successful."

"I think we could delay our departure, except, as you said…the Caid's men will now be looking for us," Fez answered.

"Perhaps there is a way around that."

Aseem looked at Timin and, apprehensively, asked a question.

"Timin, as you said, you have never done any of this before. How do you plan to learn?"

Timin smiled at this question.

"I was thinking the same thing myself. But then, I do have the perfect experience for it! I ran a secret betting parlor and constantly hid from police. We developed a series of codes to communicate where our games would be played. I had to keep all the numbers in my head for, if I wrote them down, I might be exposed. In prison, I had to learn to fight and even kill to survive. I ran a contraband business selling illegal goods to inmates. I have the perfect amount of experience for this sort of work."

"Let's get started, then," Aseem replied.

Back at his kasbah, the Caid assembled his generals in his war room. The men sat around his table, smoking their hookahs, drinking mint tea, and awaiting word from their master.

"I have word from the Sultan. The French are going to invade Morocco any day now," the Caid finally explained.

The generals immediately shifted in their seats and became quite animated.

"We must help the Sultan! We must keep the infidels from our land!" one general said.

"We will prepare our army at once!" another said.

The Caid sat at the head of his table, staring at these men, secretly wondering how such fools could have gained the rank of general.

"We will do no such thing," he finally answered.

The generals sat stunned. What did he mean, they would do nothing? The French were attacking and the Caid would do nothing?

"Morocco is like a little toy to the French. Something to be won and admired and that is all. The Sultan and his army have no chance against the machines of the French and all their money, tanks, aircraft, and rifles. They will be slaughtered like dogs!"

The generals quieted down and continued to listen.

"Once defeated, the French government will need someone loyal to them to take the Sultan's place. Someone who knows how to control the Moroccan people and can maintain law throughout the land," the Caid explained. Not looking at the generals, he began to slowly peel an orange with a silver knife.

"You mean we will not help the Sultan? But he will cut us down. Our army is no match for his."

The Caid considered this more than a minute, continuing to peel his orange, letting the generals wait for his answer.

"The Sultan has more pressing needs on his mind, such as fighting the French invaders. He won't have the time or the troops to fight us. We will control our land, make peace with the French, and gain control of

Morocco. Besides, I have already made an arrangement with the French. In fact, they sent me two hundred of their troops, along with rifles and money for our own soldiers."

"But we will still answer to the French!" another general exclaimed.

"Yes, we will play their little game. We will allow them to think they are the ones in control. We will use their troops to control the land. Meanwhile, we will be the puppet master pulling the strings. We just need to make them think we are stupid peasants who don't know any better."

The generals slowly began to understand the Caid's plan for domination.

"It is a grand plan, Sire!" one finally admitted.

"Why control our little slice of land when we can own the entire country? But first we must hunt down these rebels and exterminate them like the little rats that they are. We must have complete control of our dominion. It will be like a gift we offer the French. Their plan will be so much easier if they don't have to worry about seizing our land."

The generals now buzzed with excitement. They began to see the beauty of the Caid's plan. It would have been preposterous—and suicidal—to fight the French. The Caid already understood who would win this war. The French were already their friends and allies. The generals slowly began to understand the strategy the Caid had formed long, long ago. He would be on the winning side and in a position to gain control of the entire country. It would mean grand riches to the generals as well, and they would be given entire dominions to rule.

It would also mean the Caid would be the next Sultan and would rule Morocco with an iron fist.

Along a lonely street in Tangier sat an old building. Although its shingles were falling from the roof, it was also very beautiful. A new garden had been planted in back, and ivy trickled down from the columns on the front porch. Freshly painted white, it didn't look so old, but rather it looked lived in and cared for with love. Jasmine was planted along the sides of the building, and herbs grew wild in the front, to be picked by the many children that inhabited the orphanage.

In an upstairs room, by candlelight, Zijuan meditated on a rug with burning incense at her side. She sat cross-legged, with palms on either knee, and eyes closed. She had been like this for over an hour.

Lately, she had been very troubled. She couldn't sleep at night and her thoughts were jumbled and erratic. She began to meditate each night for an extra ten minutes, then twenty, and now an hour. Inhaling and exhaling, she used the meditation to try to find the source of her frustration. She understood that sometimes this sense of frustration, or disturbance, had nothing to do with her everyday life. It could be something in the spiritual world or associated with events entirely outside of her domain.

Yes, there was much stress in her world as news that the French would invade Morocco was on the lips of every citizen of Tangier. She tried to ignore the rumors and go about her everyday life running the orphanage. She doubted the French would care about her little orphanage. In fact, perhaps the French would be easier to deal with than the Moroccan underworld gangsters she had to strike bargains with at every corner to protect her orphans. If the French wanted Morocco, they were welcome to it.

But three nights ago, she began to have visions and see images. Negative images. Disturbing visions.

All of them included Tariq.

In one, he was in a room full of snakes with no exit. In another, he was drowning in the ocean with nobody to save him, and in another he was hanging by a cliff with one hand.

Then she saw it.

A flash. A momentary flash, but she saw it. It was there.

The flash was the face of an old man. His face was skinny but swollen, his cold eyes black and without life. On his mouth was a sinister sneer. This man was pure evil. This man had done unspeakable things in his life.

This vision had something to do with Tariq.

How was this man connected to Tariq? Was it someone that Tariq had met and was now in his life? Was it someone from Tariq's past? Tariq's life was such a chaotic mess that perhaps this man had been his father or his grandfather?

Finally, in one vision, she thought she had the answer.

The man was a shadow, his face tucked away in the corners while Tariq was attacked by a pack of wild dogs. The man remained unseen, but smirked as he watched Tariq being attacked and bitten. He rejoiced in watching the fear in Tariq's face and hearing the agony of his cries.

The man was somehow controlling Tariq. He was involved with him in some way.

He was feeding off of Tariq's misery.

But how?

Zijuan had heard nothing of Tariq for months now. Her communication with Malik and the others had grown cold, due to rumors that the Mamba was hunting them down. Several times she had sent messages asking if her assistance was needed, but each message went unreturned. It was very dangerous for her to travel, because the Caid's soldiers were questioning everyone who entered his land. If she was somehow captured, who would look after her orphans? She had to be very, very careful and not draw attention to herself.

Yet, somehow she felt she was needed; it was the how or when or where that was a mystery. Zijuan had the same feeling when she rescued those children being sold into slavery in China all those years ago. Her destiny wasn't immediately understood, but once she started on the path, opportunities simply opened up to her. The way she met Captain Basil, and he agreed to escort her and the children all the way back to Morocco without asking for so much as a dime. How she fell into inheriting this orphanage from a dying woman who willed it to her. When one is on the right path in life, when one makes the right decisions, that's the way destiny works. Things just happen.

She would keep her mind and senses open to all possibilities and signs. If she was needed elsewhere, she would make herself open to such a route and not fight or resist it. Until then, she would continue to meditate and seek more answers. She would look for clues.

Louise Owen spent many of her days at the public library, poring through books and looking for answers. She visited government offices and attended parties where she might meet politicians or military leaders.

Like Zijuan, Louise was also looking for clues, but hers were of the very tangible and physical type.

In her little cocoon in London, Louise felt claustrophobic and trapped. She couldn't confide in anyone about Charles. The situation with Margaret had grown so dire that she was starting to be shunned by some of her friends. Over months she had grown depressed and sad. But one day, she made the decision to actually do something.

Somehow, she was going to help her husband.

She started with this Lieutenant Dreyfuss. Who was he? How was he involved? For two months she searched for information about this man, but came up with nothing. Then, inexplicably, an opportunity presented itself that she thought could lead to something more concrete.

Charles had some old chums who had joined the navy, and Louise decided to start with them. There was a small cocktail party being thrown at the house of Matthew Hatrider, who was currently an officer in the navy and had gone to school with Charles.

Louise arrived at the party in traditional English attire. Her dress was ruffled and immensely tight in the middle, so much so that she had trouble breathing. Attending parties solo was nothing new to her, as Charles was often on military assignment, leaving her to fend for herself. It wasn't bad really, since most wives had husbands in the military, so attending a party unescorted was common and nobody really questioned it.

However, her circumstances made things a little more difficult. Everyone knew that Charles was missing and that Louise was having some troubles with her daughter. Margaret's little business with the bees had made its way around the cocktail parties in Louise's circle of friends. Oddly enough, most of the women were secretly proud of Margaret, as most of them had also suffered under Miss Cromwell.

Generally at these parties the women stuck to their circles, eating finger sandwiches, drinking Pimm's, and discussing the latest fashions or gossip. The men, meanwhile, retired to the billiard room with their glasses full of brandy and tins of cigarettes. Louise knew she would have to somehow make better acquaintance with Matthew Hatrider without drawing attention.

Louise intently watched the study door, and at last Matthew came out to use the facilities. He wasn't a particularly distinguished man. In fact, he was rather plain and was more than halfway on the way to going bald. He was rather short in stature and approaching pudgy at his waistline. His manner was on the quiet side, and he seemed to detest these cocktail parties. Louise knew he was a connoisseur of wine and decided to use that as her tactic for starting a conversation.

Dismissing herself, she waited outside the bathroom door, pretending to look at a painting, but secretly waiting for Matt.

After a few moments, he emerged from the bathroom and turned into the hallway.

"Oh, Matthew, thank you for throwing such a wonderful party!" Louise said, blocking his path to prevent him from escaping the conversation.

"Louise, certainly; thank you for attending. Are you enjoying yourself?" he asked, almost embarrassed. He thought his parties were boring, so he assumed everyone else felt the same.

"Of course, I always enjoy myself at your parties! We were just discussing whether the 1910 Rothschild Bordeaux was as good as the 1909 Burnsberry Pinot Noir. I, of course, prefer the Bordeaux. I understand you're quite the connoisseur...do you have a preference?"

Matthew was a bit taken aback by the question. Rarely had anyone bothered with his opinion on much of anything, much less wine, which was his passion. In the navy, he was little more than an administrative pencil pusher and was rarely included in any kind of strategic discussions. Even in his own study, while the other men boasted of service in the Boer Wars and the impending French invasion of Morocco, he was rarely included in those conversations.

He very much felt like a forgotten man.

"Uh, well, yes, both wines are excellent, of course. The 1910 Bordeaux is an excellent vintage, but I would keep it in storage for another two years until it peaks. I tend to feel the Burnsberry Pinot is a bit overrated. It falls a bit on the sweet side for my tastes, as I prefer a nice dry wine."

"Interesting. I don't prefer the 1910 at all, but the 1908 was a splendid vintage," Louise replied.

"Well, yes, you are right. The 1908 was magnificent. In fact, I just opened a bottle last week and was pleasantly amazed by how well it was maturing. It has developed a nice solid finish. There might be hope yet for the 1910."

Louise could see he was enjoying the conversation. His wife most likely thought his fascination with wines to be boring and tedious.

"You know, I picked up a few bottles on my recent trip to France. I'm going to have a small tasting with some friends, would you be interested in attending?"

He stammered a bit when presented with this invitation. Hardly anyone invited him to anything. His wife, however, was invited to almost everything, and most times he felt like a handbag being dragged to and fro.

"Which part of France?"

"Down south; Margaret's school is just outside of Marseilles. I did manage a little jaunt with David up near Avignon and picked up wines I'm especially excited to open. Not the most popular vintages, but they might present some finds."

"Oh, Avignon; I've been meaning to visit Avignon at some point. Did you visit the Palais des Papes? I've heard it's quite lovely."

"Yes, we did! It has such a lovely view of the surrounding countryside. You really should visit!"

"Well, Ellen doesn't really like France. She finds the people to be quite unusual. So, we don't make it over very often. But, yes, I would be delighted to attend your tasting."

"Lovely! Next Thursday at seven thirty at my house; it will be just a small gathering. I've also garnered some nice French cheese that will go perfectly with the wines. I look forward to having such an expert in our midst!"

"Oh, well, I'm not an expert, more of a hobbyist than anything," he said as he blushed a deep red.

"Nonsense, you should be rating wines in the *Times*, as far as I'm concerned. Their current critic is an absolute nincompoop."

"Oh, well, on that I agree. I can't believe he gave the '09 Voignier a 93. It deserved, at a minimum, a 96 and I would have given it a 97 or perhaps even a 98," said Matthew, referencing the wine ratings assigned by critics.

"Well, his oversight is our gain. I'll see you next Thursday!"

"Looking forward to it."

The two made their way back to their respective areas and didn't talk until the following Thursday. Louise did organize a wine tasting and invited two of her closest friends, both of whom had a passing interest in wine. Louise, of course, had a different, secret agenda for the party. As an administrator, Matthew would be privy to just about everything happening with the navy. She hoped he might have some information on Dreyfuss or her husband.

The party went off without a hitch. Matthew showed up promptly at seven thirty with a bottle from the Bordeaux region. In all, they tasted eight wines and six cheeses. A few of the bottles were disappointing, but there were some surprises and, overall, it was quite a success. After the party, the group retired to the back yard for a quick game of croquet. Afterwards, her friends left and Matthew was left alone with Louise, exactly as she had planned.

"Matthew, I don't want to seem forward, but a friend of mine mentioned something about a Lieutenant Dreyfuss. I was wondering if you've ever heard of him."

Matthew stopped in his tracks.

"What do you know of Dreyfuss?" he asked.

"Nothing much, something about a battle or something, but the name stuck with me. Do you know him?"

"In passing, yes, I met him on a couple of occasions."

Louise could tell he was hiding something. Although he was an expert on wines, he was quite a bad liar.

"Anything else?" purposefully pressing him.

He was shifting on his feet, obviously feeling awkward. It was as if he had something he wanted to tell Louise, but could not bring himself to discuss it.

"This is about Charles, isn't it?" he asked.

She sat in a chair, looking straight at Matthew.

"It has everything to do with Charles. Do you know anything?"

He sat down across from her, rubbing his knees with his palms, and staring at the ground.

"There are rumors about Dreyfuss," he finally answered.

"What kind of rumors?"

"That he is working with some of our merchants as a kind of hired bodyguard. There have been reports—well, rumors—that he actually attacked some villages and fishing boats."

Louise almost fell out of her seat with excitement. So, it was true! Dreyfuss was corrupt.

"Rumors? Nothing substantiated?"

"You have to understand, Louise. This is a British officer acting outside of orders. It would be a disaster if any of this were made known to the public. Besides, there is no hard evidence, just the testimony of some peasants who swore Dreyfuss attacked them without provocation."

"Has there been an inquiry?" she asked.

"Goodness, no. It's the stuff that is right in front of us, but never discussed in the open."

"And have you heard anything of Charles?"

He sighed and dug even deeper into his thighs.

"This stays between you and me, right?"

"Absolutely!"

"The order came down yesterday. I was going to share it with you tonight, so I'm glad we had this time to talk. Charles is going to be announced as a traitor to the Crown and a bounty put on his head."

Louise almost fainted at his words.

"What? Why?"

"It is all so complicated, Louise. The navy is in with the Far Indian Trading Company. They are the ones who are pushing for Charles to be declared, essentially, a pirate. The brass tried to delay this for as long as possible, but was finally pushed to make a formal declaration."

"What would the Far Indian Trading Company want with Charles?"

"I have no idea."

Louise took a moment to digest this news. The Far Indian Trading Company was the largest trading company in Britain, perhaps even in the entire world. They imported spices, silks, furniture, even precious metals from everywhere in the world, not only to Britain, but to just about every country in Europe. They were invested in timber, fishing, and probably every slice of commerce imaginable.

"This doesn't make any sense."

"I know," he agreed. He couldn't imagine Charles Owen ever being a traitor. He didn't share this with Louise, but Charles had actually protected him from a series of bullies all throughout their boarding school years. He had always looked up to Charles, and could never, ever believe he was a traitor to his country. If ever there was a patriot to the Queen, it was Charles Owen.

"Louise, I will help you in any way I can," he finally continued.

"Really?"

"I am indebted to Charles. There has to be an explanation behind this, so I want to work with you to clear his name. We just need to be very, very quiet about it."

"Yes, yes, absolutely. Thank you, Matthew."

The two shook hands and Matthew promised he would begin looking further into this business with the Far Indian Trading Company and try to get better intelligence regarding Charles.

Louise closed the door after he left and almost started crying on the spot. If the navy announced Charles as a traitor, then it would certainly make front page news. It would be a massive story. Louise knew she would be ostracized even further and banished once and for all from all circles of society. In essence, she would be considered a social leper.

Finally, she broke down and started crying, lying down against the door and allowing deep and heavy sobs to spill out of her as she buried her head into her hands. She'd tried to be so strong through all of this, but the latest news hit hard. To be publicly tried, condemned, and humiliated was just too much for her. She imagined her shame at being the juicy gossip at cocktail parties, the subject of chatter at the daily bridge games, and the brunt of jokes at the beauty parlors.

More than any of this, however, she felt complete empathy for her husband. Her heart ached for him. She wondered where he was and if he was safe. And, she also wondered how in the world such a good and honorable man could possibly be skewered like this—by the very men he trusted!

After a few moments Louise composed herself, had a spot of brandy to calm her nerves, and went about preparing a snack for David, who would be home before too long. Then, she took out a pen and paper and began writing notes on everything she had discovered thus far regarding Dreyfuss and, now, the Far Indian Trading Company. In his letter, Charles had specifically stated that Dreyfuss was massacring villages in the name of British commerce.

Immediately, she made the connection to the Far Indian Trading Company. Was it possible that they had somehow contracted Dreyfuss to do their dirty work? It did not seem plausible that a British naval commander would engage in something so unseemly, at least, not alone. It seemed he must have received orders from above, from someone very high up in the British military.

It made her mission all the more dangerous. If the leaders of the British military suspected that she knew someone, or anything, related to their involvement with the Far Indian Trading Company, they would stop at nothing to keep her quiet.

She had figured out part of the puzzle, but it still didn't help her with the most important part, and that was how to help Charles. She could never prove that the British navy was acting as a kind of thug for the Far Indian Trading Company.

Could she?

CHAPTER
— 18 —

CRUELTY OF IMMEASURABLE PAIN

Tariq grew more despondent with each passing day. Jack was nowhere to be found and Tariq's hopes for rescue were dire. He could feel he wasn't his usual self, but he didn't know why. Normally, he would be plotting an escape at every turn and looking for weaknesses within his captors. Now, he merely rode on his horse and did what they instructed him to do. He washed their clothes, prepared their meals, and readied their horses.

On the third day of their journey, they came upon a tiny village at dusk. It was a dark kind of village, set in the shadows of the mountains, and its inhabitants scurried indoors when they saw the Caid's soldiers approach. They had already been taxed and their sons recruited by force into the Caid's army. All who remained were fearful grandmothers, heartbroken mothers, bitter men, and scared children.

In this place, which had seen so much tragedy, Tariq felt especially depressed and sad. It was as if something inside of him fed off the pain of others, and he was dragged down by the weight of their despair. There was something else about this village—an odd familiarity. It was as if Tariq were being watched.

The group went to the largest house and knocked on the door. A woman answered. Skin hung off her face and heavy bags sat below her eyes. She looked very old and tired.

"Woman, we need your house tonight. Cook us a meal and remove your family," came the order from the lead guard.

The woman didn't protest. She was accustomed to being abused by the Caid and his soldiers. Quickly, her daughter, a woman of about twenty-three, and her daughter's two children scurried outside, off to a relative's house. The soldiers made themselves comfortable while the old woman went about preparing their dinner.

Tariq didn't eat that night, and he didn't sleep, either.

He lay awake, listening to the wind howl against the thatched roof, hearing the crickets chirp in the distance. He was so alone and away from his friends, perhaps it was better to just give up.

A voice from somewhere within him told him to hold out—to be strong, and never to give in to anger and sadness.

He listened to the voice and tried to calm himself by thinking of Malik, Sanaa, Fez, Aseem, Margaret, and especially of Zijuan. He pictured Zijuan patiently teaching him to read and write and cooking warm meals for him at the orphanage. He remembered her smile and how she was the first person to look after him. Thinking about Zijuan gave him hope and comfort in this depressing place.

Margaret and Alice were having the time of their lives at Saint Catherine's. Unlike their English school, Saint Catherine's was progressive, and the nuns encouraged independent thought from the students. Alice was quickly learning French, and the other girls helped her as much as possible. After lessons, the girls would run freely in the woods and vineyards, inventing new games and allowing their imaginations to run wild.

Margaret hadn't felt this happy in a long time. Yet, there was still a nagging feeling inside of her. She missed her father and until she knew what happened to him, she wouldn't feel satisfied. She hid these feelings from the others, but each night she wrote in her journal, trying to piece together the clues to his disappearance. If he was alive, wouldn't he have contacted her by now? If he was alive, surely he would found some way to let his family know he was safe. Every indication was that he had been captured by the pirates and killed. Still, that's not what Margaret felt in her heart.

In her heart, she felt her father was still alive. As long as she felt this way, she would keep searching for clues to his disappearance. In London, she had scoured the newspapers for any reference to pirate activities in the Mediterranean, especially along the Strait of Gibraltar. There had been a lot in the news, but most of it was pirates attacking fishing boats and, occasionally, a merchant vessel. A pirate captain by the name of Basil was featured prominently, but there was never any word of her father. She thought it strange that a missing officer in the British army didn't make some kind of news, but there was nothing.

The problem with Saint Catherine's was there was no access to the outside world. For months she heard nothing and was kept in a safe little cocoon. She decided that she would have to go to Marseilles to try and find some kind of news, anything that might relieve her fears.

She told her plan to her roommates.

"But that is forbidden, the sisters have strict rules about not leaving the grounds. They are responsible for our safety. If anything were to happen to us, the school could be shut down!" Sophie explained.

"I know the rules, but I can't just be kept in the dark from everything happening in the world. I've asked Sister Anne for some kind of news, but she refuses. Even my own mother won't send me any newspaper clippings. I just don't understand it," Margaret cried.

"We could go next weekend, when the sisters have their day of silence and repentance," Alice offered.

"Alice, you're not helping!" Sophie scolded.

"Yes, we could escape to Marseilles on Friday night and return on Sunday morning before mass," Inez said excitedly. "The sisters confine themselves to their quarters for twenty-four hours—they would never know we went missing!"

"No, it's madness, we'll get caught!" Sophie protested.

"It's much too dangerous for any of you to go. I'll go by myself," Margaret tried to explain.

"No, we will all go together. It is an adventure, an affront to authority, and I will not be excluded," Inez proclaimed proudly.

"I wouldn't miss it. Besides, I've always wanted to see Marseilles," Alice agreed.

Sophie, the last voice of resistance, finally relented.

"Fine then, count me in, but we better not get caught!"

Etienne readily agreed, and it was settled. The girls would make a break for Marseilles the following weekend.

"We need a plan to get to Marseilles and to return unnoticed," Inez said.

"Oh, I've got that all figured out," Sophie said, and all the girls giggled once they all heard the plan. This was to be a genuine adventure, with a great element of danger, and the girls would spend the next week almost sick with excitement and anticipation. Extensive plans were made, down to securing a map of Marseilles, finding the address of the city library, and securing enough provisions to last the journey. It was agreed they would be there just long enough to get any news of Margaret's father and would then make their way right back. There would be no tourist activities or lounging about. They were on a mission!

On Friday night, as darkness fell, the sisters of Saint Catherine's went to their quarters for solitude and confinement. The students of Saint Catherine's would be left to their own devices. Sophie devised a plan to tell the other girls that their cabin was going on a camping expedition, just over the hill, to spend the night under the stars to commune with nature and would return on Sunday morning.

The following morning before dusk, the girls left their cabin in darkness and walked for two miles to a neighboring farm. A large red barn was next to the house, and inside, there was a series of stalls with horses in each one. When the girls took their equestrian lessons, these were the horses they used. The farmer rented them out to Saint Catherine's whenever lessons were required. It was a good arrangement for the sisters, as boarding horses could be quite expensive.

Sophie had already left a note with the farmer that the horses would be used for lessons that weekend. He was somewhat of an eccentric man, and old age had dulled his senses, so she hoped he wouldn't inquire with the sisters as to the whereabouts of the missing horses. Sometimes they kept the horses for up to a week when there was a competition, so she didn't think they would be missed over a day.

Quietly, the girls each saddled a horse and together they led them out under the cover of darkness. Their timing had been exceptional, because as they led the horses away from the barn, the sun began to rise on the horizon, lighting the road to Marseilles.

All five girls mounted up with broad smiles on their faces. This felt like freedom! Soon they were flying along the road to Marseilles, dressed in their school uniforms, hair being tossed wildly, and laughing most of the way.

They would reach Marseilles by afternoon.

The Mamba and his soldiers rode through the night and into the next day. They hardly stopped for water or food and their horses were sweaty and tired from riding so hard. Sanaa and Malik were blindfolded, tied up and each was slung over the back of a horse. The ride was most uncomfortable and the ropes burned their skin. Neither could speak to the other. For hours on end, their only frame of reference had been all the sounds made by the horses. Otherwise, they were in total blackness.

Finally, they stopped.

Sanaa and Malik were brought down from their horses and their blindfolds were taken off. It was morning, very early morning; the sun wasn't even up yet. They could see their breath in the night air and it was most cold.

They were in the desert.

Someone cut the ropes on their wrists so they could use their hands. The Mamba handed each of them a shovel.

"Now dig!" the Mamba ordered.

"Dig what?' Malik asked.

"Your graves."

Sanaa and Malik looked at one another with sorrow in their eyes, and began to dig in the sand—all the while being watched and guarded by the Mamba. They were surrounded and there was no possibility of escape.

They dug for two hours, until finally the holes were just as the Mamba wanted.

"Now, tie their arms behind them and bind their ankles together. Be sure they cannot move."

Jawad and some of the other guards did as they were instructed and soon Malik and Sanaa were completely helpless.

"Good, now throw them in their holes and bury them up to their necks."

Malik and Sanaa were carelessly tossed down into their respective holes and, within fifteen moments, the holes had been filled with sand, leaving only their heads above ground. They couldn't move at all and were completely helpless.

The Mamba looked down at both of them with a smirk plastered on his face. He had some kind of needle and thread in his hand. Forcefully, he took their eyelids and began stitching them to their eyebrows so their eyes would remain open. The needle burned and the pain of the thread going through their eyelids was unbearable. It was a messy business and he wasn't very careful, or gentle, in his work. Blood dripped down each of their cheeks and mingled with the tears flowing from their eyes.

"The sun will be up in a few hours. This is a torture passed down for centuries from our earliest ancestors. As your eyes are now stitched open, you will not be able to close them. The sun gets very, very hot in the desert. At first, it will singe your eyes until they are blind. The pain will be unbearable. But, you won't be dead. You will just be blind. It will take you three or four days to die of dehydration, that is, unless the animals get you first. Your tongue will swell inside of your mouth and you will want to cut it off—but you can't. You will scream, but there will be nobody to hear you. You can pray, but I don't think your God will help you either."

The Mamba stood up, kicked a little sand into their faces, and then mounted his horse. He and the rest of the soldiers took one last look at them.

Jawad spit at them, his spittle landing on Malik's face.

Then they rode off into the distance, leaving Malik and Sanaa to roast to death.

Malik could not look at Sanaa as he could not move his head.

"I am sorry Sanaa, for I have failed you. I…I never wanted it to end like this," Malik said, his voice choked with emotion.

"This was always going to be our end, Malik. You and I are warriors; it is better to go out like this than to die of old age."

Malik managed to smile a bit—the same old Sanaa.

Yet, he also knew she was afraid. This was not a warrior's death. This was not a death in battle. This would be a slow and agonizing death of first going blind and then dying of thirst, or burns, or being eaten alive by wild animals.

"I've always loved you, Sanaa," he said.

Tears started to flow down Sanaa's cheeks. Those were the words she had waited to hear her entire life.

"I've always loved you as well, since the first day that you were brought to our tribe."

"I wish I would have done something about my feelings. I was so afraid you would reject me. Now, we are going to die," Malik said, the regret in his voice heavy enough to sink a ship.

"At least we will die together," she explained.

"Yes, but we could have lived together."

"We *have* lived together, Malik. You have been my best friend in the world."

"Sanaa, why are you so fierce? You never let anyone inside your heart, why?" Malik pleaded.

"Do you remember the day of those games when I beat you and you rejected me?" she asked.

"Yes," he replied softly.

"The pain of your rejection was so great, that I promised myself that nobody would ever get that close to me again. I would never allow myself to be weak or vulnerable so I could never be hurt like that again. I dedicated myself to being a warrior."

Hearing this made Malik hurt even more. He had allowed his silly ego to prevent him from being with the love of his life.

He had failed Sanaa. He had failed his people.

Louise Owen read the newspaper and wanted to be sick.

Charles had made the front page, but not in the way that she had hoped. He had been labeled a traitor and a pirate and would be executed if found. It went on to paint a lurid picture of him providing details of his pirating and marauding exploits. There was even a quote by an English admiral, calling him a disgrace to the Crown and all that England represents.

As she finished the article, she just wanted to hold her husband. How could he be crucified like this? He was the most honest and honorable man she had ever met. The military had been his entire life.

As she sat at her kitchen table, she heard a knock at the front door. Opening the door, she saw two men standing in front of her.

"Louise Owen?"

"Yes."

"My name is William Holdsworth and this is David Mills. We are with British intelligence. May we come in?"

"Of course."

Although she felt in no mood to have company, especially official company, she let the men in and quickly went about making a pot of tea. The men were both dressed in dark gray suits with matching black ties. A white handkerchief was prominently displayed in both of their pockets. They were identical in every way with the exception of their shoes—Holdsworth wore black ones, while Mills wore brown.

Placing the tea tray at the table, she poured both men a cup, added some cream and sugar, and then poured her own. It tasted bitter on her tongue.

After the pleasantries, the men got down to business.

"As you're probably aware, there have been some difficulties with your husband," Agent Holdsworth began. He was obviously the more senior of the two men. Aged about thirty-five, his blond hair was already starting to recede, but other than that, he was a handsome man with a narrow face and slight build.

His manners were impeccable, as was his speech. Undoubtedly this man was well-educated.

"I'd say 'difficulties' is an understatement," Louise corrected him.

"Yes, well, we're still trying to get to the bottom of all of this. I've looked up Charles's records and they are excellent. His entire military career is one accolade after another. In fact, he was being groomed to become a general. None of this makes any sense. If you have any information on his whereabouts, or any communication you have had with him, it may help me," he said, and he was convincing.

"No, I haven't had any communication with Charles. I don't understand what has happened to him, but this all has to be a huge mistake."

Louise got the feeling that this man was trying to get something from her, and he wasn't being entirely honest. Although his manners were impeccable, Louise had learned that good manners rarely translated to character or substance within a person.

"Yes, well, at this point, he has been charged with being a traitor—a most serious offense. You must hand over any correspondence you've had with Charles, and contact us immediately if he attempts to contact you, or you will be charged as an accomplice. Do I make myself clear?"

His tone and demeanor had taken on a sinister tone. When he spoke, he made direct eye contact with Louise and leaned forward in his chair to make his point.

"I understand. If Charles contacts me, I shall immediately alert the proper authorities," Louise said, obediently.

"Well, in this case, the proper authority is me. Here is my card with my address. Please do contact me with any news."

"I shall."

"Well then, thank you for the tea. It was most generous of you on what must be a trying day. We won't take any more of your time," Holdsworth said, as both men emptied their cups, put on their hats, and made their way out of the Owens' home.

"He's innocent you know," Louise said to them as they were walking away.

The men turned back around, smiled and gave a slight nod, and then continued to walk down the street.

"What do you think?" Mills asked.

"I think she knows something, I just don't know what. I can't imagine her husband didn't at the very least send word that he was safe. Still, the entire affair is strange. Keep an eye on her."

The two British agents walked down the street while Louise watched them from her window. Immediately, she threw on a shawl, headed outside, and walked briskly in the opposite direction. Afraid she was being followed, she continued to zig and zag through alleyways and parks, and even took a street car up Highgate Hill to ensure she was alone. Finally, she waited outside of Matthew's office in a park, pretending to feed the pigeons while reading a book. She knew he mostly took his lunches alone and hoped to get some time with him.

Sure enough, Matthew walked out alone at five past noon, book and lunch in hand, preparing for a little solitude while the other employees went off together without him.

Louise walked next to him.

"Can we talk?" she asked him.

A little startled, he looked over at her before talking.

"I thought I might see you given the news in today's paper."

"I was just visited by two agents from British Intelligence. They wanted to know if I'd been contacted by Charles."

"That's standard procedure. You didn't tell them anything, did you?"

"No!"

"Good, keep it that way. I haven't found out much, except that it's definitely the Far Indian Trading Company that is putting on the pressure to make this happen. In fact, my superiors aren't happy at all that a decorated British officer is having his name raked through the mud. Obviously, someone at the top of the Far India Trading Company is very nervous about Charles."

"Do you think perhaps that company has something to do with pirates?" Louise asked.

"How do you mean?" Matthew asked.

"I mean, perhaps they are the ones who are marauding and killing the competition. Not them specifically, but perhaps they have something to do with it?"

Matthew thought about this for a minute before replying.

"I don't know; it seems very far-fetched. Why get entangled in something so devious?"

"Governments do it all the time, why not companies?"

"I'll look into it. In the meantime, be very careful about who you talk with and make completely sure you're not followed whenever we visit. I'll continue to do my part to try to dig up something on what, or who, is behind this entire thing."

"Thank you, Matthew. I so very much appreciate all of your help and support. Nobody else would believe me."

Matthew smiled at this gesture. He felt good about being appreciated, as most of his co-workers, and even his boss, didn't fully realize his talents.

"My pleasure! Just be careful. The game just got a bit more dangerous."

Louise nodded, and the two quickly went their separate ways. On the way home, she stopped by the public library to check the other newspapers. Thankfully, the news of Charles was strictly local news, and none of the foreign papers seemed to pick up on it. However, there was usually a lag of a week or two, so it could just be a matter of time before the news about her husband hit the mainland of Europe.

In the meantime, she had a son to raise and a public image to uphold.

CHAPTER
— *19* —

AN UNEXPECTED DISCOVERY

Tariq and the soldiers trudged up a mountain road. They were dusty and filthy and smelled of sweat and grime. It was just getting dark and finally starting to cool.

The soldiers saw a deer in the distance and all of them began shooting at it with arrows—a few coming within inches of it, but all missing their target. Transfixed by the giant buck, they chased after it, continuing to shoot and reload.

Without thinking, just reacting to the fact the soldiers were distracted, Tariq saw this as his chance and started running in the opposite direction. He only had a head start of about fifty or sixty feet, but the terrain sloped downhill, with slippery leaves on the ground, and trees to dart in and out of. He heard the guards as they began to yell and give chase. He didn't dare look back, as he really didn't want to know how close they were to him. He ran in as straight a line as he could, making angle turns whenever possible to prevent their speed from catching him.

Down the hill they went for what seemed like an eternity. He heard a couple of the guards stumble and fall behind him, but he knew they were very close and getting closer. At the bottom of the hill he came to a clearing that led to an opposite ledge. If he could make it past the clearing and onto the mountainside, he might be able to lose them somehow.

He really didn't have a plan.

He ran as hard and fast as he could, but there was one guard who was faster than him. He could feel footsteps just behind him, maybe only ten feet, and the panting of breath. He felt the guard get closer and closer to him; he even thought he felt the wisp of a hand swipe at his back.

Tariq knew he was going to be caught. He knew there was no hope for him. Just as he was about to give up, he felt himself being lifted upwards, as if by a magical force. His feet left the ground and suddenly he was ten feet in the air, then fifteen, then twenty.

Looking up, he saw the smiling face of Melbourne Jack and his solo balloon, which was now a balloon for two.

"Didn't think I'd leave you, did you mate?"

Tariq didn't say anything; he just smiled and let out a "wahoooo." The sense of relief he felt was intense. Not just at being saved from certain doom, but at seeing his friend who had come back for him.

He looked back and saw that the soldiers had briefly stopped, dumbfounded, no doubt at the sight of a hot air balloon, probably for the first time, and also at having their prey slip through their fingers.

The balloon floated higher and higher, and the soldiers quickly began their chase after them.

"Hold onto the bar and try to lift yourself up. We're not out of the thick of it yet. We've got to clear this ledge or this is going to be the shortest escape in history! This baby wasn't made for two, so I don't know if we'll make it," Melbourne Jack said, wrestling to control the balloon.

Tariq stared straight ahead and saw what Jack was referring to. As they climbed higher, they faced a mountain ledge directly in front of them. The ledge was a mass of cracks and ledges and valleys with an almost sheer face down the side of the rock.

Trying to pull himself up, Tariq felt the balloon stop climbing as rapidly and finally begin to even out.

"Damn, it's too much weight. I'll give it full power and hopefully we can lift past it!"

Jack gave as much fuel to the balloon as possible, but it wasn't enough. The mountain ledge was getting closer and closer and they weren't going to make it.

"Can't you turn it?" Tariq yelled.

"This baby goes where the wind takes her, and unfortunately the wind is taking us right into that mountain. Sometimes there's an updraft when the wind hits the side—that might lift us over."

Jack's voice was fast and flustered and his pupils dilated with excitement. Adrenaline surged through his body as he fought his balloon, trying to push it beyond its capabilities.

She tried to rise, tried as best she could, but there was just too much weight.

Tariq and Jack were going to crash right into the side of the mountain.

The four girls of Saint Catherine's made their way through the streets of Marseilles. Being a sea port, Marseilles had one of the most dubious reputations of all the cities in France. It was notorious for thieves and confidence men, as well as pirates and thugs. It was a popular place for pirates to sell their bounty, and rarely could a night go by without the police recovering a victim of a stabbing or assault. Rarely were murders even investigated; most went into the police log as apparent suicide. The police were just as corrupt as the criminals of the city, if not more so. In fact, far too many of the beatings and stabbings actually came at the hands of the police.

This didn't concern the girls.

They made their way to the city library, a beautiful building in the heart of the city.

"Did you know that Marseilles is the birthplace of the Tarot card? It is also the birth city of such brilliant French poets as Valere Bernard, Pierre Bertas, and Andre Roussin. I find it to be even more spectacular than Paris because of the political history. Did you know that Marseilles was a proud supporter of the French Revolution and sent over 500 troops to Paris to fight the government? That is when "La Marseillaise" became the national anthem of France!" Etienne proudly stated.

"Etienne, you are giving me a headache. We know Marseilles is a great city," Sophie scolded her.

"I haven't even told you about the opera and the many museums, why…"

Before Etienne could continue, Margaret interrupted to point at hundreds and hundreds of troops walking down the street. They were walking six to a line in a proud progression. Citizens had lined up to cheer them on.

"What is going on over there?" she asked.

The other girls looked at where she was staring and wondered the same thing.

"Let's go have a look!" Alice squealed, and the girls ran to the troops.

The soldiers were of the Troupes Coloniales, really naval marines, and they looked dashing in their blue uniforms, black sashes, and pith helmets. They marched in a rigid fashion, arms at ninety-degree angles, holding their shiny bayonets.

The crowd hooted and hollered and threw rice at the troops, who dutifully ignored them, in strict military fashion.

"What is happening?" Sophie asked a bystander.

"We are sending more troops to Morocco," a woman answered.

"You girls should go see the pirates they captured. The government is always looking for reasons to send in more troops. These poor men are going to be hanged tomorrow," her husband interrupted.

"Pirates!" Inez exclaimed.

"Yes, yes, over there by the square. They are on display for all to see. You must arrive early for the hanging, because it's always quite a show and the crowds will be in the thousands," the woman continued.

The girls watched the parade until its finish and then decided to go to the square, to where the woman had pointed. None of them had ever seen a real-life pirate and they wondered if they all had wooden legs and parrots. Inez, in particular, wanted to see a pirate in the flesh, and she hoped she wouldn't be disappointed.

The square was a large area of cement, about fifty yards square, with trees and benches surrounding it. In the middle was a large metal cage surrounded by a few dozen people. Some simply stared at the cage, while others cursed at it and threw garbage at the men inside.

The girls began walking more gingerly, as they were curious about seeing a pirate, but scared at the same time. They walked to the front of the crowd to see the cage. Everyone stood about fifteen feet away, too afraid to go any closer.

There were a few men in the cage. They were dirty and beaten and wore tattered clothing. They sat facing the crowd, ignoring the insults, and simply stared at the ground.

Margaret looked at the men, gasped and turned away. She ran to the outskirts of the square and began sobbing, burying her hands in her face, tears streaming down her cheeks.

The other girls caught up to her, Alice and Sophie reaching out to hold and comfort her.

"What is it? What is wrong?" Etienne asked.

"One of those men..." Margaret stammered out.

"Yes?" Sophie asked.

"One of those men is my father!"

Charles Owen, Captain Basil, Cortez, and some other men sat in the cage. Each had been beaten, and all were dirty and smelly. French citizens had been cursing and spitting at them for days.

Charles looked ahead, his left eye bruised and swollen. He thought of his family and missed his wife and children so much. How he just wanted to be with them.

He knew he was scheduled to die and there was no hope for escape.

CHAPTER
— 20 —

TO THE VICTORS

The Caid received news of the French sending more troops to Morocco. French troops had been in Morocco for years, but this time it was different. Some locals had attacked and killed a French citizen, and now the military was serious about taking control. There was even speculation they would depose the Sultan and replace him with a Frenchman.

How odd that he had his own garrison of French Foreign Legion soldiers to command, while the French continued to invade his country.

Such was politics in Morocco.

He sat at his table, his fat belly rubbing against the side, with his right hand stroking the fat under his chin. If he could establish an allegiance with the French, then he could be in line to gain control of the throne.

His negotiations with the French general had started out innocently enough, but in their last conversation, he had made a more formal offer. The rifles and the Legion soldiers were just the beginning.

He had control of his lands, and would swear allegiance to the French flag if they would give him the Sultan's seat upon his defeat.

He would maintain loyalty to the French, give them their share of taxes, and ensure the war was quickly over.

In his mind, he feverishly dreamed of his plans for dominance and how he would conquer the Moroccan people and control his land.

He would do this by force and brutality—things that the civilized French could never perform due to their standing in Europe.

He would massacre tribes of people who opposed him.

He would force every boy between twelve and twenty to join his army and swear allegiance.

He would take control of the police and military and ensure they worked hand-in-hand with the French military.

He would raise taxes and take control of all mines, fishing fleets, and anything else. All profits would roll directly to him, and then the French.

He would shut down all schools. He preferred an ignorant population that would blindly follow his lead.

He would control all newspapers so they only spread the news he wanted.

He would institute martial law and forbid any weapons by the general population.

He would forbid anyone from owning land, with the exception of himself and some select advisors, and all other land would be sold to French citizens. In essence, a native Moroccan would be forbidden from owning land in his own country.

There would be no voting of any kind.

He would be the sovereign ruler of Morocco.

Malik's tribe was leaderless. Their numbers had been drastically reduced after the Mamba ambushed Malik and Sanaa. Packing up their tents, the tribe trudged in single file further up a mountain ridge to yet another campsite. Already, snow was starting to fall and the air was growing so cold. They still had some good soldiers, but there were so many children and elderly among them that traveling was difficult. Without Malik, they didn't have a survival plan.

They were reduced to living day-to-day with no plan for the future.

It was more than that.

Malik and Sanaa together had been their anchor. Without them, a depression fell over the tribe. They missed Fez, Aseem, and Tariq as well, who had become leaders in their own right.

They knew the Mamba was hunting them, and they all knew it would only be a matter of time before he found them and wiped them from the face of the earth.

They were defeated.

Tariq knelt on a ledge about two hundred feet above the ground but below the summit of the mountain. The balloon had crashed very hard, sending him and Jack sailing through the air, landing safely on this little cliff. The top was only about fifteen feet away, but there was no possible way he could get to it quickly. His head was woozy from the crash and he felt blood dripping down his forehead. The ledge was only about three feet in width, and two hundred feet was a dangerous drop to the ground.

Standing up, he felt the cliff behind him and a very strong wind at his face. At his feet, Jack lay unconscious. To his left, about six feet over and three feet up, the balloon was stretching by its rope and trying to fly away—the landing rope had snagged on a branch sticking out from the sheer face of the cliff. The balloon was being tugged hard by the wind, and it would be only moments before it freed itself and floated away forever.

Tariq braced himself and pushed his back hard against the rock behind him. He spread his arms out for more balance and let his fingers grip the face of the cliff.

In the distance, he watched as the Caid's guards rode to a stop just beneath him. They started shouting something at him, shaking their fists, and a couple of them withdrew their swords and started waving them at him. For a couple of minutes they stood there waving their swords, until the leader ordered a couple of them to ride around, up the cliff to the top, where the guards could easily surround their prey.

In a matter of moments, they would be captured.

The Mamba and his soldiers all sat around a massive table. Plates of food were at every corner and all types of delicacies were served. There was roast lamb and an entire sea bass filled with apricots. There were stews, soups, and salads. Six whole chickens were baked to perfection and brought to the table. Cakes and sweets of all flavors completed the feast.

The men ate and drank, and food dribbled down their lips. They laughed and sang and hugged one another.

Jawad sat with them as if he was one of their own. He had fine new silk dressings and leather shoes. The Mamba had personally given him a gold necklace which now hung around his neck.

"So, how does it feel to be the victor?" the Mamba asked.

"It feels good!" Jawad answered.

"This is only the beginning, boy. We are going to rule this land and you will have a kasbah of your own someday. Killing that rebel filth was just the start."

The Mamba was in unusually good spirits. Yes, he was still sinister and imposing, but he had let down his guard a bit to celebrate with his men. He understood how important it was to spoil them with food and fine clothes after such a hard ride.

Jawad looked around at the men drinking and eating and yelling. This is what he had always wanted for himself. This was power!

In her room, Zijuan stared at herself in her mirror. She was dressed in black, with lightweight boots tied high on her calves. Her clothes hung loosely from her body and she fixed her long, black hair into a ponytail. On her bed was a backpack with provisions she'd prepared that afternoon.

Also on the bed was a sword. She picked it up, felt the sharp edge against her palm, and swung it in the air a few times for effect. She stared at herself in the mirror, allowing the reflection of her eyes to look into her own.

Lately, her dreams had gotten more and more vivid, to the point where she could scarcely sleep. Last night's dream was the worst of them all, with Tariq finally being consumed by water as Zijuan lay grieving over his lifeless body.

She understood that he was in grave danger and she must act to somehow find and save him.

Over the weeks, she had put out word to her various contacts in the Moroccan underground to provide any news or gossip of Tariq. At last, she finally had word. A gypsy caravan about fifty miles out of town had something to do with Tariq.

She stared at herself in the mirror and eyed the sword in her hands. Her face was thin and had the look of a warrior. Her Asian eyes looked fierce and her chest slowly went back and forth as she calmly breathed in and out.

This was going to be a time of war.

This was going to be a time of blood.

Adventures continue in:

Legends of the Rif

ABOUT THE AUTHOR

The idea to write the *Red Hand Adventures* first came to Joe O'Neill while he was on safari in Sri Lanka. As he was driving along in an old jeep, under a full moon casting silhouettes of wild elephants against the jungle wall, the image of a rebel orphan in old Morocco popped into his head. While he wishes he could take full credit for coming up with the idea, it was, in reality, a story that was already out there, waiting to be told.

Joe O'Neill is the CEO and founder of Waquis Global, which gives him the opportunity for world travel and the experience of many different cultures.